MW00903233

Cataclysm

(c) Theresa Jacobs 2015

Edited by: Zane Dowling

Dedicated to Zane Dowling my friend and mentor, whose valuable guidance and wisdom are shaping me into a better author.

To my husband Duane Minshull who puts up with my tales of woe and triumph through my writing endeavors. As does my best friend Aimie Pagendam, my tired test reader.

Also to my son Mordecai, may all your dreams come true, except for the scary ones.

Special thanks to Mark Senske for his artful map making.

~1~

Forward

Usually, I would not write a forward. However, I need to tell you, this tall tale has been approximately 36 years in the making.

This story began when I was perhaps 10yrs old. I awoke in the middle of the night to see, on the floor near the foot of my bed, two glowing red eyes staring at me. It felt as though my heart stopped an I held my breath in fear. What was this beast staring at me? All I could see were two eyes, nothing more. Then a cloud must have shifted across the moon, and the eye shine went away. In its place was my cat, just sitting there looking at me.

At that very moment, the idea for this book came to life – which I can't spoil before it begins – and I carried it with me until 1992.

You will note the book starts in Oct of 1992, this is literal. I sat down and wrote the first passage 25 years ago. I would write a chapter or two and walk away for years, only to pick it up again and again.

I typed the end, of the first draft in 2003.

It sat in a drawer for another 12 years, until in 2015 when I learned of self-publishing.

Now this little book of mine, novel #1, my "pet" project, has been re-written and edited and edited again. It would not be publishable if not for the hard work that Zane Dowling has put into this book.

Please give Mr. Dowling a round of applause and perhaps help by purchasing one of his books too. I can't tell you how many times he had to read and edit and slap me on the wrist for my stubbornness. So yes, any errors left are all my own doing, but it's hard letting go of something you have tooled with for so long.

Thank you, Zane, and thanks to all my supporters and my beta readers. You all mean the world to me.

Theresa Jacobs, 2017.

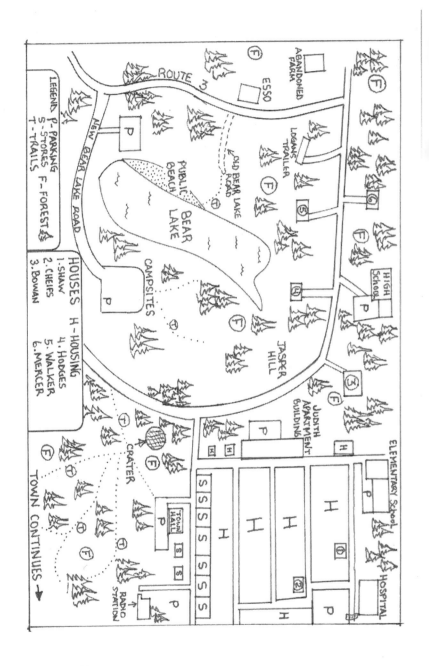

N

CHAPTERS

Rude Awakening

October 1992,
North Falls, B.C. Canada
Judith Barnes's Apartment 10:20 pm

Judith limped down the short hallway. The pain in her hip was a red-hot poker, searing her bones with every step. As she inched along, she used the wall for support. When she reached her apartment door, she slid the deadbolt back and cracked it open just enough to allow the small black cat to slip past. It slinked between her legs, as it entered its familiar domain. Judith had been living in the three-story walk up for so many years that all the neighbors knew not only her, but her cat Missy as well. Whenever she let the cat out, eventually another tenant would let it out the front doors, and at some point, back in again. She was thankful they were so kind, as it was not possible for her to run up and down three floors, so her cat could actually get outdoors.

She stooped down painfully to stroke the cat's soft fur, crooning, "Did my Missy get the nice neighbors to let her back in? Eh puss, puss?" In response, the cat scurried down the hallway and disappeared into the kitchen. Judith shook her head smiling at her pet's antics. She was grateful Missy had returned home early; there was nothing she hated more than to get into a comfortable sleep, only to be awakened by her meowing in the hallway. At her age and with her old bones aching, even the little things like getting in and out of bed were hard for Judith. Knowing Missy had plenty of food in her dish was a comfort as she inched her way back to the bedroom. As she slid under the covers, a sigh escaped her, soft and mournful as natural as the creaking of a wooden ship on a quiet sea. It felt good to stretch out her aching limbs, but she doubted the depths of her sleep tonight with her joints acting up as they were.

She fluffed up her pillow and settled back for a good hour of reading before she'd call it a night. Then she saw Missy creeping into the room. "Missy, come here puss-puss," she patted the blankets invitingly.

The cat perked up her ears when she heard her name, jumped gracefully onto the bed. It kneaded the covers, fussed and turned, finally settling on a spot, curling into a tight little ball. "Good girl," Judith rubbed the cat gently and began to doze off, the book tilted, forgotten in her other hand.

Judith opened her eyes, confused as a weight pressed heavy on her chest, and she couldn't draw a good breath. She tried to turn onto her side and found that she couldn't move. The weight was pressing tightly against her ribs. Oh no, she thought, I'm having a heart attack. As she reached up to rub her chest, her hand encountered a warm furry body. She gasped as she tried desperately to breathe.

"Oh Missy, goodness," she wheezed, "get off mommy, I can't breathe." She pushed feebly at the cat, but it would not budge. She struggled harder now to get some air into her aching lungs. She lifted her hips and tried to unbalance the cat, hoping to knock it to the floor. All that succeeded in doing was tiring her out more. Judith didn't understand what was happening to her. Why did Missy feel so heavy? The cat had lain on her many times before, she wasn't heavy. Why was tonight so different? Maybe it wasn't the cat, but really the pressure of a heart attack, and she was just mistaking the pain for the feeling of weight. She wasn't sure, but she knew she had to get the cat off of her quickly and call 911. She wrapped her thin fingers around Missy and gently squeezed, not wanting to hurt her pet. Then she started to lift her upwards away from her body. Missy hissed at the touch and dug its claws into Judith's tender flesh.

Her scream echoed off the walls as sharp claws pierced her skin. She gave up being nice and shoved the cat. The green eyes blinked and the eyelids, usually pale pink, flicked to black and then opened to burning crimson embers. Its tiny mouth stretched wide, revealing a gaping black maw. Judith's head rocked back and forth as she pushed at the thing on her chest.

Its claws grew longer and sunk deeper. As Judith wailed in pain, the creature leaped onto her face.

Stars exploded on the black screen. Sound boomed and screamed through the speakers as the little blue ship raced back and forth shooting the enemy. Doug's deft fingers flew from one button to the next as he annihilated the robotically advancing spaceships. His left foot had fallen asleep, but he barely noticed the tingling sensation; all his thoughts centered on the computer screen. He had surpassed his high score and was working on setting his new record.

"Yeah! Go…go…YES!" He jerked and jumped along with the ships' maneuvers until he heard his mother's voice from down the hall once again.

"Doug! Now please," Brenda yelled louder.

"Okay, I'm coming." He quickly disposed of three more ships, hit the pause button, and tossed the controller onto his cluttered desk.

Doug headed downstairs to the kitchen and rounded the corner just as his mother was walking out the opposite side into the living room. "What's up?" He asked before she could disappear.

Brenda stopped mid-stride and turned to look up at her son, who at eighteen towered over her by a few feet. "Can you please go find Sneezer honey? I called, but he didn't come in. There is another storm coming, and after that huge storm the other night, I want him to be safe."

Doug nodded, pulled on his Nikes and a light fall jacket, and stepped out into the cold mountain air. He made sure the door closed tight behind him so it wouldn't blow open and let the heat out. He stood for a moment in the darkness, watching the trees overhead as they swayed in the heavy wind. He loved hearing the calming song of soft creaks and rustling leaves and inhaled the deep sweet scent of autumn. As he stepped away from the back door, the motion sensor clicked on, and he started calling out to the cat.

"Sneezer! Here kitty!"

Not seeing any movement, Doug walked further out into the yard. Leaves crunched underfoot, and the cold wind pierced his thin coat. He shivered and rubbed at his arms, then let out a shrill whistle to attract the cat. He stopped at the end of the circle of light and braced himself before stepping out into the darkness. It seemed to smother him as he focused off into the distance, allowing his eyes to adjust until he could make out the silhouette of the mountains that rode the skyline. Then he scanned the yard and caught a glimpse of a small dark shape disappearing behind a large unruly holly bush.

"Hey, come here Sneezer," he yelled running after the cat. Normally the cat was in before dark; he didn't know what had gotten into Sneezer tonight.

"Yeeooowww!" A cat screeched from behind the house in the other direction.

Doug jumped and spun around, his heart pounded from the sudden noise. He could have sworn he saw the cat go under the bush. He followed the sound back toward the house and, as he peered around the corner. He saw Sneezer crouched low, teeth bared, hissing and spitting.

"Hey silly," Doug soothed the cat as he reached down to pick him up, "it's only me." As soon as he scooped the cat into his arms, the hissing turned into a low rumbling purr. Doug patted the stiff fur back down into place.

As he walked past the Holly Bush talking to his cat, a low growl came from within its confines, and a pair of glowing red eyes watched them enter the house.

☐

The next morning the sun hid behind a mass of gray clouds. A cold autumn wind blew across the small town, bringing the smell of dry leaves and snow down from the mountains. Doug whipped his bike daringly off the dirt road that led from his farmhouse out onto the highway. The ground was still covered with frost, and it looked as though the sun wasn't going to be coming out to make the day warmer. He'd worn gloves but neglected to wear a hat, and now he regretted it as his ears burned from the cold. He pumped his legs harder to make the short trip to school, that much faster.

He swung into the school parking lot and hitched up to the bike rack. He then stood on the edge of the yard watching his peers as they laughed and jostled each other about before the routine of the day started. Noise from behind brought him out of his trance, and he turned to see Katlin rushing up the field towards him. When she got within arm's reach, he rubbed the top of her head, which he knew she hated but could never resist doing.

"Stop that!" Katlin brushed her long black hair out of her eyes and gave Doug an ineffectual swat. Her tiny, five-foot, ninety-pound frame was no match for him, but he was always willing to let her get in a few mercy shots. He noticed her brow furrow just before she looked away in thought.

"Crazy news, huh?"

Doug shook his head, "What news?"

"Haven't you heard?"

"Guess not," Doug replied looking perplexed, "heard what?"

"You remember our old library teacher Mrs. Barnes?"

"Of course, she was our librarian for eight years, Kat."

The first bell rang out over the schoolyard and chaos ensued as students swarmed towards the doors like an angry mass of bees. Doug ambled behind the crowd waiting for Katlin to finish.

"She was murdered," Katlin blurted.

Doug was taken aback, "Who would kill an old librarian? And whatever for?"

As he opened his locker, a couple of classmates acknowledged him as they passed by. Doug nodded or lifted his hand to them, but carried on unloading his books.

Katlin leaned against the lockers, her bright azure eyes exploring his face in wonder as she waited. "Rumor has it that she was mutilated, and her eyes and tongue were missing."

Closing his locker door and securing the latch, Doug scoffed, "Really, and you believe that? Come on Kat," he rubbed her head again, "you know this town and its rumors. You better get going, or you'll be late for homeroom; we'll talk later, okay?" He turned to his friend, who had just walked by, "Hey Gar, wait up." As he stepped away from Katlin, he saw the disappointed look on her face. "Meet me in the cafeteria ok." Then he raced off after Garry and first class.

Throughout the day, Doug heard many different versions of Mrs. Barnes death or murder as the talk went. A couple of girls in his Biology class were whispering about how her heart had been ripped out of her body, and that blood and gore covered the room. During study break in the library, a group of students argued over different versions of the tale, one said her head was missing, another that her face was mangled. They all claimed to have the most informed source on the subject. Quite frankly it was making him sick. *What is it about a murder that intrigues people so much?* He thought. Not to mention she was a sweet little old lady. Everyone knew and loved her.

Then he wondered how Katlin had heard about it. It wasn't like her to gossip.

An hour later while standing in the lunch line, Doug scanned the crowded cafeteria. His eyes slipped easily over the heads until they stopped on the long raven tresses that belonged to Katlin. He grabbed his food and headed to the corner table where she sat.

"Hey, how's your day going?"

She grunted around a mouthful of coleslaw, swallowed, then wiped her lips before speaking. "Ah the usual crap," she complained. "Mr. Foster is giving me flack again about my grades. So I'm not very good at math," she shrugged angrily, "who cares. I totally make up for it in the rest of my classes."

"If it's going to interfere with your graduation why don't you get a tutor? I'll be your tutor for free," he said jokingly, though he was thinking how lucky it is that math is his strong suit.

Avoiding eye contact, Katlin watched her fork as she pushed food around on her plate. She was positive that Doug did not know she had a crush on him. They had known each other since kindergarten but became close friends in the second grade. She had always been smaller than the rest of her peers. Add quiet to that, and you have the perfect combination as bully bait. At least that's what some of the older boys thought until Doug showed up, saw them pushing the little girl around and became her savior. Katlin peeked through her bangs at him. His full lips brought on a sudden yearning for him to grab her right then, and kiss her. Heat rushed from her stomach and straight to her cheeks. She kept her face dipped low and gave him a noncommittal shrug.

Doug, lost in his own thoughts, never noticed the signals that Katlin was throwing out to him. "By the way, where did you hear about Mrs. Barnes? I've been hearing weird stories all day."

"Yeah," she grimaced at the memory of some of the gross things the other kids were saying. "I've heard plenty of those myself." She shook off the thoughts. "Well," she confessed. "I overheard Bobby Salinger this morning when I was waiting for you."

"Well then let's go find Bobby and see what's up."

"Whatever for?" Katlin asked, wondering why he was suddenly so interested.

"Because it just doesn't sound right that's why. I mean her tongue and eyes missing? Come on, I want to hear it from him directly." The rumors reminded him of the game that they played in English class where one person would make up a sentence and whisper it in the ear of the person next to them. Each person passed it on as they heard it and by the time it traveled to the last person in the class, the sentence would be completely different from the original tale.

Katlin paused for a moment not sure if she wanted any more details than she'd already heard, but she wanted to be with Doug, so she agreed.

They found Bobby Salinger hanging out in the smoking area, his back against the wall and a smoldering cigarette jutting from his jet-black lips.

There weren't too many kids in the small community that tried to rebel as hard as Bobby did. Having the chief of police for a father and a mother who died of cancer years earlier, made him defiant.

"Hey," Doug greeted Bobby.

Bobby squinted as smoke billowed up into his eyes. He ignored the smoke, better to look tough rather than remove the offender. "You look like you want something. A chunk of hash maybe?" He smirked knowing these two goody-goodies weren't looking to buy anything from him.

Katlin stood self-consciously beside Doug, keeping her head low, gnawing at her lip.

Doug got to the point. "I want to hear about the murder of Mrs. Barnes."

"I've already told about a hundred people today. Why should I tell it again?" Bobby crushed out his cigarette under the heel of his boot.

"Because I'm asking nicely."

"Ah, what fucking difference does it make," Bobby replied more to himself than to them. "I heard the old man on the blower talking about it. He didn't know I was home, or he would have made sure that I wasn't listening in. But…" Bobby paused to light another cigarette and offered the pack to Doug, who shook his head no. Bobby scratched at his spiky black hair, "Where was I? Oh yeah…so anyway, I heard him saying how he'd never seen nothing like it before, how her body was so flat… like empty…like no bones or nothing. Fucking strange man." He put the cigarette back in his mouth, closed his eyes and rested his head against the wall.

"And? That's it? No who done it? Or how or why?" Doug queried.

Bobby just shook his head. It was clear to Doug that Bobby had said all he was going to, and they learned nothing new from the conversation. He thanked Bobby for the story and led Katlin away. Once they were out of earshot, he took her hand. "Well, that was hardly worth the effort. But I think I should walk you home for a while, just to make sure you're safe.

Katlin smiled at his concern for her. "Fine with me," she said, "as long as you promise you'll stay for dinner."

"Would I ever pass up free food?"

The bell rang, and they parted, agreeing to meet up after school.

CLUELESS

Chief Salinger sat behind his oak desk studying the crime scene photos. The lines in his brow seemed deeper as he picked at a hangnail with his thumb. The pictures revealed nothing new to him as he spread them across the desk. His stomach tightened when he came to the photo of Judith Barnes, retired school librarian, now unrecognizable. Her body an empty sack of flesh. No bones, aside from her skull, no blood, just skin. Her empty eye holes, the eyelids now useless flaps that sagged grotesquely, stared back at Salinger. Challenging him to decipher how a person could die so brutally.

Turning away from the grizzly pictures, he replayed the scene he walked through that morning. Trying to see something inside his subconscious that the pictures did not reveal. He had been at home asleep when the call came in. The caller, Judith's friend, Lucy Walker, was in such hysterics that his dispatcher Millie had a hard time understanding her. Millie was able to calm her down just enough to get the words murder and the address. Then she contacted Salinger at home, and he rushed right over to the crime scene.

When he saw what was left of Mrs. Barnes, he understood why Lucy was hysterical. As soon as he entered the bedroom, he noticed that the body looked odd, there was no blood spilled. She was emptied, he could think of no other way to describe what he had seen, other than the body was emptied. Her nightgown was torn open in front, and her body no longer had any substance. Her body consisted of mere flesh; she appeared sucked dry of blood and organs. Her mouth hung open in an eternal scream revealing a gaping black hole.

Salinger opened his eyes to the clouded sky outside his window, he felt nauseous remembering the scene. The lack of clues to such a horrific murder left him scared. To make matters worse, the Mayor was out of town on one of his notorious "off the grid" fishing trips and wouldn't be back for at least a week. So now, Salinger was stuck with the added burden of notifying the town's people without causing a panic.

He ran his hands through his hair and thumbed the intercom. "Millie?"

"Yes," she responded quickly.

"Get that new reporter over here A.S.A.P., then notify the men that we have an emergency meeting tonight at six p.m. sharp."

"Right away, Sir."

He turned to the computer. Its dark screen ruined the quaint country feel of his office, like some ghastly Cyclops head, and he cringed as he clicked it on. He was actually lucky to have the computer. With all the government cutbacks, he was down to four constables and needed the extra resource to run a town with a population of five thousand people. Now he wondered how he was going to split up two twelve hours shifts plus run a murder investigation and hoped he would find a solution somewhere in the computer. He had to have a game plan by the meeting tonight. He brought his attention back to the matter at hand and focused on the computer screen, entered his password that took him directly to the secured police network. Where he could access criminal files, known suspects, and profiling systems that helped the police do their jobs in the new era of computer technology.

Salinger spent an hour on his computer running through all the possible channels to aid his investigation, but none of the cases he found even came close to what happened to Judith Barnes. He now stood at an impasse. He needed to keep his community safe from whoever had done this horrendous act, and yet at the same time, he couldn't let word get out about the exact nature of the death. Time was running short; he had to get a statement together for the reporter, plus contact the coroner to find out the results of the autopsy.

First things first, he picked up the phone and hit speed dial. As the phone rang in his ear, he silently prayed that Dr. Woodhouse would have something good for him.

North Falls General Hospital, 2:00 pm

Dr. Grover Woodhouse stood clucking his tongue at the body that lay opened on his table. He'd been seen death in such variations in his forty-odd years as a Medical Examiner, but never had he come across anything of this magnitude. His head fell in disgust, as he pushed the microphone away from his face. When he concluded his findings, which unfortunately were very little, he wanted to scream in frustration, but decorum and his on-looking assistant would not allow him the luxury of such an outburst.

"Clement," he called over his shoulder, "get those samples wrapped up, we're shipping her out."

Hal Clement gave no reply as he began preparing the body for removal. One day he would take over for Dr. Woodhouse, and the entire show would be his. It wasn't that he didn't like the old doctor; he just felt that it was time to make some much-needed changes in the small town. Until then, though, Hal kept his mouth shut, his nose clean, and worked hard to finish his apprenticeship with the old fellow.

When the phone rang, Dr. Woodhouse tore off his gloves and answered it. He told his assistant, Maria, at the front desk, not to let any calls through except for Chief Salinger himself. "Hello, Charles."

"Hi doc, any news?" Salinger cut right to the chase not in the mood for small talk.

"My findings are inconclusive, so I'm having her shipped to Vancouver. Maybe they can find something with their high-tech gizmos'."

Salinger swore silently to himself. If Dr. Woodhouse didn't have any answers for him, then that meant his investigation was going to be further delayed. "Can you tell me anything at all Doc? Was there any physical evidence left behind that can help us?" He needed something to go on, anything at all, no matter how insignificant it may be.

Dr. Woodhouse cleared his throat before answering the chief. He hated that he couldn't understand this case himself. "I found no solid evidence that I can report," he paused then added. "I'm sorry son. All I can tell you is that some unknown force removed everything from inside her body. With the exclusion of her skull, the remainder of her bones, blood, eyes, all her organs, even her brain ..." he paused as he heard the deep intake of breath on the line. "I can't tell you how because such a feat is impossible."

Salinger couldn't believe what the doctor was telling him, she'd been sucked clean? "Okay, help me understand one thing Doc," he said, more frustrated than before, "Judith Barnes was brutally murdered by some strange means and yet there was absolutely no trace evidence on her person? And we found nothing in her house?"

The doctor didn't have an answer, but he explained what he did know. "The only marks on the body were from her cat, on the chest where it dug its claws into her flesh. Although the claws seem wider, and longer, than that of a cat." He shrugged to himself. "It's an odd one that we can't answer, and it may not even have any bearing on this case anyway. I did a scraping from the throat, and body cavity, and ran the swabs through extensive testing. We came up with a substance that could not be identified. That's also being sent away for further tests. Until we hear back from the labs, we're stumped." Dr. Woodhouse explained all this as calmly as he could, considering this case had him as jittery as the chief. He looked back over his shoulder to where Clement was carefully zipping up the body bag, and a shiver ran down his spine.

He prayed that he would never see another body in such a state again.

On the other end of the line, Salinger began sweating. He felt the room closing in on him. How was he going to explain this to his men? And, what in the world were they getting into? He thanked the doctor for his time, hung up the phone and resumed picking at his hangnail deep in thought.

Lucy Walkers Residence, 4:00 pm

Lucy puttered around her small one-bedroom bungalow. She didn't know what to do with herself now that Judith was gone. Tears welled up in her eyes again, but she pushed them away and focused her attention on the dust rag in her hand, meticulously rubbing at her decorative crystal animals. She had been Judith's housekeeper, aid and closest friend for the last ten years. She had been the unfortunate one to find the body that morning. Lucy pushed the memory of the horrible sight out of her mind; she wanted to remember her friend for the kind lady she had been and not some grisly horror mask.

As she absently rubbed at the figurines, she allowed her thoughts to wander back to a couple of days before, when she and Judith took a road trip to Chilliwack. They spent the three-hour drive talking. Judith was a wonderful older woman filled with fascinating stories of mountain life before the village of North Falls had grown into a town, and the hardships her family endured farming the land. In the end, Judith always ended up talking fondly of the children she taught at North Falls Elementary. Not being able to have children of her own, all her love went out to the ones that she saw every day at the school.

Lucy recalled the spark of life Judith had as they shopped for Christmas gifts recently, well mostly they window shopped, as neither woman had anyone to buy for, save each other. Nevertheless, they had a fun day in each other's company. Lucy realized she was staring off into space and shook herself free from the memory before it could return her to the unwanted memory of finding her friend. She reached for the next figurine and, as her hand closed over it, a creak came from behind her. She screamed dropping the delicate crystal to the hardwood floor, where it shattered. She swung around expecting to see a madman coming at her covered in blood, a butcher knife poised to strike. As she turned, however, there was no one there. Her heart pounded so hard it felt like it was going to explode right out of her chest. The creaking came again, this time right at her feet. She looked down and saw the cat sitting on the floor watching her intently.

"Oh God, do I feel stupid." Lucy placed a hand over her pounding heart. "Sorry Missy, I am just so used to having the house all to myself."

She had forgotten that she took Judith's cat that morning. Rather than see it carted off to the pound by the police; she would take care of it as her friend would have wanted her too. It felt strange talking to a cat, but Lucy was so lonely now, that it was soothing. Her parents were both long dead, and now her good friend Judith was too, tears welled up in her eyes. The cat rubbed up against her legs purring softly. Lucy reached down, picked it up and moved to the rocking chair next to the window.

"Poor Missy," she said to the animal stroking its fur. "You must miss your mommy. I know I do." Lucy rocked back and forth in the chair cradling the cat, trying to soothe both of their losses.

North Falls High, 4:30 pm

Although school ended at 3:30 pm, Katlin had basketball practice, so Doug promised to wait for her. Usually, she would walk home, she was one of those people that enjoyed it, but now it wasn't safe, and her parents worked until 5. So, Doug was being a good friend and keeping her safe. He met Katlin on her way out of school. As she approached, he tossed his arm over her shoulder, and they headed across the field to where Doug's bike was chained to the rack.

She looked up at his chiseled face, her heart raced, and as heat ran into her cheeks, she said, "You know I could have gotten a ride with one of the girls."

"Are you trying to get out of the dinner you promised me?" He straddled the seat on his bike as if it was a Harley. "Besides, don't you think this will be more fun than riding home sitting next to a chatty girl? Hop on." He smiled shamelessly while tapping the handlebars.

Her eyes widened, and the gray clouds reflected in them, "Are you kidding? We haven't done that since we were kids!"

"Come on," he winked, "just like old times and I promise I won't drop you." He crossed his heart then held up three fingers like a Boy Scout.

Katlin could never resist his smile. Even though she trusted him, she was afraid to perch precariously on the edge of the handlebars as they rode downhill to town. She wasn't about to let him see her fear, though. So she threw her book bag over her head and secured it to her back, then jumped up onto the thin crossbar.

"Ready?" He asked.

"Okay, just please take it easy going down the hill. I don't want us to fall into the traffic; I'm not as light as I used to be."

"Please!" Doug shook the front of the bike back and forth to show her just how light she really was and that he was in complete control. "You're way too light. It feels like you're not even on the bike yet." He continued to tease her.

Katlin turned her head and glared at Doug. "Alright! My ass is getting sore already can we please just go!"

"Here we go!" He took off pumping hard across the grassy field. When they reached the roadway, Doug kept the bike on the rough pebbled shoulder. He stayed as close to the ditch as he dared without worrying about dumping them into it.

Katlin sat above him gripping the crossbar hard enough to turn her knuckles white. As they approached the top of Jasper Hill, which would lead them down into the town center, Katlin's heart began to pound. This was the part that she was afraid of, and she squeezed her eyes shut when the front tire tipped downwards.

Doug smiled, the cold autumn wind rushing over them as they picked up speed. He knew Katlin was scared, but they'd be fine as long as her hair didn't block his vision. He slowly began to apply pressure to the brakes, not wanting them to go too fast downhill, but, as he gently squeezed the brake lever, the cable snapped.

"Oh shit!"

"What?" Katlin yelled back over the whistling wind. She could feel the bike picking up speed and wished he'd slow down.

"Hold on tight Kat we just lost the brakes!" Doug lowered his feet to the gravel hoping to slow their descent somewhat with the friction.

Katlin gave up the pretense of being brave and screamed.

Doug's feet began to get sore after only seconds of dragging them across the ground. Their progress had slowed slightly but not nearly enough to save them from a nasty spill. The cars that sped past honked their horns in warning to the speeding bikers.

Doug spotted a dirt road up ahead on his right and had an idea.

"Hang on we're going to get away from this traffic!" He yelled to Katlin, who was already holding on for dear life and needed no direction to do so. If she could grip the handles any tighter, she would bend the bars. She had stopped screaming but had kept her eyes shut tightly against the world that was speeding past.

"Watch your feet, I'm making a sharp right turn ahead!" Doug informed her.

Katlin didn't have time to allow that thought to register before she felt the bike swerving. She opened her eyes now, thinking if they were about to crash into something, perhaps she'd be able to jump clear.

The bike hit the dirt road at high speed, and Doug lost all control. They sped across the gravel, headed straight for a deep ditch. Doug knew if he tried to pull away from it, they would go into a skid, which would put them across gravel. He allowed the inertia to take them where it may and silently prayed for the best.

As soon as the front tire left the road, the bike dipped. Katlin screamed as the force flung her off the handlebars and into the trees. Doug held on for dear life and tumbled headlong into the ditch, bike and all.

The world spun in circles over Doug's head, an endless gray sky ominously threatening to turn darker. Now stopped, he dizzily lifted his head off the ground, his legs tangled in the bike's frame. Pushing it off, he stood up gingerly and assessed the damage. His jeans were ripped down his left leg, and he could clearly see blood seeping from a scrape.

"Kat! Hey, Kat!" He called out. If anything bad happened to her, he'd never be able to forgive himself. Assessing the area, he spotted her book bag lying near where the tree line began. "Kat?" He called out as he climbed out of the ditch moving into the Pines.

"Doug! I'm over here." Katlin called over to him, "Come and see this."

Doug raced forward and stopped suddenly, in awe of what he was seeing. Through the trees was a large impression in the ground. It was at least twenty feet across and nearly six feet deep in the center. The hole was bowl-shaped, and Katlin was inside.

"What do you think did this?" Katlin asked. Then as she glanced up at Doug, she noticed for the first time that he'd been hurt. He was favoring his leg, and it was covered in blotches of blood. "Oh, my god! Are you alright?"

He waved her concern away. "I'm fine," he tugged at the torn jeans exposing a clean part of his hairy thigh. "It's just scraped really. But what about you? Are you hurt anywhere? I'm so sorry for the accident, it…I…I didn't know the brakes were bad, or I wouldn't have taken the chance." Doug stammered, feeling even worse now that he saw just how far from the road she had been thrown.

She looked down at herself; there was not a scratch on her. "I was scared when we were going down the hill but then after we crashed," she giggled, "it was kinda fun. But I got off lucky and landed in the soft grass. And when I got up, I saw this weird clearing through the trees." She clucked her tongue, "I'm sorry you got hurt, though. But, hey, look at this cool crater, what do you think?"

Doug surveyed the area before him. He had to admit that it was odd. The hole was perfectly symmetrical, the bottom surface was smooth - rock free, almost as if a giant ball rolled back and forth until it left a perfect indentation. "Who knows," he shrugged. "I've never seen anything like this around here before. Do you think maybe we had a meteor strike?" Doug looked up into the sky as if it held the answer.

"But wouldn't that be the talk of the town? Like how could we have a meteor and no one know about it? This can't have been here long, or people would know. Hum, it's definitely odd how it's so smooth."

Doug bent down touched the edge of the crater, he didn't see any scorch marks, although he didn't know anything about meteors, he figured it would be hot enough to burn the earth. "I wonder if it happened last week during the big storm we had."

Katlin squinted up at him, pondering the idea.

He gazed down on her upturned face. "I don't know if you guys felt it, but there was crazy thunder, and at one point our house shook." He shrugged. "We just chalked it up to that. But maybe it wasn't, maybe a meteor did hit?" He reached out his hand for Katlin. "Here let me help you out of there." As he was helping her crest the side, a shimmer of light near her foot caught his eye. Once she was beside him, he got to his knees, leaned over the edge and picked something up.

"What is it?"

Doug turned it over in his hands and held it out to her. "I don't know it looks like a fish scale …only much bigger." They watched the green scale turn iridescent in the dull afternoon light, and as Doug tipped it on his finger, he tapped it with his thumbnail. "Whatever it is it's as hard as a rock."

"We'd better go," Katlin looked up at the sky, "it's getting dark."

Doug nodded and slipped the scale into his pocket. They crossed the ditch, tidied themselves up as best they could, and began the walk into town with the mangled bike.

☐

Police Station, 4:45 pm

      As Sally McKinney stepped from her Ford Ranger, her short tweed skirt rode up the back of her shapely thighs. She grabbed the matching tweed jacket from the passenger seat and pulled it on over her thin blouse. The temperature had dropped to ten degrees Celsius, as the day passed into late afternoon. She entered the police station mentally going over her list of questions. She stopped at the counter and waited patiently for the portly woman behind the counter to stop typing. Sally couldn't help but evaluate the woman before her. With unchecked disdain, her lip curled at the bad ashy-blonde dye job, the unkempt 80's perm, and the pale rosacea covered cheeks. Sally rolled her eyes, living here was like taking a vacation in hell.

      Millie purposely ignored the young redhead woman that was standing before her. She was not happy with all the out-of-towners coming to North Falls and taking away the local folks' jobs. It had only been a few days since her dear friend Wanda's retirement party. For the last fifteen years, Wanda was the local reporter, and Millie missed her already. She was not oblivious to the dirty looks the young, beautiful woman was giving her and delayed addressing the new reporter.

Sally could see what was happening here already, getting flak from the locals was just what she needed. "I have an appointment with the chief," Sally said holding her anger in check.

Millie stood up from behind her desk without saying a word, threw a dirty look at the redhead and went through a door that led deeper into the station. As she left, Sally rolled her eyes and stepped away from the counter, taking in her surroundings. She noted the beige walls, hard plastic orange chairs, and fake potted plants that needed dusting. *Yuck*, she thought, *what a dump, they should just lock the prisoners up in here that'll punish them.*

Suddenly Sally regretted taking this position. She knew that leaving Vancouver was going to be a real adjustment, but she had no idea how boring small-town living could get. She was used to the fast-paced life, chasing leads and cornering the lower levels of society. That had been her fun. Her train of thought was interrupted when a door clicked shut from behind her.

Chief Salinger came out of his office to welcome the new reporter to town and to give her a quick tour of the police station. But he was not prepared for what he saw. The woman standing in his small waiting room was stunning. Her wavy red hair shone in the fluorescent lights. She was wearing a tight-fitting short skirt with a slit running up her thigh, and although she wore the matching jacket, he could still make out the shape of her ample breasts. He had paused only for a couple of seconds, but both ladies sensed his hesitation.

Millie, who was behind the chief, turned and stalked off to the break room to get a fresh cup of coffee.

Sally, used to men's reactions to her looks, ignored it and extended her hand.

Salinger stepped forward taking her soft hand in his own. "Welcome to North Falls. How long have you been with us?" Usually, he would have gotten right to business, but he was so struck by her beauty, it felt wrong not to make small talk first.

"One week and enjoying every peaceful moment," Sally replied ruefully. Her trained eye noting his finger held no wedding ring.

Salinger picked up on her sarcastic undertone and chose to ignore it. If she didn't like the solitude of country life, then that was her problem, not his; he had more severe issues to deal with. Remembering why he had brought the reporter here in the first place, he let go of her hand and gestured for her to follow him.

"Our operation here is rather small I'm sure, compared to Vancouver." He gestured into rooms as they moved passed them. "Here is our break room, a couple of offices that our constables share, two interrogations rooms."

Sally glanced in as they went by, they were barren gray rooms each with a bolted down metal table and two chairs. There were no two-way mirrors or wall cameras. She frowned; it was so Mickey Mouse. Taking a deep breath, she thought, *what have I gotten myself into. I never should have agreed to fill in here, her eyes moved towards the chief, even if it is temporary.*

As they entered the chief's larger office at the end of the hall, he finished his spiel, "the holding cells are in the basement of course."

Needless to say, Sally was unimpressed; she did, however, enjoy watching the lanky chief move smoothly from room to room.

As Sally took a seat in a guest chair opposite his desk, he watched her skirt ride higher up her thigh. He moved to the safety of his own chair behind the desk feeling glad to have the distance between them. Only then did he get to the matter at hand. "The first thing I want is for you to announce on air, that a curfew will be in place as of this evening," he held up his hand to ward off the question that was poised on her lips. "Please just let me talk, and then you can ask your questions."

Sally nodded in agreement opening her notebook. "Go ahead."

Chief Salinger sighed and leaned back in his chair. "We have a serious situation on our hands here. Ms. McKinney, I know you've heard we had a murder in town this morning. Hell, it's a small town; I can imagine everyone already knows about it. However, I don't want Mrs. Barnes' death flaunted around like a damn parade. She was a pillar of the community."

Salinger paused and ran his hand through his hair trying to ward off his frustration with the situation. Confessing to a reporter that he had no suspect was the last thing he wanted, on the off chance she'd run with it and scare the whole town. How he wished the mayor was here, this should have been on his plate. He saw Sally staring at him waiting for the rest of the scoop, so he resumed. "We know for a fact that she was murdered, but we have no conclusive evidence that leads to a suspect, and I fully intend on taking good care of the people of this town. That is why I want everyone off the streets by ten p.m..

Constables will be patrolling the town, and anyone caught out after curfew will receive a hefty fine. This is not a joking matter, and we expect full cooperation," he tapped his finger on the desk. "I also want anyone who spots suspicious behavior or sees a stranger around, to notify us immediately. I don't want any more people to get hurt so everyone will have to understand the situation here and take extra precautions until this is resolved." His deep brown eyes bore into Sally's. "Your job is to get that message out to them, repeat it as often as necessary on every television and radio station."

Sally finished writing and flipped her notebook back to the beginning where her questions were written. "Fine," she answered, "I'll get that on the news as soon as I get back and I'll run it every hour until you give the word to stop." Sitting straight-backed, she began, "Can you tell me how Mrs. Barnes died?"

"Not at this time, no."

"I've heard that the killer left no signs of forced entry. Do you think she was killed by someone she knew?"

Salinger's jaw almost hit the floor, and he thought. *How did she hear about that? None of the details of the investigation have left this office unless it leaked from the hospital? But that doesn't feel right either. Damn, she is getting under my skin already.* "That is still under investigation," he replied, checking his anger. He knew it would do him no good to blow up at her, or to ask her to reveal her source.

"Well then, is it true that all her bones were missing, except for the skull?"

"Jesus! Where did you hear that? No...never mind, you know I can't answer any of these questions while the case is still being investigated." Now he was perturbed if the reporter found out so much about the death already then who else knew. Or, more importantly, who was talking?

"Haven't you heard the rumors that are all over town, Chief," Sally asked bluntly. She could tell by the look on his face that he hadn't, so she decided to enlighten him. "People are talking, and it's not pleasant. I would like to get some real answers and deliver them to the people, maybe then they'll be reassured." She threw in the last comment as though he wasn't doing his job efficiently.

Salinger stood up from behind his desk towering over Sally. "I cannot tell you anything about the case right now. Get the curfew out, and I'll call you when I have information to give."

Sally snapped her notebook closed, she didn't hide her anger the way he had. "Fine, I'll get your message on the air. But let me tell you something Chief," she leaned over the desk bringing her face close to his. "If you end up with half the town on your doorstep, you only have yourself to blame!"

She turned and stalked out of the office leaving Salinger sweating and definitely hot under the collar.

The Mercer Residence, 5:00 pm

Shadows fell across the yard drawing long dark ribbons of the looming night. The chains on the swing creaked in a sing-song rhythm as Jennifer swung lazily back and forth. *I could do this forever*, she thought, as she glided through the crisp air, watching the leaves flutter in the tree above her.

Her day-dreamy feeling was interrupted by her step-mother's high-pitched voice. "Come inside!"

"Aww…a bit longer?" Jennifer whined.

The wind seemed to hold its breath, as the voice hollered shrilly from the kitchen window. "Get in here now!" Then the window slammed shut.

Jennifer jumped off the still moving swing. As she flew through the air, she pretended she could fly. She landed with a thud seconds later and shuffled her feet in the tall grass as if that would slow her ascent back to the real world.

As she sauntered aimlessly past the old shed, she heard a soft mewling. She moved to the old wooden door and put her ear against it. Sure enough, the noise was coming from inside. She grasped the rusted metal handle and pulled. The door didn't budge. She looked around for something she could use to pry the door open; convinced that there was a scared little kitten inside waiting for a strong, brave girl just like her to come along and rescue it. She spotted a rusty old car door that had been placed strategically to hide a missing board in the wall.

"That must be how it got in, silly cat. Maybe it'll come out there, too." She talked out loud as she pulled the car door forward. It was heavier than she thought and fell with a loud thud. She winced in fear and glanced back to the house hoping her step-mother hadn't heard the noise. Jennifer knew that Alice was going to be mad. She may even get a whooping, but she had to save the kitten. She could hear Alice call again. She ignored the calls as she got down on her knees and peered into the dark hole.

"God damn it! Where did that girl get off to now!" Alice grumbled. She looked out the small kitchen window but couldn't see her step-daughter anywhere. "Shit!" Alice tossed the towel down on the counter she went to put on her coat and shoes. "Making me go out into the cold and fetch her from her damn fantasy land, I'll bruise her behind!" The screen door slammed as Alice stalked out into the yard searching for her step-daughter. She looked around the darkening yard and saw no signs of her.

"Jennifer!"

Where could she be? She was beginning to worry now. Jennifer never left the yard. Guilt welled up in her chest. *I should have kept a better eye on her; she's only ten after all kids do wander. Oh, fuck, what if some weirdo came in and took her? No that can't be I just heard her whining a minute ago.* Alice pushed that panic away. *I have to find her before dinner. Rick will be home soon. What am I going to tell him? How can I explain this? I'll have to ground her for sure to save getting smacked up by Rick again.*

"Jennifer!" She yelled louder cupping her hands over her mouth. As her eyes moved around the yard, she noticed the car parts around the shed had been moved. "Damn it, she's gone and hid away on me, well I'll show her what hiding will get her!" Anger replaced the worry as she stalked towards the shed.

"Jennifer, I know you're in there now come on out!" Alice grumbled as she pulled on the stuck door. When no answer came from inside Alice began to wonder if she was wrong, maybe Jennifer wasn't hiding maybe something did happen to her. The panic seized her once more. "Listen, honey," she said softer now, pressing her ear up against the door. "I know you're in there. I'm not mad. I just want you to come out and get cleaned up for supper; your daddy will be home soon."

Still, not a sound came from the shed.

Fear and anger mixed and Alice pulled on the door handle as hard as she could. It creaked and groaned, but the door only opened a crack. She braced one foot on the wall of the shed and used both hands to wrench the door, suddenly, something let go, and Alice fell back slamming painfully into the ground. "Ooff!" The air rushed out of her lungs, and pain spread across her back as she fought for air.

"Aw fuck," she moaned, the door handle had come off in her hand. Rolling over she lay on her side waiting for the pain to subside and her breathing to return to normal. Then she spotted the hole in the wall and crawled over to it.

Squinting into the darkness but seeing nothing she knew that she'd have to stick her head into the hole. There was no possible way for her to fit her whole body in the hole, but if she could just see what Jennifer was up to, she may be able to coax her out. Alice grimaced; she did not want to put her head inside there. It was dark, and all she could think about were spiders and mice, her throat closed up, and she gagged. Muttering curses under her breath at her stepdaughter, she steeled her will and pushed her face up to the hole.

Inside she could make out the shape of a shoe.

"Jennifer," she said as calmly as possible, holding back both her anger and her fear, "you are not in trouble okay. Please just come out, and we'll forget this ever happened. I promise I won't tell your daddy either." Alice pleaded with the girl, but still, there was no response. She had to try a different tactic. "Fine then, you want it the hard way! If I have to come in after you, there'll be hell to pay little missy! I don't appreciate you scaring me like this."

Damn you girl for making me afraid. Alice pushed herself forward until her head went right inside the shed; dust flared up from her movements and tickled her nose. She wiggled harder until her shoulder blades came up solid against the outside wall. That was as far into the shed as she was going to be able to get. As she tried to see where Jennifer was, she realized her own body was now blocking the only light source.

"Jennifer?" Her voice sounded hollow and foreign. Something was wrong here; Jennifer hadn't moved or said a word at all this entire time. Plus, she just noticed that the foot was turned at an odd angle, surely Jennifer wouldn't sit so still in such an awkward position for so long. Alice was trying to figure out a better approach to getting into the shed when movement caught her eye. All that concerned her at that moment was mice. She was afraid that a mouse would run over and bite her unprotected face, and she began to hyperventilate.

~ 50 ~

Out. I've got to get out of here, Alice thought until two large red eyes appeared in front of her face. Fear transformed her body to stone, her bladder let go, piss coursed down her legs, and she screamed.

PLANS

Doug leaned his bike up against the stone wall of the City Hall building, as Katlin did her best to straighten up her clothes and try to look presentable. The walk to town took them fifteen minutes longer than riding would have and the sun had set. It was five o'clock now, and the city workers were starting to exit the building for the night. Some of them muttered hellos as they passed by, and others clucked their tongues at the messy state the kids were in. Doug was, after all, the son of the mayor's head secretary, and he wasn't representing himself well at the moment.

Doug ignored them as best he could and opened one of the glass doors for Katlin, and then followed her into the wood inlay foyer. The main floor was a large open room with a bank of counters for the public works department. Stairs at the end of the hall ran to the upper two floors, with the mayor's office being at the top with the best view. He held the rail as they made their way carefully up the stairs to where he expected his mother would still be working away. Katlin stayed close to his side for support in case his injured leg gave out. When they reached the top of the stairs, his mother looked up from her desk and gasped at the sight of their dishevelment.

"Doug!" Brenda stood up moving quickly around the desk to inspect her son. Grabbing at his torn pants, Doug winced when she brushed against his skinned leg. "What on earth happened to you?"

"I'm okay mom," he said shaking his leg to dislodge her grip. "The brake line on my bike snapped, but we're fine."

Brenda stood up glancing at Katlin. "What do you mean, we?"

Doug knew instantly that he'd made a mistake, now he'd never hear the end of the fact that he endangered Katlin's life.

Katlin stepped forward to Doug's defense. "It wasn't his fault Mrs. Bowan, honest."

Doug placed a protective hand on Katlin's shoulder. "I talked Kat into riding on my handlebars and then as we came down Jasper Hill I lost my brakes, and we had a spill. It's nothing to get excited about. It was just an accident." He tried to shrug off the incident, or at least make it sound harmless to his mother.

"Well, what are you doing here anyway? You should be at home."

"I'm taking Katlin home, to see that she makes it safely…" he wondered what his mother thought of Mrs. Barnes murder, but he decided not to remind her of the additional danger and played it off as nothing special. "She invited me to dinner if that is okay with you?"

"So you've heard the news then," she shook her head, "it's a terrible situation, that poor lady."

The kids silently nodded in agreement.

"How are you going to get home after if you plan on staying there for dinner?"

"Well, I'm sure Doug could stay in the spare room." Katlin blushed at her quick proposal. "If, of course, that's alright with you and my parents," she added sheepishly.

"Is it okay mom?"

Brenda sighed and sat back down behind her desk. She felt weariness pull on her muscles after a long day's work, which always seemed to triple in volume whenever Mayor Wainfleet took off on his fishing trips. Now it looked as if she would be spending the night alone out on the farm. The idea wasn't comforting, but she didn't feel right about asking Doug to stay home just because she was afraid to be alone. So she agreed. "Find out from Katlin's parents if you can stay as soon as you get there. If they say no, I'll come get you after dinner. Perhaps I'll call a friend over for my own slumber party if you're not coming home." The very idea of having a friend over cheered Brenda up considerably. It had been years since she'd had anyone stay with her.

"Thanks, mom," Doug kissed her softly on the cheek. It tugged at his heart knowing how lonely his mother really was. She was an independent woman and tried not to show it, but he knew. He looked into her eyes to convey his love for her, but at that moment Brenda was staring at the pretty young girl she knew was stealing her son's' heart.

☐

Police Station, 6:00 pm

Chief Salinger entered the small conference room, the constables were already there waiting for the meeting to begin. They were talking raucously, some of them joking about the murder and the chief couldn't believe what he was hearing.

"Enough!" Salinger yelled.

The room fell into silence as the shocked officers turned towards the chief's uncharacteristic outburst. Raking his hands through his hair, Salinger sat at the head of the table. The officers squirmed in their chairs, giving each other worried looks.

"We have a serious situation on our hand's gentlemen, and I'd appreciate it if you could set aside the childish humor and behave accordingly."

Constable Jim Crow was the first to speak up, his chestnut colored eyes bore the honor and pride that his Indian heritage bestowed. "Has the coroner's office given us any leads?" His voice was heavy with the Cree accent.

The other three constables moved restlessly in their seats, unaccustomed to so much pressure. One of the perks of living in this small mountain community was that nothing ever happened. This murder had them all scared and baffled, and the last thing they wanted was for the town to perceive them as incompetent idiots.

The chief carefully looked at each man before him to let them know he was serious. Most of them had been working with him for at least ten years, all but Mark Duncan. He was a local youngster that had joined the force only three months previous and was still in his probation period. Salinger had planned out the next 24 hours and knew it was not going to be easy.

Clearing his throat, he began to lay out the facts. "I spoke to Dr. Woodhouse this afternoon, and the results of the autopsy were inconclusive. The Doctor stated what we already knew; the bones were removed by some type of force, possibly suction. All the internal organs are gone, eyes, and brain matter also. How that was done…they have no idea; it's not possible. They are working hard to provide us with some answers." Salinger licked his dry lips and continued as the group of men gave each other worried glances. "I also checked the crime reports online and turned up nothing that even remotely matched our problem here. The first thing we are going to do, to ensure the safety of the townspeople, is to enforce a ten-p.m. curfew. Anyone on the streets past that, without good reason, is to be escorted home, fined, or arrested. Is that understood?"

All heads nodded in silent but unified agreement.

"We are alone in this gentleman; I want the situation kept under control!"

A throat cleared from the far end of the table. Mark Duncan raised his hand like a school kid. The chief nodded for him to go ahead and speak. "I was wondering …ah…are we going to stay on patrol duty all night Sir?" His voice cracked with embarrassment at the question, but he had to know how they were supposed to work all night without any breaks. Plus, he'd promised Debbie he'd stop in after his shift tonight for dinner.

With that cat out of the bag, the others piped up with their plans for the night. "Hey, yeah! The kid is right chief. I've been in since six this morning, when do I go home?" Jeff Baker complained.

Bob Wiley's voice, which had a constant whine to it, spoke up even louder. "It's not fair chief. I'm the seven to eleven shift, and here I am missing sleep, and for what some flippin curfew meeting. It ain't right."

Salinger stood up quickly, his chair flew out from behind him and tipped over with a loud bang. "Now listen up! I know we are all overworked already, but yes we all have to put in more time until this killer gets caught!" He pointed towards the window, his finger shaking. "We can't have our friends, families, and children out there walking around waiting for some wacko to pick them off one by one. You all saw the results of Mrs. Barnes this morning. That was not some random murder. It was strange and quite frankly, damn scary. Don't forget that I too have a son at home who is relying solely on me to take care of him. So don't any of you dare complain, or you can leave right now, and I'll get someone else to replace you."

Wiley leaned into Baker, whispering, "Ya, a son he never sees."

As Baker was about to retort, Millie pulled the door open without knocking and poked her head into the gap. "Chief, I just got a call from Rick Mercer; he says his wife and daughter are dead."

Salinger cursed under his breath knowing he didn't have time to waste, turned to his Constables and barked out orders. "Baker and Wiley, you start patrol immediately. Watch the people on the streets, look for anyone out of place, and if you don't recognize someone check them out. I don't care if they are tourists or just passing through and stopped to take a whiz, find out for sure and bring 'em in if you have to. Crow, you cruise the highways, same thing, watch for strange cars or unusual activity. Duncan, you're with me. Millie, get Dr. Woodhouse out to the Mercer's house on the double, I want this crime scene done right."

Mark Duncan winced at the thought of going out to the crime scene. He felt his stomach flip at the idea of seeing dead people. It would be his first live, well *dead*, crime scene, and he didn't think he was ready for it yet. With a shiver running down his spine and a lump in his throat, he followed the chief out into the night.

Katlin giggled as Doug made faces from across the room. They were clearing the table, while her mother was putting the finishing touches on a chocolate mousse that looked divine.

Jean glanced her daughter's way, hearing the muffled laughter. "Hurry up Katie; we want our dessert while it's still fresh." Jean Shaw teasingly swiped a dab of whipped cream on Katlin's nose as her daughter passed by with her arms full of dirty dishes.

Katlin laughed and set the dishes in the sink. She wiped the cream from her nose and sucked the cream from her finger. Just then she noticed Doug was watching her, and she blushed at the sudden realization that he had a particular look on his face she had never seen before.

Doug had mixed feelings. On the one hand, he suddenly realized how innately seductive Katlin could be. On the other, he saw her as he always had, kind of sisterly. He watched the family with envy as they played and missed having a father when he saw how well Katlin and her parents got along. Unloading his dishes too, he went back to join everyone at the table.

Katlin's father, Randolph Shaw, was a geeky kind of fellow, but very generous and warm. He always welcomed anyone into his home and had the philosophy of 'the more, the merrier.' He even insisted that Doug borrow a pair of his track pants, and tossed the ripped in jeans in the trash. "Dig in everyone," he said with enthusiasm as he scooped a significant portion of the chocolate mousse for himself.

They finished off the desert in no time, and Doug sat back rubbing his full stomach. "That was delicious Mrs. Shaw."

"Please Doug how many times do I have to tell you, call me Jean." She smiled at Doug as she stood up to clear the dessert plates. In her heart, she felt that someday her precious daughter would be married to him. Jean always liked Doug, he was a decent young man, and she'd be proud to see them make a life together. "Come and help me, Randy," she goaded her husband. "I think the kids should be left alone to relax now.

Randolph grinned knowingly. Getting up he gave his wife a light pat on her behind and laughed at her girlish giggle.

Doug didn't have to turn around to know what was happening; this was a regular occurrence in the Shaw household. Katlin's parents loved each other and were not afraid to show it, no matter who was around or where they were. He had seen many such displays of affection, when he was younger, he found the situation quite embarrassing. Now, however, he enjoyed watching them have fun. He hoped to someday have the same kind of love that was free and open and would last forever.

Katlin moved into the family room and clicked on the television. "Come here," she called to Doug.

"Oh man," Doug complained. "I ate more than my own weight I think." He plopped down on the couch raising Katlin up a couple of inches.

"I'm so glad you're here with me," she cooed not paying attention to her channel flipping. Something, however, caught Doug's eye.

"Hey wait," he grabbed for the remote as Katlin flipped the channels, "go back a bit."

She withheld the remote and flipped the channels slowly backward though her eyes were not on the screen until the moment he said: "Stop." On the local channel was a reporter that she had never seen before, a fiery redhead with bright green eyes.

"She's pretty," Katlin said with a mix of jealousy and envy.

"Yeah, shhh."

"What is it?"

"I don't know listen."

They listened as the reporter, whose name they missed, was talking about a curfew for the town. Katlin and Doug looked at each other with raised eyebrows. The woman on the screen said, "I repeat that Chief Salinger is placing the village of North Falls under strict curfew. You must be off the streets no later than ten p.m. this evening. The chief has advised that anyone found out on the streets after ten will be fined or arrested, if non-complainant. Please inform your friends and relatives of this curfew to help spread the news, and our broadcast will be repeated on the local channel through the night."

Katlin clicked off the set. "I'll go tell mom and dad, you should call your mom too. What is happening?"

Doug shook his head, "I don't know, but from the sounds of that announcement, Mrs. Barnes' murder was as bad as the rumors we heard today. I'll go call mom right now. Actually, I'm kind of worried about her being out on the farm alone now; maybe if she wants, I'll go home instead of staying here tonight."

"Um, yeah. I mean if you think your mom may need you then yeah of course." Katlin brushed past him quickly to hide her disappointment. Even though she understood his apprehension, she really was hoping that he'd stay overnight. It would be the first time that he stayed at her house, and she was thrilled at the thought.

Doug stood chewing his lip as the phone rang. It was picked up on the third ring. "Mom?"

"Hey, what's up? Is everything okay, I thought you were staying over there?"

"Oh yeah, everything's fine here I was just wondering if you saw the news?"

"No, I was listening to music actually. What's going on?

"Chief Salinger has set a curfew for ten o'clock tonight. Should I come home? I'm sure Mr. Shaw would drive me back."

"A curfew, really?" Brenda paused, wondering what was happening. With the mayor being away she was left out of the loop. "No, no, it's okay Margaret is on her way over right now. We have already planned a little slumber party of our own." She was touched that her son would have given up staying the night with a pretty young girl to come home and babysit her old ass. She almost laughed at the thought but held it back.

"Well, if you're sure then I'll stay here and come home tomorrow. Love you and be careful okay."

"Hey, I love you too, sparky and call me in the morning, don't try and walk all the way back up here I'll come get you, ok."

"K, bye mom."

"Bye, sweetie." Brenda blew a kiss into the phone at the last second hoping he heard it. She was glad that he called but missed him already. He was turning into a well-rounded young man right before her eyes, and she knew that sooner rather than later, she'd be alone permanently. She shook the melancholy thoughts away and turned from the phone to prepare for her friend's arrival.

Doug's hand was still resting on the telephone when Katlin came back into the room. When she saw him slumped with worry, she felt compelled to comfort him. She stepped up behind him and wrapped her arms around his muscular shoulders.

Doug turned and embraced her, glad to have such a kind and caring friend.

Bowan Residence, 7:45pm

Brenda peered into the darkness beyond the windows, fear lapping like waves at her heart. Everything will be okay, she told herself. Doug is perfectly safe where he is, and Margaret will be over within the hour. Glancing at the clock again and seeing that only ten seconds had passed since the last time she looked, she moved into the brightness of the kitchen to get a glass of wine, sure it would help take off the edge. It was close to eight p.m., and everything was quiet as one would expect in the countryside. She was so used to having Doug around making noise that the silence was making her jumpy. One would think that turning on the television would relieve the tension brought on by the silence, but she thought she heard noises from outside. She turned the volume down and listen intently only to hear normal night sounds, crickets chirping, wind howling through the dying leaves, owls hooting and the wolves baying at the moon. So, she had to content herself with pacing from the living room to the kitchen and back again while she waited.

Brenda jumped and nearly spilled her wine onto her lap when she heard the sound of a car pulling into the driveway. Running to the window she peered outside, relief flooded in when she saw Margaret's' Volkswagen. She stood watching the dark, slender figure step from the car.

Now things will be fine, Brenda thought opening the door for her best friend.

FEAR

Constable Mark Duncan had done the very thing he vowed he'd never do, he threw up at the crime scene.

Chief Salinger was gracious about the incident. "It's alright Duncan," he placed his hand on his constable's shoulder, "it happens to everyone with their first body, even me."

"That was not just a body Chief," Duncan replied, the horrific scene still fresh in his mind. "That was a child." The images of her sunken and pale skin would not leave his mind. Neither would the step-mother's face, her empty black eye sockets, her flesh a loose puddle under her clothes. He knew that sleep would be difficult tonight.

Salinger poured two generous glasses of brandy from the Mercer's well-stocked pantry and passed one to Duncan. "Drink this. It will take the edge off, and don't give me any crap about drinking on duty. I need this as much as you do and no one's going to blame us for it after what we've been through."

When they first arrived on the scene, Rick Mercer was in hysterics. Dr. Woodhouse had to sedate him and have him sent away to the hospital. Duncan felt sorry for the man; losing both a child and spouse to murder would be devastating. He downed his drink, and the images left his mind for a second, as the drink reminded him that feeling is a natural part of life.

Salinger knew the feelings of burden, anger, and fear that Duncan was going through, for he felt them just as strongly. Right now, his anger was mostly directed at Sally McKinney who tried to shove her way onto the crime scene earlier. She had arrived only moments after they had the scene secure; how she had found out about it so quickly he didn't know, but he intended to find out.

"Damn her all to hell," he whispered sharply.

"What Chief?" Duncan looked up from his drink, his eyes wet with unshed tears.

"Nothing," he smiled reassuringly. "Come on; let's wrap up here so we can get out onto the streets and help find this psycho." Salinger swallowed his drink, quickly and headed outside.

They left the Mercer's immaculate kitchen and locked the door securely behind them. Salinger felt hollow as the door clicked shut. The scene had been gruesome, both bodies still haunting him. After Dr. Woodhouse had removed the bodies, they had spent a couple of hours combing the area for clues, only to come up empty-handed. Salinger gave one last look at the shed as he walked through the dark yard. A slight movement along the bushes caused his heart to race. He drew his gun automatically and placed a restraining hand on Duncan's shoulder.

Duncan, startled by the chief's grip, gasped and almost tripped over his own feet. He looked in the direction that the chief was facing, seeing nothing he raised his eyebrows in question.

"Shh!" Salinger hissed and pointed in the area where he saw the bushes move. They stood still listening to the wind as it rustled through the branches. After what felt like an hour to Duncan but in reality, was only thirty seconds, the movement came again. Salinger lifted his gun pointing it at the shadow that formed on the shed wall. "Freeze! Police!"

A small black shape flew out of the bushes racing towards them. Duncan jumped back, tripped over his own heels and fell flat on his ass.

"Jesus Christ! A fucking cat," Salinger lowered his gun back into its holster, "I almost shot a fucking cat," his breath rushed as his heart pounded. "Are you alright?" He looked at Duncan still sitting in the damp cold grass. The chief felt like an ass now, he was too jumpy, and he knew that could be dangerous. If it had been a person what would he have done, shot them without warning? These murders were affecting him worse than anything ever had. He just had a strange feeling about this one. He extended a helping hand to his constable, wondering if the drink was a good idea after all.

Duncan took the chief's outstretched hand and wondered the same exact thing, though he wasn't about to say it. All he wanted right at this moment was to go home, shower and drink a bottle of tequila of his own. He dreaded the long night ahead. When all was said and done, they still had to go back to the office and begin the long, arduous job of filling out endless mountains of paperwork. Although right now, filling out forms would be a blessing as long as it kept him safe in a well-lit office. He had to admit he was scared stiff.

Lucy Walkers Residence, 9:30 pm

Lucy jumped, and the rocking chair creaked. Startled by the noise, she let out a small cry and gripped the wooden arms in fear then realized that she had fallen asleep. *Just a dream*, she thought, *poor Misses Barnes*. Lucy gagged as the horror of it filled her mind. She had to stop herself from thinking about it. The scene was atrocious, and she knew it would be one she'd never forget. She stood up from her chair clutching her stomach; she needed to get some sleeping pills from the bathroom. Maybe then, she would be able to lie down and get some proper rest.

Glancing at the clock above her collection of glass trinkets, she saw that she had been asleep in her chair for hours. Her small bungalow lay in darkness, for she had nodded off when it was still light outside. Oh my, she thought, the shock from this morning must have worn me out. She felt so alone at that moment, unlike any loneliness she had ever felt before. She was used to life alone, her only friend was Judith Barnes, and she preferred it that way. The whole town thought she was a crazy old spinster, living a quiet life. Lucy was not a popular lady, too skinny and unattractive. She cleaned apartments and tended to people's homes when they were away. Everyone trusted her implicitly, but no one ever tried to get to know her. She was reserved and kept all her relationships on a business level. With the exception of Mrs. Barnes, who had taken to Lucy even when everyone else turned her away. No matter how many times Mrs. Barnes insisted in her quiet librarian's voice, "Call me Judith dear." Lucy would address her as Mrs. Barnes, out of a deep respect for her elders. Now she longed for that friendship back. There would never be a replacement for her friend. That hurt most of all.

Lucy flipped on the bathroom light moving directly to the toilet to relieve herself. When she caught a movement in the mirror, she froze. Her heart thumped into her throat as two red glowing eyes stared at her from down the hallway casting their reflection in the mirror. She stumbled backward and slipped on the pink bath mat. Her feet tangled together causing her to lose her balance and fall sideways. Lucy saw the porcelain toilet rising up to meet her face but knew it was too late; she hit it hard, and darkness flooded her eyes.

Blood began to flow from a deep gash along her hairline; it quickly soaked through the mat. She fought to keep the darkness at bay. Something inside her told her that if she did not get up this instant, she would die.

A scream formed on her lips as the glowing eyes moved around the corner. When she saw it was the cat she closed her eyes and licked her dry lips. *It's just the cat*, she thought. Her pounding heart slowed considerably. She felt the presence of the cat as it moved closer to her. She reached for it knowing she was not alone in her time of need. However, something didn't seem quite right. She heard a slurping sound and a shiver raced down her spine.

Lucy opened her eyes slowly, and dizziness brought a fresh wave of nausea to her stomach. With great effort, she turned her head slightly towards the sounds. The cat was inches from her face lapping up the blood. As she looked into its eyes, she knew the cat was evil. The red glow came not from the light catching the cats' pupils but from deep within its soul.

Then it licked its lips, appearing to grin, and its mouth opened strangely.

She hissed at the cat in an attempt to make it move away, and the cat hissed oddly in response. Pain rippled through her head, and she felt faint again. "Nooo," she moaned groggily.

Then the will to live returned to her, bringing a strength she didn't know she had. "No," she yelled in defiance. "Get away from me!"

Ignoring the fierce pain, she knew she had to run.

She stood too fast and had to make a quick grab at the counter to keep from falling back to the floor. Lucy kicked the cat as hard as she could into the corner, though it seemed heavier and meatier than average, and scrambled out of the bathroom, running as fast as she could on wobbly legs.

The cat gave a high-pitched screaming growl of outrage at losing its tasty meal and turned after her, not far behind.

The house lay in darkness; a faint circle of light from the bathroom illuminated the hallway. Lucy's head pounded, and bile rose in her throat. The very idea of some horrendous monster chasing after her was enough to make her believe she had hit her head a little too hard. She couldn't help but wonder if right at this moment she was laying on the bathroom floor bleeding to death, or deep in a coma. This all felt too much like a nightmare. Still, she had to drive on; she had to get away.

She braced herself against the wall chancing a quick glance behind. Terror gripped her heart as she saw the cat crouched on its hind legs ready to pounce. She screamed and pushed herself from the wall and raced blindly towards the front door. She knew the layout of her house well enough to get around in the darkness.

Lucy flailed her arms as her foot hit the edge of the couch and she went down hard on her knees. Gasping for breath, she scrambled to get back to her feet. Her left hand slipped under the cushion, which caused her to slide forward. As she threw her weight towards the couch, she felt a burning pain in her right ankle. She looked back and saw the cat's mouth had somehow, impossibly, opened wide enough to engulf her ankle. The pain grew unbearable. Terror overrode her senses, and she reached out to grab the first thing she could. Her hand closed on a glass figurine, a ballerina poised in a graceful pirouette and she stabbed the fragile glass towards the animal. Screaming like a banshee, she poured all her fear into that one moment. The figurine came straight down just as the thing looked up. The tiny pointed toes of the dancer penetrated one of the glowing red eyes causing the creature to release its acidic suction on Lucy's leg.

The cat rolled around on the floor, a green pus looking liquid seeping from its eye as it wailed a high-pitched screech. Lucy could now clearly see the mouth full of pulsating suction cups, like those of octopus tentacles.

"WHAT ARE YOU!" She cried out but was not going to wait around to find out.

She now knew what had happened to Mrs. Barnes, she had to get away from it and find the chief, to warn him.

☐

The Mercer Residence, 10:00pm

It was dark as Sally McKinney finally left the Mercer farmstead. The chief had kicked her out when she approached him, but he hadn't seen her hanging around the woods watching them survey the scene. Now she hurried across the gravel driveway looking skyward at the ominous clouds low overhead, bringing the promise of rain. Shivering, she rubbed her arms through the thin Tweed coat that did nothing to dispel the cold autumn air. Sally realized that she had not been prepared in any way for mountain living, not only had she underestimated the townspeople but also the weather.

Tomorrow I'll go and buy some warmer clothes, she promised herself as she hopped into her Range Rover. She had parked in a hidden pullout some ways down the road. Sally cranked the heater to full blast only to be welcomed by more frigid air. As she reached out to turn the heater down, a call came over the police scanner. She pulled the hand scanner out of her purse and turned up the volume.

The chief's assistant, Millie's voice sounded whiny over the scanner, grating on Sally's nerves. "I don't like that woman," Sally mumbled, then shook her head and admonished herself for being petty. Just because Salinger is sexy is no reason to be spiteful towards this helpless hick town woman. Sally chuckled softly at the thought of Millie having a fling with the chief as if that would ever happen. She listened as one of the constables reported that everything was looking right in town. Disappointed, she hit the gas in anger, tore out of her hidey-hole and, with a rain of gravel flying behind, headed for the highway.

As Sally sped down the empty highway, she thought about what she was able to witness before the chief noticed her there. She saw Mrs. Mercer's body lying on the cold ground outside of the shed, her head disappearing inside. And, the way the body was so flat against the ground was the oddest thing of all, it appeared as if a great weight had fallen on top of the woman crushing her flat. Yet there were no signs of blood on the body or ground around her. *Very strange indeed*, she thought.

As she crested the steep hill, an unexpected form flashed passed her vision on the roadside. "What the hell!" Sally yelled and stomped on the brakes causing the truck to pull over the centerline. Correcting her angle, she came to a complete stop on the soft shoulder and glanced in her rear-view mirror.

Standing on the side of the dark road behind Sally's Rover was a skinny woman, her thin gray hair hanging over her eyes. The woman sprinted to the stopped vehicle.

Sally reached over and made sure the passenger door was locked. There was no way she was going to let a stranger into her truck with these murders happening. Of course, being new in town, everyone was a stranger, but this person was frightening, to say the least. She watched the women as she closed in. She noticed that the women didn't have a coat and was smeared with dirt or possibly blood.

The women reached the door and pulled at the handle when it did not open she looked down and saw that the lock was engaged. As she lifted her head to gaze into the interior, Sally saw the gaunt, pale face and blood-stained cheeks.

"Please, open the door," the woman pleaded.

"Who are you?" Sally asked through the thick glass, the only thing keeping her from harm, which at the moment was not reassuring.

"M....my name is Lucy Walker. I live just over the ridge. Please, we must hurry and get help."

When Sally heard the name Lucy Walker, she immediately made the connection to the death of Judith Barnes. Lucy was her housekeeper. Sally unlocked the door, allowing Lucy to jump in with a blast of frigid night air.

"What happened to you? Were you in a car accident?" Sally asked the shivering woman and scanned the area to see if the woman's car was in the ditch nearby.

"No, uh ... I don't have my car." Lucy replied through clenched teeth, she wasn't going to explain that she had to run from her house, without her keys or purse. "I was uh..." She wasn't sure what to tell this stranger. "I was attacked in my home," she pointed through the trees to where her little house stood. Can you take me to the police station? Please hurry!" Her eyes searched the darkness.

"Is he following you?" Sally's heart rate escalated at the prospect of seeing the killer first hand. A vision of breaking the top story and getting back to the big leagues in Vancouver suddenly lifted her spirits, and she considered dropping her passenger off and coming back to check it out. She slammed the lever into gear and hit the gas.

Lucy turned her head and watched the road spinning away behind them. Seeing nothing around, she replied. "I don't know if it followed me or not."

Sally lifted her foot slightly off the gas pedal. "What do you do mean, it?"

"What?"

"You said, *it*." Sally glanced at Lucy and seeing her bewildered look repeated what Lucy had just told her. "You said, I don't know if *it* followed me or not. What do you mean *it?*"

Lucy turned her eyes away from Sally; she could see that already she had been mistaken about trying to warn people. They would think she was crazy and lock her away for the rest of her life. She sat silently watching the dark road in the side mirror. "Please just take me to the chief ok."

Noting the blood on the woman's head, Sally said, "I think I should drop you at the hospital first."

"No!" Lucy shivered and glared at the redheaded stranger. "I need to talk to Charles. Now!"

"The chief's not at the station right now," Sally said, then she saw the look of horror on Lucy's face, knew she said the wrong thing. "Hey, look," she soothed, "I'll drop you off at the station, you can file your report there, and one of the other officers will help you until the chief gets in. At least there, you know you'll be safe. Alright?"

Lucy chewed self-consciously at her lower lip and conceded to Sally's idea with a nod of her head. Anything was better than going back to her own house, that thing might be lying in wait anywhere along the way.

They drove back to town in silence, each thinking their own jumbled thoughts about the horror that was happening in North Falls.

The Bowan Residence, 10:00 pm

Brenda Bowan laughed as her friend Margaret flopped back onto the plush couch. They'd both had too much vodka and, despite the events going on, they were giggling like a couple of schoolgirls while spinning tales about old high school boyfriends. They met each other ten years ago when they both started working at City Hall. Margaret was in the town planner's office and Brenda as the mayor's personal assistant. Most of the town folk treated Brenda like she was Mayor Wainfleet's spy and completely avoided her. While others continually plagued her in the shopping mall or grocery store, with their problems, as if she had the power to aid them. Anyone who cared to take the time and get to know Brenda knew that she was an honest woman and a decent regular citizen of North Falls.

Margaret was recounting a love scene that she once played out with a young man, and Brenda was hanging on every word. "Ooohh….he was HOT! Girl, let me tell ya, I haven't had action like that in…." she paused, rolling her pale blue eyes back to think about it. "I'd say six years. And they've been long years too."

They both laughed, agreeing that the "good lovin," had been few and far between in the past few years. Especially for Brenda with her own young man in the house to think of, plus she hadn't wanted a serious relationship since the passing of her husband not long after moving to North Falls. Sure, she had the occasional fling, but always short-term and Brenda deterred them from getting too close. Margaret, on the other hand, was single and carefree. Her only worries were work and which way to flip her short cropped blonde hair. Brenda loved her friend, and instead of envying her, Brenda decided long ago to live vicariously through Marg's wild experiences. They got along wonderfully in this fashion.

Leaning forward Brenda grasped her friends' hand. "Thank you for being here with me tonight, I know that you probably had to cancel a hot date."

Marg slipped closer to Brenda, placing a comforting hand on her shoulders. "Don't be silly. In this dead zone of a town, all the cute ones, I've already had." Marg ended in a deep voice pretending to be a man, making them both laugh so hard that they almost spilled their drinks. Margaret stopped laughing, lifted her head and looked towards the curtained window. "Shhh," she whispered placing a manicured finger over Brenda's lips. Brenda hiccupped sat up straight and looked nervously at Marg.

"What?" Brenda whispered back. Then turned towards the window where Marg was looking.

"I thought I heard a noise from outside," Marg replied quietly and stood up to move towards the curtain.

Brenda followed behind her friend, all the laughter gone from her now as her throat seized tight with fear. *Jeez*, she thought, *now I do wish Dougie were here.*

They moved stealthily across the floor, both women listening carefully as the wind gusted outside. Soft music floated through the room from the stereo. Reaching the window at the same time, they stood on each side, looking at each other trying to decide the next move. Should they take a chance of peeking out and seeing a large ax-wielding man standing there waiting to kill them? Or should they wait silent as church mice, to hear defined footfalls in the brittle grass?

Marg made the first move; she quietly clicked off the floor lamp standing beside her. Now the light would not reflect on the window when she looked out. Giving Brenda a thumbs up, Marg gently parted the edge of the curtain, lifting it only inches away from the window so that if there were anyone out there, they would not notice the slight movement.

Brenda clutched her drink, as though it would be a good weapon, should the situation arise for her to need one, and held her breath as Marg looked outside. "Well?" She breathed silently.

Marg waved a finger to signal for another minute. Then Marg dropped the corner of the curtain and smiled at Brenda. "Just a fucking cat!"

"OH GOD! You realize you scared the life out of me," Brenda said, patting her heart.

"Hey, me too," Marg countered. "I'm the one who heard the noise after all. Jeez, if we left our safety up to you we'd be dog meat already!"

Brenda swatted playfully at her friend. "At least I'm not paranoid and hearing every little kitty in the neighborhood...Ah fuck." she finished.

"What?"

Brenda glanced around the living room. "Have you seen Sneezer at all tonight?"

"Come to think of it, no I haven't."

"Let's go see if that's him out there, I can't leave him out, or he may run off, and then Doug will never forgive me." Brenda moved towards the kitchen to retrieve their coats.

☐

The Salinger Residence, 10:00 pm

Bobby Salinger squirted a glob of Gel into his palm carefully swiping it through his jet-black hair, pushing and pulling at it until it stood up on his head in all directions. Perfect, he thought, slapped his sticky hands across a damp towel, and then went to his room to finish preparing for the night he had planned. The telephone rang faintly under the heavy metal that blasted from his bedroom. He slid down the oak railing and leaped through the sparsely furnished living room grabbing the phone off the hook on the kitchen wall.

"Yello!"

"Bobby, what took you so long to answer the phone?" Chief Salinger's angry voice bellowed over the lines.

"Oh…hi dad. I was in my room listening to music and didn't hear the phone. What's up?" He asked wiping a smudge of gel from behind his ear.

"Listen, I'm not going to be home until very late, or maybe not at all, but with everything that's happening around here, I don't want you staying alone. Can you call a friend and have their parents come pick you up?"

Bobby turned and looked at the time on the microwave. "Dad, do you realize that it's 10:00 already? And I have a car ya know."

Salinger sighed rubbing a nervous hand through his hair. He was stressed enough with everything happening, the last thing he needed was the added worry of his son. Times like these, which were rare in North Falls, magnified the loss of his wife. Since her death a few years back, the chief would have delegated jobs to his constable's and been home already. Tonight, that was not an option, he had to be with his men. "Look, I know very well what time it is, and I know you have a car, but I don't want you on the streets alone with the curfew in place. I would personally come home and drop you off somewhere, but I can't leave right now. So please just call around, get with some people, then call me through dispatch and let me know where you'll be."

"Sure dad. No Problemo...I'll call you back soon."

"Ok, and Bobby..."

"Yeah?"

"Please be careful. Bye."

Hmm, that was strange, Bobby thought. *He never seems to care that I'm home alone most of the time. Oh well, this is working out even better than I'd planned.* Bobby smirked and rubbed his palms together like an evil mastermind, then he called his friend Kevin.

Bobby and Kevin devised a plan on how to get away from both their parents and get a bush party started. Then Bobby called back to dispatch, and Millie put him through to his father. He told his Dad that he'd be spending the night at Kevin's house, and promised to check in again the next afternoon. Salinger agreed with his son, Kevin was a good kid, and he knew his parents as decent people and felt safer knowing that his son was not going to be home alone under the current circumstances.

As soon as Bobby got off the phone with his father, he set about making numerous other phone calls to all his friends from school and asking them to pass along the message to their friends. "This is going to be the best party ever," Bobby said to the empty house as he raced upstairs to finish preparing himself for the wild night ahead.

☐

The Shaw residence, 10:30 pm

Katlin was checking her email on the shared family computer, while Doug cleaned up the scrabble game they just finished. She leaned over the keyboard her dark hair falling softly onto her pale hands as she typed in her password. There was the usual "junk" email, which annoyed her, and she deleted. The next email was entitled "Party" as the subject.

"Hey, check this out," she called over her shoulder

Doug tossed the tiles haphazardly into the box and pushed the lid on top of the jumbled mess. "What is it?"

"I received an e-mail from a girl at school." Katlin read the letter out loud while Doug stood over her shoulder reading along with her.

Party Tonight at Bear Lake. Use old side logging road for safety and be SURE to have a solid and confirmed cover! Everyone who's anyone will be there tonight starting at 11:00pm. B.Y.O.B. And Don't Get caught!!!!

Katlin turned her chair slightly towards Doug; he was standing so close that she could smell the sweetness of the cola that he was drinking earlier. Looking into his almond color eyes, her heart skipped a beat. *Damn it*, she cursed herself, *stop thinking like that he's your best friend for Christ sake.* Clearing her throat nervously she asked him what he thought of the party.

Doug moved to a chair along the wall beside Katlin's desk. He braced his muscular arms on his knees resting his chin on his hands. "I don't think it's a good idea, Kat. I mean look at what's happened here, not to mention that there is a curfew. Do you have any idea how much trouble everyone would be in if we got caught? And besides how on earth would we get there? Ride our bikes? That's like at least ten miles, in the dark, plus it's cold."

Katlin deleted the message, then she went directly to the delete file and dumped it as well. She made sure the message was gone entirely from her computer, that way if any partygoers ever got caught no one would know that she had the information about it.

"You're right," she said. "We don't need any of that hassle in our lives right now, not for some stupid party where a lot of assholes from school will end up. Ok so now what do you feel like doing?"

Doug grabbed Katlin's hand. "Let's go to the den and watch a movie, a comedy preferably."

In The Night

Rita Mae Logan took a long swig from the greasy cup as she rubbed the sweat from underneath her saggy breasts. While her husband, Harlan banged loudly through the dirty kitchen, swearing at god only knew what, and slamming the small cupboard doors. Rita Mae continued to ignore his complaints, as she always did and shushed him loudly when the news returned from commercials. She sat on the nicotine yellowed couch and waved her hand up and down as she tried to quiet Harlan. He grabbed a bag of cookies and sulked into the living area where he plopped sullenly beside his three-hundred-pound, toothless wife.

When the story about the death of Judith Barnes ended, and the reporter gave the curfew orders, Rita Mae really flew into a rage. "How dare they tell us what we can and cannot do!" Her voice echoed around the small space. "Just who do they think they are? Do they come out here and help us when we have troubles? NO! All the cops around here do is cater to these whiny rich people and ignore us poor folk. Those assholes, I'll show em' a thing or two!" Rita Mae's face grew red with her tirade and spittle flew from her mouth as she got louder.

Harlan knew there was no point in trying to talk sense into Rita Mae at times like these. She enjoyed her tantrums as much as he enjoyed his. As a matter of fact, just watching this beast of a woman rant and rave was making his cock grow in his pants. He leaned over and grabbed a fist full of her short-permed hair, pulled her head back and climbed onto her wobbly round belly.

"Shut up women fore I shut you up!" Harlan yelled into her reddening face.

"Oh, you thinks yous a tough man do ya. Well, come on you little FUCK! Show me what you got." Rita Mae wrapped her wide hand around Harlan's' throat while spreading her legs for him to work his way easier between her monstrous thighs. She loved it when he got rough.

Just as Harlan was about to give Rita Mae a stinging slap for the pleasure of it, a crash from outside stopped his hand cold in mid-swing.

Rita Mae pushed herself forward knocking Harlan to the floor as she looked at the front door. "What the fuck was that?"

"Well, how the hell should I know?"

"Go look dumbass!"

Standing up, Harlan adjusted his withering penis. "Juesus women, why the hell don' you get off that lazy ass and do somptin' for a change."

Rita Mae scowled at Harlan as he walked over to the door. "Don't be such a chicken and just look wouldya."

"Huh," Harlan grunted back, "hold your hat." He shoved the front door open into the dark night.

Rita Mae leaned over trying to see past him, too lazy to even stand from her spot on the couch.

"I don' see not'ing out here." Then movement from the high grass that surrounded the trailer caught his eye. "Uh wait a sec. Ah, it's just a cat."

"Well then fuck face, shut the bloody door, you're lettin the cold in."

"Here cat. Come here cat," Harlan called out to the animal that was crouching out by their dilapidated car.

"What the fuck! I don't want no stinkin' animals in here. You're enough to deal with," Rita Mae hollered.

Harlan stepped out of the trailer disappearing from view. He grew up with a cat and suddenly kind of missed having one. Even though Rita Mae would never allow one inside, perhaps he could feed it, and pet it in the yard. If he could coax it to stay.

Tall dry weeds surrounded their small trailer; they blew softly in the cold night wind sending chills up Harlan's back. Behind him, dim light shined through the open trailer door. Standing where the grass began, Harlan peered into its depth. The grass stretched out in front of him for only a few feet, before it hit the edge of the Forest. The light of the full moon waxed and waned between the fluffy grey clouds, making visibility low.

He began to shiver through his thin shirt. Parting the grass in front of him he called out to the animal that lurked in its depth. Poor thing must be hungry, he thought. He could still hear Rita Mae yelling at him from inside the trailer. Shivering with the cold now, he decided to give up on the cat. As he turned to go back in, he noticed two red eyes staring at him from underneath the trailer.

"Now how on earth did you get over here kitty?" He bent down and reached his hand out towards the cat. Noise from behind him caught his attention. As he turned to see what it was, there was a loud screech in his ear. Harlan jumped, and something thudded against his back hard enough to knock him off balance. He rolled landing on his side facing the underside of the trailer.

Rita Mae stopped yelling when she heard the thud and a scuffle from outside. Pulling her bulk across the couch, she inched her way to where she had the best view of the door. Still, she could not see directly outside. Leaning as far over the couch arm as her weight allowed, she called out. "Harlan! Stop fucking around and get your ass in here, mister!"

She stopped and listened, peering at the dark slab of night through the open door. She no longer felt the cold air as her heart pumped with fear. She held her breath trying to see if she could hear Harlan sneaking towards the door. All she heard was some odd sucking sounds. *What the hell is he doing there, sucking himself off!* She thought wryly. *Ya, he wishes.*

With a grunt of exertion, Rita Mae hauled her body off the couch. She inched her way left for a better view out the door. Still, all she saw was blackness. Her weight shifted the trailer as she moved slowly towards the narrow opening.

"Harlan, you ass, if you jump out at me I swear I'll rip your cock off!" Satisfied with her warning, she wobbled closer to the door. She put her hands on either side of the open door to help support her weight. What she saw when she looked outside nearly stopped her heart.

Harlan, or what was left of what used to be Harlan, lay in a puddle of flesh and clothes.

Retching, Rita Mae threw her hands over her mouth and without her arms for support, she fell headlong out into the dirt. She narrowly missed the cinderblocks they used as steps and landed with a thud, and a curse, in the square of light from the doorway.

Spitting dirt and blood, she pushed herself onto her side away from the Harlan puddle and yelled, "What the fuck? Harlan?" She poked at his clothes, and they sloshed like jelly under her touch. Her stomach flipped again, but her breath was taken from her when she saw the multitude of red eyes glowing from underneath the trailer.

Rita Mae's screams pierced the quiet night as a team of screeching cats rushed towards her.

☐

Bowan Residence 10:45pm

Sneezer wouldn't come in when called, so Brenda and Margaret both threw their coats on and headed out into the cold night. Stepping away from the porch, leaving its glowing light behind, Brenda flicked on her flashlight. "Where did you see the cat?"

"Over by the bushes," Marg answered pointing past the lawn.

Holding hands, they moved as quietly as possible across the cold grass. Even though they were together, both women felt nervous about being outside in the open. They walked slowly scanning the area for the cat.

"This is silly you know," said Brenda. "We're acting like a couple of schoolgirls sneaking out for the night."

Marg laughed. "Yeah but it sure beats hanging at home on a Friday night."

Brenda rolled her eyes at Marg, letting go of her hand. "Well that may be so, but I'm not going to be caught holding your hand like a chicken."

"Brock, brock," Marg laughed as she made chicken noises. "I was only letting you hold my hand cause I thought you were lonely or something," she continued to tease Brenda.

"In your dreams woman."

"Yeah, I know you don't flip that way."

"Shhh…" Brenda stopped near the holly bush. She lowered the flashlight so she could see underneath its dense leaves.

Marg crouched down looking at the spot where the light was illuminating the ground, then shook her head and whispered. "I don't see anything. But I hear it. Sounds like it's coming from deeper inside. Wait, why am I whispering?"

"So we don't scare the cat. Silly," Brenda whispered back.

"Well, it's your cat. Why don't you just call it?"

"I've got the heebie-jeebies, that's why," Brenda smiled, uneasy about using a normal voice out in the dark yard. "Here Sneezer, come on kitty. Come here Sneezer," she snapped her fingers a few times trying to draw its attention. What she thought was odd, though, was that she knew Doug had brought the cat in before he left. Unless the cat had gotten out when Marg came over, she reasoned to herself. She listened for a moment hearing no more noise, she crouched down shining the light as far under the bush as she could reach. All she saw was darkness. She grabbed the lower branches and lifted up the leaves to try and get a better view. Glowing red eyes stared out at her.

"Ahh!" She hollered and fell backward on her ass in the damp grass. Her teeth clicked together and rattled her head, almost biting her tongue. "Shit!" She rocked up to her heels, her behind now wet.

"What is it?" Marg asked rushing to help her friend up.

"Damned cat!" Brenda exclaimed wiping a hand across her pants. "Scared the life out of me is all. He's hiding under the bush, and when the light hit its eyes, they glowed, and it just startled me."

"Oh. Well if he's still close to the house, why don't we just go in and let him come home on his own then," Marg suggested. The cold night air was penetrating her thin fall coat, and she knew that couldn't be good for the both of them. "You'll catch a cold now that you're wet."

"Yeah you're right we'll leave him out here. If he's too stubborn to come in where it's warm, then it's his own fault."

In agreement, they held each other close and headed cautiously back to the protection of the house, the two of them now shivering in stereo. At this point, neither of them were worried about the cat or the murderer; warmth was the first priority.

Bobby Salinger found it hard to take his time driving along the rough dark lane toward Bear Lake. He was in a hurry but his anxiousness to arrive and get to partying was overridden by the realization that it was best to take his time rather than get stuck and ruin the fun ahead. Riding shotgun beside him was his best friend Kevin, who had lied to his parents saying that he was staying at Bobby's house. So far, the plan was going off without a hitch. Turning left onto an even narrower road, the branches scraped against the side of his car. "Shit, I forgot how overgrown this road has gotten."

"Ah don't worry about it Bobo, it won't ruin your paint these are just saplings," Kevin reassured him with a wave towards the darkness.

"What the fuck do you know, butt breath, you don't even own a car!"

Kevin sulked in the bucket seat. He hated it when Bobby called him names or belittled him. He knew it was just a tough guy attitude that Bobby put on along with the piercings and tattoos, so he shut his mouth, as he always did, and ignored the remark.

Bobby noticed the silence for what it was, and as a way of apology punched Kevin in the shoulder. "Come on cheer up buddy, we're going to a party remember! Are you trying to bring us down, or what?"

Kevin pulled back and punched Bobby's arm in retaliation. "Not on your life pal. I'm ready to rock and roll!" He let out a loud whoop as they rounded the last bend and saw that there were already people milling around a bonfire.

"Looks like they started without us," Bobby said pulling the car off the road and into a clearing. He parked up near some bushes so no one would block him in. They climbed out of the car and hauled out a couple of cases of beer that Kevin had swiped from his old man.

Bobby yelled out. "Helloooo…. I'm here….and I gots beer!"

A few hoots and whistles met them from the darkness, but they weren't close enough to the fire yet to make out who was already there. It looked to Bobby as if about six or seven people had made it out before him. It was a shock with the curfew on, but at the same time, it was encouraging because that meant more kids would sneak out later on. Raising the case above his head, he hooted back to the group. Then two figures separated from the others and walked towards them. Bobby squinted into the dark. Nudging Kevin, he said, "Isn't that Sheila?"

Kevin raised his hands over his brow to cut the glare from the fire. "Yup it looks like it, and if that's Sheila, then the other one must be Mindy. I wonder what they want?"

Bobby grinned from ear to ear, showing off his white teeth. In the dark, against his black lips, he looked like evil itself. "What do you think they want butt wad? My tool." He demonstrated by squeezing his crotch.

Kevin groaned. He knew Bobby was no virgin, but he still was, and he wasn't happy with the prospect of losing his to either of these girls. Kevin tried to look nonchalant as the girls approached swaying their hips, their tight jeans leaving nothing to the imagination. He couldn't help but notice that neither girl wore a bra as their massive breasts bounced freely.

Sheila and Mindy could have been mistaken for sisters if the whole town hadn't already known them. Both girls had long blonde hair, slim but full figured and were the same age, only a month's difference in birthdays. They were sought after, and had, by most of the seniors in school. What the girls had in looks they lost in personality, they were shallow, rude, and got whatever they wanted. They became fast friends because no other girl in school could stand either of them. Now they were looking for fresh meat.

"Hey, Bobby how ya hanging?" Shcila asked coyly, rubbing her hand across his leather-clad arm.

"To the left."

Both girls laughed at his answer, while Kevin just stood there feeling uncomfortable. Bobby wrapped his arm through Sheila's, the slightly buxomer one, pulling her towards the bonfire. Mindy not wanting to be left out grabbed Kevin's hand and followed behind.

Kevin allowed Mindy to hold onto him, not wanting to cause a scene even though her hand was hot and sweaty and her overpowering perfume made him want to gag. Once they reached the fire, Kevin shrugged his hand away from Mindy under the pretext of opening a beer for her. Which he did, then stepped off to talk to another friend from school.

Mindy wasted no effort to stop Kevin and moved in on Bobby. Standing on the opposite side from Sheila, she began rubbing herself against Bobby's warm leg. Bobby looked at Sheila on his left, Mindy on his right and thought, *right-on, tag-team tonight*. Quite pleased with himself he guzzled his first of many beers while squeezing Sheila's ass with his free hand.

Police Station 11:00 pm

Sally pulled into the police station and double parked in front of the main doors. Lucy did not want to go inside until the chief arrived, so they sat in the dark listening to the radio while they waited. After about a 45-minute wait, a police car pulled in. With just a glance, she saw the chief's logo on the door and knew it was Salinger. Sally turned off the ignition and moved around to the passenger side to assist Lucy safely out of the Rover. "Steady," Sally braced Lucy to make sure she wasn't dizzy from the bump to her head.

While Lucy accepted the help, she also continued to insist that she was okay, but when she saw the chief, she began to cry.

"Now what?" Salinger mumbled to himself, running his hands through his hair, he was ready to be done with the redheaded reporter, who so far had been nothing but a nuisance. As Duncan slowly clambered out of the car, the chief shut off the engine and watched Sally through the rear-view mirror standing by her Rover waiting for him. *If things were only different,* he thought, *maybe we could have gotten together.* Shaking off that thought, he decided it best to stop stalling and got out of the car. Duncan was now holding Lucy who was inconsolable. "Ms.McKinney," he greeted her without warmth. "Would you care to tell me what exactly is going on here?"

Sally pursed her lips and gave a slight shrug, motioning to Lucy. "You'll have to ask her. I picked her up on the highway near her house, and she won't tell me a thing." Her stare bore into the chief's, "I did try, honestly."

Lucy's breath hitched as she tried to talk but she couldn't seem to stop crying. Duncan rubbed her shoulders and wrapped a protective arm around her feeling better himself for having someone else to care for.

"Come on," Salinger motioned, "let's get inside where it's warm. Then we can figure out just what is happening." He led the group into the police station, where he knew the brightness and warmth would help everyone feel safer, especially Lucy.

Once they got Lucy seated in the chief's office, Duncan wrapped a blanket around her shivering body and Millie hustled off to make fresh coffee for everyone. Sally sat quietly waiting for things to calm down, hoping she could learn some new information. Millie brought them each a fresh coffee and a warm cloth for Lucy's head, then hustled back to her desk.

"Duncan, can you start the paperwork for the Mercer's crime scene. I'll be back to help you as soon as I can." Salinger closed his door and moved behind his desk pulling out a pad to take notes. "How do you feel?" He asked Lucy, taking a quick sip of his much-needed coffee. Lucy was silent for so long that the chief voiced his concern for the gash on her head. "I think you should go to the hospital and have that looked at," he said.

Lucy shook her head. "I will go later," she smiled self-consciously at the handsome chief, "I must get this off my chest."

Salinger nodded gently and leaned into the desk, encouraging her to speak. "Can you tell me what happened to you?"

Taking a deep breath, Lucy closed her eyes and began to recount her story. "Well, I guess I fell asleep in my rocker, and when I woke up it was dark. I went to use the washroom, and when I clicked on the light, there were two glowing red eyes in the mirror. They scared the bejesus outta me, and I fell." She held the cloth to the wound on her head and glanced quickly from Sally to the chief.

"Are you sure you're up for this?" Salinger asked again.

Lucy sighed. "Yes, thank you." She twisted uncomfortably in her seat.

"Please continue," he prodded gently, needing to hear what happened, but also thinking a hundred different thoughts simultaneously.

"I...I'm not crazy. I know what I saw, and it's not going to sound good. I know this is going to be hard to believe but please just hear me out," Lucy stammered nervously, as her gaze flickered between the two. "When I was lying on the floor I heard a strange sound. I opened my eyes and Mrs. Barnes cat, Missy, was there..." Lucy stopped as her throat constricted with the memory of that horrible beast. She took a deep breath and a sip of coffee.

"Anyone have a smoke," she asked. Even though she had quit smoking four years ago, now she needed one more than ever. Sally silently handed Lucy a cigarette from her purse. Lucy fiddled with her smoke as she talked, occasionally taking a deep draw from it. "It wasn't a cat though, I just know it. The way it looked at me..." her breathing became stilted, and Sally placed a comforting hand on her back. Lucy resumed, "it had things in its mouth, look," she swiveled in her chair and lifted her ankle to show the raw area where the creature had clamped on. Then she started to cry again thinking of Mrs. Barnes being eaten by that thing.

Sally's eyes widened at the marks on Lucy's ankle, as the chief peered over his desk clucking his tongue. Neither knew what to make of her injuries, but the cat not being a cat was a bit far-fetched.

Lucy saw the grim looks in their eyes. "Well, I can see that neither of you, believe me, so…."

"Please Lucy, I know you are under great strain right now, we all are," Salinger tried to reassure her. "I'm going to have Constable Duncan take you to the hospital now, and I will personally go and investigate your house." He led Lucy to the door, supporting her by the arm, the blanket still wrapped around her.

"Duncan!" He yelled into the outer office.

The constable rushed in, and Salinger instructed him. "Take Lucy to the Hospital, then come back here and finish your report."

"Right away Sir," Duncan replied as he took Lucy's arm, and led her out of the chief's office.

Lucy's voice called down the hall, "Watch for the cats!"

Salinger sighed and turned around only to find Sally standing directly behind him. The momentary mixing of their breath was somewhat intoxicating for each of them, but propriety stepped between them and each adjusted their position by stepping back at that awkward moment.

"Ms. McKinney, I want to thank you for bringing Lucy here, but if you'll excuse me, I have a lot of work to attend to," he hoped to dismiss her quickly but had a feeling it wouldn't be that easy.

Sally remained planted firmly; she wasn't going to let him push her out again. Not after everything that had happened tonight. "I'm going with you," she stated matter-of-factly.

"What?"

"You heard me right. I'm going with you. I want some answers, and I think this town deserves them as well." Sally stood rigid, arms crossed.

Salinger rubbed his hand across his brow; exhaustion was already seeping into his bones. He knew it was going to be a long night. "I'm afraid that is impossible Ms. McKinney. This is an investigation, civilians are not allowed."

Picking up her purse from the chair she flung it over her shoulder as she stormed past the chief. "If you're not going to allow me to come along voluntarily then I'll just be in your face every time you turn around. I'm a public servant just like you; so, I'm going to do my job, with, or without your cooperation."

Rushing after Sally, Salinger grabbed her arm angrily spinning her around to face him. Millie stood up from behind her desk when she saw the scene being played out before her.

Sally yanked her arm out of his grip. "How dare you! Do you want me to tell the people what Lucy reported?"

Words faltered on his lips, he couldn't believe that she would use Lucy's story against him. "Don't you threaten me lady or I will have you arrested for obstructing justice." He hoped his threat would move her to back down; however, when the steeled look in Sally's eyes did not waiver, he knew he was in for trouble. He could have her thrown in the tank for the night, but he knew that would only add fuel to her fire, and he didn't need the hassle right now. Defeated he said, "Fine come with me as long as you promise to stay out of my way."

Sally finally looked away and pretended to adjust her purse on her shoulder trying not to gloat. She knew if she persisted, she would win but she was not going to screw it up by hurting the chiefs' pride.

Salinger saw the look on Millie's face. "Don't you start!" He held up his hand. "Just let me know if anything else happens." That said he led Sally out to his patrol car.

☐

Main Street, 11:45 pm

Heee…check out the legs on that one!"
Constable Wiley giggled as he pointed to the well-lit
department store across from where they sat eating
doughnuts. Constable Baker elbowed Wiley in the
ribs causing him to cough out part of his long john.

"God Damn it! Now look what you did!" Wiley
whined as he surveyed the mess at his feet.

Baker shrugged off Wiley's complaining. For all
he cared, Wiley could choke on his long john. It was
bad enough driving aimlessly around town let alone
being stuck with tubbo, Wiley. So far, the streets had
been quiet. They had watched all the townsfolk as
they headed home late from work, then continued to
cruise the roads seeing no one. After a couple of
hours of this Wiley began complaining he was hungry
so they had stopped at the late-night coffee shop,
which had no customers due to the curfew, and got
some coffee and doughnuts before the owner closed
up for the night. Now they sat in the empty parking
lot of Kmart while Wiley cracked meaningless jokes.

"Well," Baker said, "we might as well call up
Crow and see how he's making out."

Wiley laughed, "Yeah that poor bugger gets to be
alone in the wilds, what's he going catch a bunch of
trees!"

Baker gave Wiley a dirty look as he set down his coffee to reach for the radio mic. *What an insensitive bastard*, he thought. He pushed the button and spoke directly into the mic. "Unit 2, this is Unit 3 come in." Releasing the button, he waited for a response.

Wiley was silent, anticipating Crow's response.

"Ten-four, this is Unit 2, go ahead," Constable Crow's voice crackled over the radio.

Wiley leaned over Baker and grabbed the mic from his hand. "Hey, Crow! How's it going out there?"

Baker gave Wiley a dirty look but knew that any attempts to get the mic back would be futile, so he let Wiley talk.

"Boring as a visit to your mother," Crow replied stoically.

"You wish my mother would let you in her house."

"What's the matter, Wiley? Truth hurts?"

Wiley was about to retort when Chief Salinger's voice broke into their conversation. "Quit pissing around."

Baker jumped at the sound of the chief's voice, and Wiley willingly handed the mic back, he didn't want to be the brunt of Salinger's anger. "Sorry Chief," Baker, responded meekly.

In the patrol car with McKinney seated beside him, Salinger rubbed his brow as he avoided her heavy gaze. "Listen up, this is important. Ms. Walker was attacked tonight, and I want unit 2 to meet me at her house now. "You got that Crow?"

Crow clicked his mic. "I'm about five miles East, past the radio station, so I'll turn back and meet you there Chief."

"Unit 3, Baker and Wiley, you are to take over for Crow. Come West as so far, all our troubles have been out this way. Make sure people are staying inside their houses, we don't want any more incidents tonight." He purposely left out the fact that he was not alone, he didn't need to explain the already sticky situation over open airwaves.

"Oh great. I bet he heard us talking and wants to punish us by sending us out on Crow's duty," Wiley complained.

Baker shifted the gear from park to drive and said. "Hey, I'd rather drive around the empty streets looking for people, than go poke around a crime scene for hours with the chief."

Wiley nodded. "Ya, I guess."

North Falls General Hospital 11:45

Constable Mark Duncan pulled his cruiser into the hospital parking lot. It was almost empty this time of the night; the staff always parked in the rear of the building. He stopped in front of the emergency doors, expecting only to be here long enough to make sure Ms. Walker got checked in okay and then he'd be heading back to the station. On the trip over Lucy had been quiet; she hardly spoke at all only to answer a few of Duncan's' questions, which he kept light. He stayed away from anything that had to do with what was happening in town and never once asked her what form of trouble had befallen her. He could sense that she was distraught, and he did not want to disturb her more. Duncan knew that she'd talked to the chief, and he would be fully informed as to the situation later. Although he did want to know who had hurt her, he knew he'd have to be patient.

"Here we are," he said to her. Lucy didn't move at all, her eyes stayed locked in a stare out the window. Duncan stifled a sigh and stepped out of the car into the cold night. He moved around to the passenger side of the car and opened the door for her. Taking her arm gently he helped her out of the car. She came willingly but moved as if in a trance. The blanket was still wrapped around her shivering form. The constable placed an arm around Lucy's slender shoulders and led her into the hospital.

The fluorescent lights glared off the pale puke colored green and white tile floor. The waiting room was deserted and silent except for soft voices emanating from a television mounted on the wall near the ceiling. Duncan steered Lucy to a seat, where she sat down as soon as the back of her knees touched the blue vinyl. He walked over to the check-in window and peered through the glass. No one was in sight, so he rang the buzzer to alert them of his presence.

A nurse dressed in a pale pink uniform peered around a corner into the small cubicle. When she saw it was a police officer, she came to the window immediately. "Hello Mark, what's up?" Living in a small town had its advantages; many knew each other by name. The disadvantages were that everyone also knew each other's business, which could cause havoc at times.

Mark Duncan smiled at the pretty young nurse trying in vain to remember her name; it wouldn't come to him, so he smiled thinly at her. "I need to check in a patient tonight," he replied. Looking over his shoulder at Lucy, he told the nurse her name and said only that she had a head wound that needed attention. The nurse came around the counter and walked over to Lucy, as she walked past Duncan he noticed her name tag read Ms. Claiborne, *stupid*, he thought to himself, *some policeman I am, can't even notice the obvious.*

Ms. Claiborne knelt in front of Lucy and gently parted her hair away from the dried blood checking the wound. "Well she'll most likely need stitches," she said as more of a diagnostic note than anything. "Come with me, dear." She took Lucy's hand in her own and turned to Duncan. "Can you tell me what happened?"

Duncan cleared his throat. "Actually," he said, "I don't know, Ms. Walker talked to the chief, and he had me bring her in. Sorry." He shrugged.

"Ok, don't worry we'll take good care of her here. Do you want me to call the station later to let you know how she's doing?" Ms. Claiborne asked him.

"Yes, please do I…" Duncan stammered, he hated having to talk about Lucy with her standing right in front of him, even though she hadn't said a word herself. "I don't think Lucy has anyone else right now." He turned to leave then thought he should say something to the kind nurse. "Uh…Ms. Claiborne?"

The nurse had turned her back to him and was leading Lucy down the hall towards the emergency room. "Yes," she asked stopping and looking back at Duncan.

"Thank you." He tipped his hat towards her then turned and left.

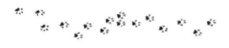

Midnight

Bear Lake, Midnight

The party had gotten into full swing; there was raucous laughter, plenty of drinks sloshing around, some necking and heavy petting. There were even a few - who were new to drinking - that had already passed out. The bonfire blazed brightly in the otherwise dark clearing, sending gray plumes of smoke ever skyward. Kevin had stayed clear of Bobby and his girls for the last hour and, luckily for him, Bobby was too preoccupied to notice. He hung with his other friend Clem, on the opposite side of the fire. Kevin laughed at a joke Clem just told, but his laughter turned into a groan when he saw Bobby and the two girls coming around the fire towards him.

"Hey, Kev!" Bobby yelled, approaching with a girl under each arm.

Oh great, Kevin thought, *he's coming to pawn one of them off on me*. When they got close, he noticed that both Sheila and Mindy were piss drink. Bobby looked a pretty soused himself. "What's up?"

"Me and these two lovely ladies here," Bobby said, causing the girls to giggle, "we're heading off into the trees for some privacy. Care to come along?"

Kevin shook his head; he knew this was going to happen as soon as he saw Sheila and Mindy. "Um…No thanks. I've kinda had too many beers if you know what I mean," he winked cryptically, hoping it would be enough to satisfy Bobby.

"Are you sure?" Bobby asked, then squeezed Shelia's large breast causing her hard nipple to push against the thin cotton sweatshirt. "There's plenty to go around."

Sheila squirmed against Bobby, her other breast pressing warmly against his side. Just then her hand snaked down over his bulging crotch.

Seeing this, Kevin blushed and hoped it was dark enough that no one would notice. "No really, go ahead and have a good time."

"Come on Bobby, I'm horny," Sheila moaned. "Forget him I think there's enough of you for the both of us. Right, Mindy?"

Mindy leaned past Bobby so she could see Sheila and said, "Oh yeah, there is definitely enough here for two." Then she tugged on Bobby's arm pulling them both towards the dark woods.

Bobby laughed as he was being led away; he couldn't believe his luck. *If I'm even luckier*, he thought eyeballing four bouncing breasts, *they'll do each other too*.

Kevin watched them walk off into the Forest. *He'll get a disease, I just know it.* Tired of all the smoke from the fire and the slight headache the beer gave him, he began to wonder why he even came to this party and only hoped he could find a ride home soon.

Lucy Walker's House, Midnight

As Chief Salinger's car rolled into Lucy Walker's driveway, both he and Sally, immediately noticed that the front door of the house was wide open. Dim light spilled from somewhere deeper inside. Sally unbuckled her seat belt and reached for her door handle. Being a seasoned reporter, she was accustomed to jumping into situations head first, but the chief had other ideas.

Salinger grabbed her wrist to get her attention. "Please?" He paused for a moment looking at her perfectly manicured hand, acutely aware that he had just felt something he hadn't felt in a long time, then he looked her in the eye. "First, we wait here for backup. Then my constable and I go in to make sure the perpetrator is gone." He couldn't help but notice how warm and soft her skin was. More than that, he noticed she did not resist his grasp. Heat rushed into his stomach, and he quickly released Sally's arm. Salinger sat back to watch his rear-view mirror for headlights.

Sally straightened herself in her seat and crossed her arms. She too had gotten a fluttering in her stomach, although she wasn't sure if it was from Salinger's touch, or because she was hoping to see the killer first hand. She didn't argue with the chief about his making her wait in the car, as long as he remained with her. They sat in silence contemplating each other. After what felt like an eternity, constable Crow's car pulled into the driveway behind them.

Salinger climbed from his car to meet up with Crow. He threw a look back to Sally, she had rolled her window down slightly to eavesdrop. But she could only make out a deep rumbling, the words had no distinction.

"Shit," she cursed under her breath; she hated being left out.

As their conversation ended, Salinger approached the passenger window and ducked low to see into the car. "Stay right here please, lock the doors and roll up this window." From behind him, constable Crow said something, as Salinger turned to reply, Sally saw them both releasing the leather clasps on their holsters. Turning back to Sally the chief said, "We'll be right back out, and then I'll let you in to look around once it's safe. If you spot anyone honk the horn, and I'll come out. Okay?"

He did not feel good about this and wished he would have left her back at the station. It had been a long time since a woman made him feel so conflicted and he just wasn't sure which idea would cause him more grief, leaving her out, or letting her in. It was distracting, to say the least. He watched Sally through the windshield as she leaned over the driver's' side to lock his door. She had to lean far over to reach, and her short skirt rose high exposing her silky thigh. His eyes drew towards her face when she moved back to roll up her own window. *Did she see me looking? No, it's too dark out here for her to tell what I was looking at.*

Behind him, Crow cleared his throat. "Ready sir?"

Salinger placed his hand over the revolver at his hip. "Ready Constable. Let's take it slow and careful."

"You can count on me Chief," Crow replied. He was no jokester, and that was why Salinger trusted him out on his own patrol and why he wanted him as back up here.

They moved slowly up the front walk, watching every angle of the house. They went up the front steps flanking the open doorway. Salinger nodded his head, and Crow crouched low as they stepped over the threshold, guns in hand.

Following procedure, they moved stealthily. As they entered the living room, Salinger flicked on the main light so they could see every corner clearly. The room was small, with a 32" TV on a simple console table. She had an old VCR player on a shelf with a selection of romance movies. Beside that, a curio cabinet housed some of her more valuable glass figurines. The room was pretty sparse and simple, with just a few knickknacks here and there. The coffee table was overturned, and Salinger noticed blood and another strange substance on the floor, near the couch. He pointed it out to Crow, who looked at it and nodded confirmation that he saw. Something had definitely gone down here.

There appeared to be nothing else disturbed here, so they moved on towards the hallway. Approaching the bathroom silently, and quickly waved his hand forward. Constable Crow understood the signal, rushed past the open bathroom door, and pressed his back flat against the wall on the opposite side of Salinger. Crow gave the negative sign that he saw no one in the bathroom as he had run by. Taking a deep breath, Salinger stepped into the bathroom doorway aiming his gun chest level. Crow was immediately crouching near Salinger's knees, his weapon also aimed into the empty room.

☐

Logan's Trailer Midnight

Baker and Wiley got back into their patrol car after checking the perimeter of the high school. "Fuck me," Wiley complained, "this is going to take all night."

Baker sat behind the wheel giving Wiley a rest from driving. Trying to ignore him, though, was like avoiding your own face in the mirror. "No, it won't take all night," he said as calmly as possible, then thought, *I would have to shoot myself if I had to spend that long listening to you.* "Look, there aren't that many farms out here, most of the people live in town. And besides," he said, the tiredness of having to point out the obvious showing heavily in his tone, "the chief and Crow are just around the bend at Walkers. They're close by if we need'em."

"Oh yeah! Fuck you!" Wiley exclaimed. "You're not the one who got a shotgun pointed at his nose."

Baker couldn't help but laugh.

"It's not funny, I almost peed my pants!"

"Stop! Or I'm going pee my pants!" Baker snorted, laughing so hard that his coffee filled bladder pushed painfully against his belt. "Well, what do you expect? It's the middle of the night, and there has been a curfew set, people are cautious." Baker nudged

Wiley's shoulder. "You should be thankful that people are careful and don't open the door to strangers."

Wiley threw his partner a dirty look. "Still I could have had my head blown off, and you think it's funny. It wouldn't be so funny if it happened to you, would it?"

"Oh, clam up. Hodges was just protecting his family."

Wiley huffed, slouched down in his seat and watched silently as the dark trees flew past his window. The car slowed down as Baker steered into an almost hidden driveway. He suddenly sat up straighter. "Where you going?"

"We have to check everybody. Chief's orders."

"Not them, too?"

"Yes, Wiley - even them."

"Fuck me." Wiley moaned. He hated the Logan's. They were a couple of foul-mouthed, dirty people and he had a run in with them a couple of years ago. Harlan had pissed on Wiley's shoes and when Wiley took a swing at him Harlan's fat wife, Rita Mae, flung her body at him knocking him to the ground. It was a scene that left Wiley both humiliated and intimidated by the Logan's.

Baker said nothing. He knew what had happened. Everyone in town knew. But, no one ever dared mention it in front of Wiley for fear of getting on his bad side.

The car rolled along the dirt track announcing their pending arrival at the trailer with the crunch of gravel. The Logan's rusty trailer looked like it had been abandoned for years, as it always did, but the two Constables knew different. As they turned toward the trailer, the headlights threw shadows over the trees, and they saw cats scattering every which way.

"What the hell," Wiley shouted. "Have they started a cat farm out here?"

Baker shrugged, too busy staring in awe at the cats. There must have been an easy hundred cats running around, hiding under the trailer, disappearing into the thick grass, fleeing the headlights as quickly as they could. He stopped the car at the end of the trailer. It sat boxy and silent lengthwise in front of them, so all they could see was the narrow window where the kitchen area was located. They could not see from this position that the front door was standing open. Putting the car in park, Baker turned to Wiley and saw that his face was pale. He poked at Wiley. "Not afraid of cats, are you?"

Wiley jumped at Baker's touch. "No!" He reached for the glove compartment where they stowed the flashlights. He tossed a flashlight at Baker, catching him off guard it bounced off his leg and rolled under the seat.

"Ah, what did you do that for?"

Wiley grinned. "Hurry up; you don't want to miss all the action." Then he opened his door and stepped out onto the gravel, leaving Baker hunched over digging for the flashlight.

Baker had to unbuckle his seatbelt so he could get a better reach under the seat. "There you are," he said as his hand closed over the cold steel. As he sat up and pushed the car door open, he heard Wiley scream. It was loud and piercing, almost like a woman's, yet not quite – more like when a man gets knocked hard in the nuts, and it sends his voice up a couple of octaves. Baker flung the door wide and raced towards the sound. Dust kicked up under his feet as he skidded around the side of the trailer. "Wiley?"

Wiley stood stock-still holding his arms straight out from his sides. His breath hitched in and out of his throat, and a low rasping sound followed each exhalation. "Don't bloody move," he said to Baker.

Baker wasn't sure what to do. *Has Wiley lost his mind, what the hell is he standing so strangely for?* He took a cautious step forward. His heart was still racing from the awful shriek that only a moment ago made him think Wiley had been attacked. Switching on his flashlight, he shined it on Wiley's back. Seeing nothing out of the ordinary, he took another step towards him. "What's wrong?"

Wiley turned his head to Baker's voice. "Shine your light on the ground at my feet."

Still not comprehending what had happened to his partner, and unsure if he wanted to find out, Baker slowly moved the light over the ground around Wiley's feet. What he saw, where Wiley's black police-issue shoes should be, was a miscellaneous jumble of clothing, which may, or may not, be a blanket and a deflated pink child's swimming pool. Baker looked quizzically at the man and thought, *that's it; Wiley's finally lost his marbles*. "What man? So, you stepped in someone's garbage, did a rat bite you in that pile of junk?"

Wiley hadn't moved the entire time, but his arms were getting heavy and beginning to shake. "Are you fucking blind?" He yelled, "THIS IS NOT GARBAGE!" Then he pointed to the mess under his feet, finally letting his other arm drop to his side. "I happen to be standing in what used to be…" he huffed trying not to vomit, "Rita…fucking Mae…fucking Logan. And, if you don't mind helping me out of…her…it…WHATEVER! I would appreciate it very much."

Baker's mouth dropped open. Now he could see it. What he thought was a pink pool and a blanket, was actually what was left of a person. He moved the light up to the head. Sure enough, he saw hair, a nose, and a sagging empty mouth. Wiley was standing about where her oversized stomach used to bulge outward, now it sunk in with the weight of his body, burying his shoes under loose flesh wrapped in a blue dress. Baker turned his head and puked, gagging and gasping for air.

"Help me," Wiley was on the verge of freaking out entirely, he needed to get out of Rita Mae, but he couldn't move alone. With each small movement, he could feel her empty flesh squishing under his feet, sliding him around like a giant slip-n-slide. He would never be able to eat anything soft again.

Baker stood up wiping the mess from his face. He didn't want to look at the ground anymore, afraid of what else he may happen to recognize in the oozing pile. He kept his eyes locked on Wiley and moved closer to him, shuffling his feet along the ground so he wouldn't end up in the same boat as his partner. He reached out and firmly grasped Wiley's out-stretched hand. Locking eyes, they both nodded.

Wiley squeezed Baker's hand tightly and jumped towards him. Baker pulled at the same time, and his feet came off of Rita Mae's deflated skin causing it to ripple in loose waves. Finally, clear of the body, Wiley gasped for air. "Oh gross-gross-gross," he shuddered. "What the fuck happened to her?"

Baker shook his head. "I don't know, but we'd better radio the chief right away and tell him to get out here ASAP."

Wiley looked at Baker. "Something bad is going on."

☐

Shaw Residence, Midnight

Katlin sat up, as the movie came to an end. She picked up the remote and pressed rewind then turned the lamp back on. If her parents knew they had been sitting in the dark so close together, while sharing a blanket, they would probably ban Doug from their house. *But, what they don't know can't hurt them*, Katlin thought glancing over at Doug. It had been wonderful sitting so close to his warm body. Her heart hadn't stopped pounding, even as they moved slightly away from each other. She wasn't sure how Doug felt about her, but she noticed that his face was a bit flushed.

Doug stood up and stretched his back. "Hum, not a bad movie. More geared to little kids though, don't you think?"

"Yeah, but it was cute, and Robin Williams is always funny, even when he plays an old lady," As she took the movie out of the VCR, she made sure to bend at the waist, so her butt was up in the air. *Was Doug looking*, she wondered and hoped that he was. She felt her cheeks redden at her own audacity. Turning to face him she asked, "So...what do you think is happening out at Bear Lake?"

Doug's face was beet red, he couldn't help but look at Katlin's behind when it was right there in his

~ 136 ~

face, and he liked what he saw. He hadn't thought of her in a sexual way, until tonight. When they snuggled up on the couch, and he felt her breast push against his arm or her sweet breath on his neck. He knew things were getting a bit risky with her parents being home, but he just couldn't help himself. He wanted to feel more of her, and he could tell from the signs Katlin gave out, that she felt the same way. As a matter of fact, when he began to have those thoughts he realized that Katlin had been giving him hints for a long time. He was just too stupid to notice before. Knowing that she wanted him as much as he wanted her made him a little uncomfortable, it would mean that their friendship may change, or even end if they tried anything.

Now that she brought up the party, he figured she was planning something. He shrugged his shoulders and acted as normal as possible, "I don't know, everyone will be drunk by now I guess," he looked at the clock, it read 12:00. "People might even be headed home."

"No way! It's just midnight they won't give up this early." Katlin smiled at Doug and wiggled her eyebrows up and down.

"You're nuts for thinking it."

"Ah…come on! My parents are sound asleep now. We can sneak out with the car, then we don't have to worry about freezing our butts off."

"I don't know Kat what if we get caught?" Doug was worried; he didn't want to be grounded for the next millennium. However, he definitely did not want to be away from Katlin now that the new feelings crept up on him.

Katlin pouted at him and stuck her hands deep into her jean pockets, so the waist pulled down showing her belly button. "Please? It would mean we'd have privacy. Out in the woods. No adults." She knew that'd get him. What guy could resist being alone in a car deep in the woods with a cute girl?

Doug's cheeks got hot again when he thought about the possibilities of being alone with Katlin. He wondered if she knew he was a virgin. *She must, she has been my best friend forever; she knows everything about me. Just as I know everything about her and I know she's still a virgin, so there's nothing for me to be scared of. Yeah right, only messing our friendship up,* he scolded himself.

"Well?" She prodded

"Ok," he said, "but if it gets too rowdy, we're coming straight home."

Raising her arm to salute him, she said, "Yes Sir!" She rushed around the room tidying up their mess, and they got geared up to go.

Lucy Walker's Residence, 12:30am

Sally sat in the dark car shivering as she watched the house closely. The chief had left the front door open when they went in, and she hadn't seen any movement for a while. Why haven't they let me know what's going on yet, she wondered. She glanced around the dark yard making sure nobody was hanging about. Sally opened her door and stepped out of the car. The cold night air swept under her skirt and again she wished she'd had time to run home and put some long pants on. She pulled her jacket tight around her neck and shivered as she headed for the front door.

She approached the steps listening for any sounds coming from inside Lucy's house. Hearing only the voices of the chief and his constable, she figured it was safe to proceed. Not wanting to startle the men, she knocked on the doorjamb as she entered. It wasn't much warmer inside because the door had been open for so long that the cold air dispelled any heat there may have been. "Hey!" she called out as she walked into the cozy, yet slightly disheveled, living room.

Chief Salinger stuck his head out of the bathroom with an irritated look on his face. "I thought I asked you to wait in the car?" He came down the hall towards her.

Sally stood her ground. "It's bloody cold out there, and you didn't come back to tell me it was safe. I took it upon myself to come in seeing as I didn't hear any gunfire," she replied. Then she noticed the spot on the floor where it was dark and wet looking, broken glass gleamed in the puddle, and a crystal ballerina figurine lay near the couch. "What's that?"

Salinger walked over to the mess. Bending down, he picked up the crystal figurine. Sally stood watching him over his shoulder. Holding the crystal between two fingers, he twirled it, and a green goop dripped from the broken off legs. Bringing it close to his face he sniffed the substances to see if it had any odor. "Uhh!" He exclaimed dropping the figurine back to the floor. "I've never smelt anything like that before."

"Any ideas as to what happened here Chief?" Sally asked as she looked around the room for her own clues.

"Sorry but I can't reveal anything to you regardless of what we have or have not found, you shouldn't even be here." Salinger stood up and walked back towards the bathroom where Crow was busy gathering evidence. He was trying his best to ignore Sally and the fact that she could be compromising his investigation, not to mention his job if anything went wrong tonight.

Sally followed behind him she had no intention of leaving his side and losing the first big break that might occur at any moment. When they entered the bathroom, though, she felt her stomach tumble at the sight of all the blood on the floor. Sally put her hand over her nose to cover the coppery scent as she watched the men stepping carefully around the mess.

"Anything," Salinger asked Crow.

Constable Crow shook his head. "This blood came from Ms. Walker's head, I'm sure of that, but there is something strange here," he pointed at the floor.

Salinger crouched down as best he could in the cramped space, trying to see what Crow had pointed out. "Yes, I see it. Do you have any bags on you?" He asked his constable.

"No sir."

"Sally would you please go to the car and get my evidence kit out of the trunk."

Without asking what they found- she knew he wouldn't tell her anyway- she held out her hand for the car keys, which he passed over wordlessly. She returned a couple of minutes later with a black briefcase. "Here," she passed it to the chief.

Taking the case from her, he opened it up removing the tools he needed and using tweezers picked up a small hard scale that lay on the edge of the blood. Placing it in a plastic bag, he held it up to the light to get a better look. It was about the size of one of his fingernails. As he turned it, it shimmered in the light like pearls, and iridescent colors reflected on the surface changing from green to blue to red.

Sally clearly saw the scale when Salinger held it up, and she wondered for the first time that night if what Lucy had told them about the cat being something other than a cat was true. She shivered again, but this time it was not from the cold.

The old station wagon bumped over the rough road. Katlin sat in the middle of the bench seat as close to Doug as she could get without interfering with his driving ability. She felt cozy and safe beside him but still felt a little frightened by the darkness surrounding them. This wasn't her first after dark-parents asleep- excursion, however, it was the first time she'd gone into the woods alone with a boy. Excitement mixed with fear and coursed through her veins; she was so unbelievably nervous that she actually trembled.

Tree branches appeared out of the darkness like the banshee come to howl their cries, as they screeched themselves against the car. It wasn't the first time along the way that Doug wondered just what they were doing out here. It was cold, dark, and, he had to admit, kind of spooky. *What if the party has already broken up,* he wondered. *Then we'll have to travel all this way back alone.* He pushed that thought away. *Just don't worry about it,* Doug told himself as he felt Katlin snuggle a little closer, *she must feel the same way I do after all it is lonely out here.*

They both breathed a sigh of relief as they rounded the last bend and could see a roaring fire with a group of shadowed figures moving around it. "See, I told you they wouldn't quit so early," Katlin said nudging Doug in the side as he pulled into an open spot on the grass.

Doug turned off the headlights then keyed off the ignition. He turned and faced Katlin. In the dim car, her face was covered in shadow; her long dark hair looked like a shroud around her frail figure. "Um…I just realized we don't have any alcohol."

Katlin adjusted herself to face Doug. Her hand found it's way between the open zipper of his jacket and touched his warm chest and said, "Who needs it? We won't be getting out of the car."

"Oh!" Doug cleared his throat, shifting uncomfortably behind the steering wheel. "But if anyone saw our headlights they might come over to check out who showed up so late."

Katlin smiled slyly at him. "That's ok; we'll be in the back anyway. No one will see us there; they'll just think we're in the crowd already." Without waiting for confirmation from Doug, she climbed into the back seat and began wrestling with the clasps that would release the backrest and fold down into a carpeted style bed.

Doug was both shocked and excited; who was this aggressive creature whom he thought he had known so well? Deciding to jump now and ask questions later, the rapid beating of his chest demanded it, and he climbed awkwardly into the back where Katlin sat waiting for him.

The Logan's Trailer, 12:30am

Constable Baker whirled around as a crash erupted from behind. Turning, he expected to see Rita Mae's deflated body lumbering up off the ground after him. His heart thumped fiercely in his chest as his light cast a feeble glow through the darkness. Beside him, Wiley jumped too. They saw nothing. Then the door to the trailer swung back, banging loudly against the siding.

"Jesus-Fucking-Christ!" Wiley exclaimed. "I almost had a heart attack." He clutched at his chest as though it was happening.

Baker was still shaking from the obtrusive noise, yet made damn sure to keep his light pointed high away from the mess on the ground. "You're not the only one," he said. Then he placed his hand on Wiley's shoulder; it was more to calm himself, but he hoped it would seem like a gesture to calm Wiley. He wanted nothing more than to get the hell out of there. "Let's go call the chief before we head into the trailer to check it out."

Wiley turned to Baker an incredulous look on his face. "What do you mean, check it out?"

"We have to secure the crime scene, Wiley." It wasn't like he wanted to go into the trailer either but it was their jobs after all.

Wiley shook his head. "No fucking way buddy! If you go in, you're going it alone." Seeing Bakers eyes widen, with both shock and fright, he was racked with guilt. "Aw! Don't' give me that look, Baker. I just walked into what used to be a person. Literally! A very fat person," he added "but still! There is no way in hell I am going into that trailer, you can just wait until backup gets here or go alone." With that said, Wiley turned his back on Baker and headed for the car.

Baker was just about to call Wiley a chicken, that always got Wiley's goat when from out of the corner of his eye he saw something move towards his partner. "Wiley!" He shouted.

Wiley began to turn with a rude comment on his lips when something slammed into his back knocking him off his feet.

Baker hadn't seen what jumped on Wiley, only a dark shape that had come flying out of the tall grass and hit his partner square in the back. As he called out, he noticed movement all around, completely surrounding them. It was the cats, hundreds of cats.

Baker stopped dead, *what the hell is going on?* He thought as he watched the cats forming a circle around them it was like there were in sync with each other. Sweeping the beam of his flashlight in a full circle he saw without a doubt, they were entirely surrounded by cats. His light reflected off their eyes causing them to shine blood red in the night. Off to his left, Wiley began screaming. Baker moved slowly keeping his eyes on the closest animals trying to discern their intentions. *Surely cats don't attack people?* He called out to Wiley, who he could hear whimpering quietly. "It's okay, they are just cats, they're not going to hurt us ok." Baker listened, but Wiley didn't reply. *What if I'm wrong? No that's crazy*, he told himself as he pushed the thoughts aside. The cats followed Bakers movements as he inched towards his partner. They crept closer and closer. Then without thinking, he broke into a run.

That was all the creatures needed, they howled in unison, tearing up the darkness with their eerie cry.

Baker fell to his knees under the weight of the cats that leaped upon him. As he struggled, he could only watch in terror as they seemed to melt before his eyes. The fur molted, bubbling like flowing lava, the ears slipped back becoming a part of the moving flesh. Their jaws opened wide, revealing rows upon rows of tiny suction cups that reminded him of octopus tentacles. The resemblance to cats all but vanished as they now stood up on two hind legs. The front paws transformed themselves into small claw-like hands, which opened and closed in what appeared to be an expression of pleasure. The things writhed in a teeming mass upon him. Their jaws opening wide to receive their victim.

He kicked, punched, and scrambled to get away from the hellish beasts, knowing his very bones were about to be sucked from within his flesh. He distantly heard Wiley screaming too, and knew at that moment that this was the end for everyone.

Bear Lake, 12:30pm

Sheila grabbed her bra off the tree branch and pulled it back on. She hadn't noticed the cold when they were fooling around; none of them did, but now that they had finished and were sweaty, the cold became more pronounced. She hugged herself and shivered. "I need to pee."

Bobby nestled closer to a still naked Mindy, hugging her body for warmth. "Sure thing babe," he said to Sheila, "just be quick about it, I'm not done with you yet!" He promised her as he rubbed Mindy's bare legs causing her to giggle.

"Yeah, yeah, I'll believe it when I see it," Shelia retorted, pointing out his now flaccid penis. Although they did have a good time for a few minutes, Bobby just didn't last as long as she hoped. With all the experience he claimed to have, she expected a longer run from him. *Oh well*, she thought, *maybe the second time around will be better.* She didn't mind too much, though. After all, Bobby was a hunk.

Shelia made her way carefully through the dark woods. She didn't want to go too far and get lost, but she had to make sure that she was far enough away so they wouldn't hear her peeing. When she could no longer hear their voices, she knew she had gone far enough. Glancing around first to make sure there were no other partygoers in the area, she dropped her pants and squatted over the dry leaves. She let out a sigh of relief as urine flowed between her feet. She inched one foot over more as the pee sprayed out in a wide arch, not wanting to get any on herself. A twig snapped from somewhere off to her right. Sheila turned and peered into the darkness. Seeing nothing, she returned to the task at hand. Another snap came this time closer. "Hey! Don't come any closer, I'm peeing here." She called out into the darkness.

There was no response.

"Ok!" she called as she stood up pulling on her pants. "It's not funny you guys. I'm all done so you can come out now." She waited, listening for Mindy's distinctive giggle. All she heard in reply was the chirping of crickets. The night suddenly seemed much darker, and quieter than before. She was no longer drunk and began to question why she had come out here in the first place. *Well*, she thought, *if it's not Bobby and Mindy trying to scare me, then it's just one of the other drunk kids being stupid.* She shrugged it off, *I don't care.* And with resolve, she moved back the way she thought she came.

The moon moved in and out of the clouds. Sometimes Sheila could see bare trees silhouetted against the night sky, and then the moon would hide, and she'd be plunged into blackness. A couple of times she tripped over roots or walked into low hanging branches. Whoever had been out in the woods when she was peeing was following her, she was sure of it. Branches snapped behind her, and her heart pounded in her chest. She stopped and called out, "Hello? Who's there?" Every so often, she would yell for Mindy, but she knew at this point she was hopelessly lost, and the sound of her voice in the darkness was weakened by fear.

The noises behind her got closer, and she peered into the dark, hoping to see another person, even if they were a dick head, but all she could see were endless dark trees. "Hello? Come on guys, quit fucking around!" Her heart pounded. She now heard leaves rustling all around her. Goosebumps prickled her arms, and she shivered. The movements were getting louder and closer. She couldn't take the fear any longer, just needing to be with people again, she gave up and ran blindly, deeper into the deadly woods.

Mindy sat up pushing Bobby aside. His hands groped for her bare breasts. She didn't bother to stop him, even though she really wasn't in the mood to be touched anymore. "What is taking Sheila so long," she asked quietly, mostly to herself.

Bobby released Mindy's breast when he noticed she was no longer into it, sat up beside her and reached for his clothes. "I don't know. She's a girl," he replied unconcernedly.

Mindy gave him a dirty look. *Men are all the same,* she thought, *all they want is sex then it's goodbye baby.* She stood up and hastily began to gather her clothes. She stepped into her pants. "Well I think she got lost and we need to go look for her."

"Nah...I bet she went back to the party to have another beer," Bobby said. Then seeing the worried look on Mindy's face, he felt bad. "Ok, look why don't we go back to the party and see if she's there, then if not, I'll help you look for her."

That did not make Mindy feel any better, she knew that Bobby didn't care what happened to Sheila, he probably wanted to get away from them both and drink some more. "Promise me you'll help?"

Bobby took her hand. "I promise." He said and led her back to the bonfire.

Bear Lake, 1:00am

Doug was sweating heavily. Unsure which he needed more, to stop and breathe, or continue sucking on those delicious lips, he chose the latter, of course, and let the air be damned. He couldn't believe what was happening to him. His hands roaming freely under Katlin's shirt felt large and clumsy as they made out, but he really didn't care. Suddenly he was overwhelmed with uncontrollable feelings of love for her. He wondered why he never noticed how much Katlin wanted him, how much he wanted her. Thanks to his mother's excellent rearing, he never thought about girls this way. She always encouraged him to wait for marriage, but now, in the heat of the moment, all her words were gone from his head. Right now, his love for Katlin told him that what was happening tonight was right, for the both of them.

Doug was well aware that Katlin was pressing her hips against him, while their lips were locked, her tongue rolling around his. She grabbed the back of his head yearning to draw him closer as she pressed her mouth firmly against his. He fumbled with Katlin's zipper, needing to touch her moist heat, sure she won't stop him. She did not. As his hand encountered her soft down, he could already feel the moisture coming from within her depths. Katlin gasped with pleasure at his touch. Her eyes closed, her mouth opened slightly, she breathed harder before swallowing past a tremble. His fingers delved deeper, and just as they reached her wetness, his excitement about to culminate prematurely, a scream echoed through the woods breaking their spell and curdling the moment. Doug bolted up, yanking his hand away from Katlin. He moved so quickly that he banged his head on the roof of the car.

Katlin struggled to get her pants zipped up so she could crane around to see what was going on. "What the hell was that?"

"I'm not sure." He scanned the darkness around them, as he rubbed the bump forming on his head. In the distance, he could still see the fire and the other kids milling about it, but could not make out anything that was going on from within the fog covered windows. His gaze moved to Katlin, and guilt and shame washed over him.

Katlin felt his eyes upon her, and she frowned. "What's wrong?"

"I'm sorry."

"Sorry for what?"

"What I tried to do to you."

Katlin laughed and snuggled into Doug's chest; he may have lost his desire, but his heart was still pounding. "I'm not sorry," she stated matter-of-factly.

She tilted her face up to his and said something she never thought she would get to say to him. "I love you, Doug."

Doug's heart skipped a beat, and he suppressed a nervous chortle by turning away, she loves me. His emotions distracted him, and his head spun with these new conflicting feelings. He looked deep within himself before answering her. They had been best friends for many years. He trusted her with all his fears, and secrets, and he enjoyed her company. Then he reasoned, well maybe that's what love is. Looking down to meet her eyes, he responded, "I love you, too, Katlin." He knew at that moment that nothing was ever more accurate.

They hugged each other, so happy at that moment they forgot all about the earlier scream. All of the sudden, though, all hell started breaking loose outside. Doug released Katlin from his arms, and they moved to peer out the steamed-up windows. Though their view was blurred, they could see the kids near the fire had gathered together, some were shouting, others screaming, and crying.

Doug pulled himself over the back seat, turned, and helped Katlin out. "I think we'd better see what's going on."

Getting out of the station wagon, they linked hands and moved towards the commotion. Pushing his way through the crowd, towing Katlin along behind, he recognized most of the kids from his school. When they made their way to the front of the crowd, they both saw Bobby Salinger standing over a girl who was on her knees puking and wailing. Doug wasn't sure how someone could throw up and cry and the same time, but this girl was doing a fine job of it.

"What's going on?" He nudged Bobby.

Bobby's eyes were wide, and his face was drawn, he looked at Doug then into the crowd of kids around them. He bent down, careful to stay clear of the vomit, and placed a comforting hand on Mindy's back. "We found Sheila. Oh man..." he wiped at his eyes, "She's dead. God, she wasn't half a step away from the clearing, and there she was." He shook his head as if that would wipe the vision of her hollowed-out body from his memory.

Murmurs, and gasps of shock swept through the crowd. A girl shrieked, "I want to go home." Some echoed agreement, while others were speculating on what happened and, of course, a handful of brave guys wanted to not only see the body, but also tramp off to find the killer.

Bobby stood up and shouted, "Hold on guys! The last thing we need is to do is get ourselves lost out here in the woods. We all need to get out of here!

Is there someone who will make an anonymous call to the police?"

"Hey, you can't tell us what to do!" Someone yelled back. That comment was followed with hollers of the agreement, some booed and others agreed with Bobby. A tall kid from the back called out. "Your dad's Cop! You should be the one to call him after we all get the fuck outta here!" That caused more heckling from the peanut gallery.

Katlin tightened her grip on Doug's hand. "I think we better leave."

Doug agreed with her, and they turned to leave but were interrupted when Mindy started screaming. "How can you people just leave? Shelia's dead, do something! Call the police!"

Bobby turned and grabbed her by the shoulders giving her a rough shake. "Stop it!"

Mindy took a deep breath but couldn't stop crying, as she said, "This is all your fault."

"What!?" Bobby was stunned, "Listen, I'll take you home, but you have to promise you won't tell anyone we were here tonight."

Mindy couldn't believe what she was hearing. Did he really expect her to just walk away and leave

Sheila, her best friend, out here alone? "We have to tell someone."

"No," Bobby continued. "We act like there never was a party. As long as no one gets caught, they'll never know we were here. It's sad, yes. But, Sheila went missing, and that's all anyone needs to know. No one will get in trouble, and people will start searching for her. Eventually, they'll find her; I guess," Bobby shrugged. He didn't like his own plan much but had no other solution to their problem.

"NO!" Mindy screamed at him, causing some of the stragglers, who had begun to disperse, to stop and stare at them. "I will not let her family think she is missing. Can't you imagine what that would be like for them! Besides, the killer is out here now, and maybe the cops can catch him."

"Shit!" Bobby yelled. Why did this have to happen? He wondered not for the first time in the last hour. *I just wanted to have some fun, but now I'm in a shit load of trouble. My dad is going to kill me.* He glanced warily at Mindy. She stood staring at him with fresh tears running down her red face, and suddenly he felt responsible for Sheila's death.

He patted Mindy on the arm. "Come on then, I'll take you home and make an anonymous call to the police. Ok? Now let's see if Kevin is still kicking about and get the hell outta here."

Seeking Answers

Sally sat in the patrol car shivering and rubbed her arms while she waited patiently for the engine to warm up so she could turn the heater on. Chief Salinger had ordered her to remain in the car again, after receiving a mysterious page from Millie, and he needed to use Lucy's phone in private. Even though she tried to weasel her way into the investigation, the chief continued to push her out. Sally watched as Salinger and Crow stepped out the door and continued to talk on Lucy's front steps. They didn't seem to be affected by the cold at all, while she felt chilled to the bone. She flicked the heater to full blast and felt the hot air pump out with welcome relief. Her eyes flicked up to the review mirror as a few cars sped down the highway beyond Lucy's driveway. *Odd*, she thought, *that looked like a lot of people out past curfew.* Her eyes flicked to the men on the porch, and she could tell from the angle of the trees that they weren't able to see the road. Then the thought flitted away as Salinger stepped off the porch, heading her way, and her concern for the investigation returned.

Salinger opened his door, and a cold wind whipped through the car stealing away Sally's heat.

"Whoa...hot enough in here?" He turned the heat down.

"Not for us city folk," Sally grimaced. But she didn't want to talk about the weather, what she wanted was for Salinger to stop holding her off. She wanted some direction as to where the investigation was going. She wanted to be around to break it wide open. Unfortunately, Salinger knew what she wanted, and he could care less about her career. "What are we going to do now?" She stared straight ahead, purposely avoiding his gaze.

"You are going to go home and sleep, or eat maybe. Whatever you want, but you're not following me around all night." Sally tried to speak, but he cut her off. "Look, as you can plainly see there is nothing to be gained by following me around." He sighed. "Just what do you think you are going to gain by getting caught in the middle of some ruckus between my constables and the murderer? The best thing for everybody is for you to go home and get some rest."

Sally stared out her window into the darkness beyond. The moon, trapped behind some heavy dark clouds for the last fifteen minutes, or so, moved into view. It illuminated the pines around Lucy's house. *It really is lonely out here*, Sally thought and shivered again. She didn't feel like arguing with the chief anymore tonight. She wasn't tired, but she was worn thin, and she knew that if she stayed in his presence much longer, they'd end up fighting. "Sounds good to me." She agreed.

Salinger shrugged he had too much to worry about without trying to figure out what she was up too. Along the way, he occasionally let his eyes wander over Sally's legs and felt the familiar stirrings in his groin. She made it easy for him to sneak a peek every so often with her face turned towards the passenger window. "So, where exactly do you live?"

"Uh…on Lafayette Drive." She turned, taking in his handsome profile for a moment before prodding. "I would've thought you cops would know everything about me. Don't you make it your business to check out new members of your community?"

"Ha-ha. Even if you are a pain in the ass," he retorted. "I didn't bother to check out your file. I've got better things to do."

"Well, it's comforting to know that I still have some privacy around here." She watched him as he drove. "Thanks for bringing me along. I'm sorry for all the trouble I caused you, but I really think that if we work together, I can actually help you with this case."

Salinger shot her a look of disdain, then turned back to the road, raising his eyebrows in disbelief of her audacity, thinking her statement quite laughable.

Sally rolled her eyes in response to the look Salinger gave her. "I'm serious, you are way understaffed, and I can do some legwork, or research, whatever you need."

At the mention of her legs Salinger smiled, *yeah, I got some legwork for you to do*. But, he kept his silence; she was, after all, trying to make peace. "Maybe," he said noncommittally. "I'll see what comes up." He smiled and bit his lip, at the inside joke he just made.

Sally resumed staring out the window. They soon reached the edge of town and quickly arrived at her house. "Thank you," she said quietly as they drew into the driveway. She was about to open her door and step out when she realized the mistake they both had made. "Um…my truck is still at the station."

Salinger slapped his forehead. "Ah, shit I forgot all about it. Well let's go get it then," he said threw the car into reverse.

Sally smiled at Salinger's obvious discomfort. Either he was as worn out as she was, or he liked her more than he let on. Sally hoped for the later. She liked the chief, even though he was a pain at times. She felt that given the right situation they could actually make a go of something real. "So, now that we have to spend another…oh," she frowned at her watch, "ten minutes together. Can you at least tell me what you sent Constable Crow off to do?"

"You never quit, do you?"

"Nope. That's why I'm a reporter."

"Fine, but," Salinger lifted a finger for emphasis, "everything that you've seen tonight, or whatever I tell you must remain between us. This is not information for the public at large. I will give you a proper statement that you can release tomorrow. Okay?"

"Sure thing Chief." She mock saluted.

"Promise me, and this will be our test for how much further I let you into the investigation."

"You have my word." This could be the break she was waiting for. If she proved he could trust her, she'd be golden.

Salinger sighed, praying that by letting her in he wasn't hanging himself. If he was being honest with himself he had to admit, he actually needed help. He didn't want to admit it, but he did. "We've lost contact with two of our constables, and I've sent Crow off to hunt them down," he informed her.

Sally was dumb-stuck. They had lost two constables? How do two police officers disappear, she wondered, then thought about the scene that she glimpsed at the Mercer house. "So, you sent one officer out alone to find two? That doesn't seem like a wise move." As soon as the words fell from her mouth, she regretted them. Insulting Salinger wasn't going to get her anywhere. "I'm sorry," she apologized before Salinger could reply. "It's just, this whole thing is crazy." She wrapped her arms protectively around her waist.

Despite Sally's reassurances, her comments cut Salinger to the bone. He knew full well the danger that his constable was facing, and yet they still had their jobs to do. Being two constables short was not helping matters any. "Constable Crow is a tracker, not to mention the smartest, strongest man I know. I have full confidence that he'll do his job quickly and safely. He'll find my men and report back to me," Salinger assured her in no uncertain terms as they pulled up to the quiet police station. "Please," he almost begged her as she opened the door to leave, "Get in your truck, lock the doors, and go straight home."

Sally wanted desperately to say some comforting words to Salinger. Actually, she felt like taking him in her arms and holding him at that moment. But knew this was not the right time. "You stay safe too. Charles." She dug her keys out of her purse and gave Salinger a parting smile before climbing into her own cold truck.

Salinger sat watching her leave, both relieved that she was out of his hair and afraid he might never see her again.

Bowan Residence, 1:00 am

Constable Jim Crow employed every bit of wisdom he learned from his grandfather as he drove cautiously along the dark highway. He glanced down all the logging roads that cut through the woods. They were only used now during hunting season; the logging industry having moved on to more lucrative and fertile fields. He was looking for signs of the missing patrol car and its occupants, trying desperately to get a bead on where the other constable's last stop may have been.

Why Baker hadn't called in their stop, Crow had no idea. The routine was that they were to call in their exact location at each stop, and in fact, up until about forty-five minutes ago, they had followed the procedure to the letter. The chief told Crow the last report was from the Bowan residence. Crow figured he would begin with Mrs. Bowan to see what had transpired between her and the men.

He called his location to Millie at the office and stepped out of his car. As he approached the front porch he noticed a slight movement of the curtains, someone was watching him. He knocked firmly on the door.

"Who is it?" A female voice asked, muffled by the closed door.

"It's Constable Jim Crow, Ma'am."

"How do we know you're a cop?" Brenda asked, feeling little security through the securely locked door.

Margaret stood beside her friend holding Doug's baseball bat close to her breast. "Make him show some proof," she whispered.

"Yah, where's your badge?"

"It's me, Jim Crow from the North Falls Police. And damn it, you both know who I am," Crow repeated for the second time. If they hadn't been drunk, they might have recognized his distinctive Cree accent.

"It may be a trick of some sort; if you were a real cop you would have thunk of that! There was already two cops here before you, so what do you want?" Margaret yelled through the door.

"Yah! What do you want? We'll call the cops if you don't go away!" Brenda yelled through the door and then giggled drunkenly.

Crow counted to ten to calm his nerves. "Listen," he called out, "go to the living room window and look out, I'll be standing there with my badge up and prove who I am. Okay?" Without waiting for a sarcastic reply from inside, he moved around to the front window and waited. He felt like an ass standing out in the cold holding up his badge, but it seemed to be the only way he was going to get access to their information, however little they may have, it would still help.

Margaret slapped Brenda's side. "See I told you it was him."

Brenda's mouth fell open. "Liar! You said it was the killer and scared the stuffing outta me!" Then she punched Margaret's arm for hitting her first.

"Alright!" Margaret laughed as she danced away from another punch that Brenda threw at her. "You'd better open the door and see what he wants."

Brenda smiled wanly as she opened the door. "Sorry, Jim."

Constable Crow stepped into the warm house, closing the door behind him. "I think you two had better lay off the sauce for the rest of the night."

"What brings you here anyway?" Margaret asked. She watched the smooth lines of Crow's face as they pulled into worry lines. "I mean…" she stumbled thinking that she said something to upset this normally composed man. "Baker and Wiley had just been out to check on us already, is everything alright?"

"That's actually why I'm here," he said clearing his throat he didn't want to frighten the ladies any more than they already were.

Brenda and Margaret looked at each other questioningly. Brenda was the first to voice her concern, sobering up quickly, "What do you mean?"

"Can you tell me the exact time that the constables left?"

Brenda looked up at the clock that hung on the wall above the couch, it read 12:59. Then she thought for a moment before she answered. "I'm pretty sure it was 11:45ish." She looked at Margaret for confirmation.

Margaret shrugged and nodded and resumed watching Crow as he took notes. "Did they do something wrong?"

Crow stopped writing and looked up instantly, his eyes bore into Margaret's, the pale blue of her eyes halting him for a moment before responding curtly. "No."

"Uh," Brenda elbowed Margaret, indicating to knock it off. "Well, what's going on? They showed up, told us to stay inside, checked the perimeter of the house and left."

"They couldn't have been much longer than ten minutes," Margaret interjected trying to get Crow to look at her again. She kind of liked the spark of excitement she felt as he looked at her the first time, but he disappointed her by continuing to scribble in his book.

Crow closed his notepad and turned to leave. "I'm just following up. Why don't the two of you turn in for the night?" He was about to slip out the door when he felt a warm hand press into his. He looked down and watched in silence as Margaret slipped a small piece of paper into his hand. He knew what would be on it, and without a word, he stuck it in his pocket. He didn't want to be rude, but he preferred the olive toned beauty of his own Native women. He gave a slight nod and resumed his search for the two missing constables.

☐

Police Station, 1:20am

Chief Salinger wearily tossed his jacket over the back of his chair and with a deep sigh plunked down hard behind his desk. When he entered the station, Millie looked exhausted. Salinger knew that he was pushing everyone too hard. He knew that if he didn't solve these grisly murders soon, he'd have no choice but to call in the Royal Canadian Mounted Police from Vancouver. That was a call he was not yet prepared to make. He was about to ask Millie for a cup of coffee when she came waddling through the door carrying a steaming cup of the potent brew for him.

"Ah, what would I do without you, Millie?"

Suddenly, as if in response to his question, the office lit up with the shrill sound of a ringing phone. Millie rolled her eyes; she already had cauliflower ear from all the people calling in to complain about the murders. Not bothering to leave the chiefs office, Millie grabbed the phone extension directly on his desk. "North Falls Police, how may I help you?" After a minute of silence, the blood drained from her face, making it paler than it already was, "Please hold," she covered the mouthpiece and handed it over to the chief.

Salinger took the phone from Millie and, without a word, she scuttled from his office. "Salinger," He said. He heard a faint gasp, then rasping sounds like something being rubbed over the mouthpiece. He waited knowing that if they had not hung up yet, they were not about to.

A disguised, but unmistakably female voice came over the line. She spoke quietly and struggled in a tear-choked voice. "There has been a murder. Bear Lake clearing. Please hurry."

"Who…" was all Salinger was able to get out before the line went dead in his hand. "Damn it!" He slammed the phone down half-cocked on the receiver before composing himself and righting it. He moved from behind his desk and raced out of his office. "Millie?"

"Got it!" Millie yelled out holding up a piece of paper that was still warm from the printer. "Route 3, Esso station payphone," she read off the location to Salinger.

Hearing the commotion, constable Duncan had already come out of the office where he was busy filling out reports. "What's up?" He asked.

"Let's roll Duncan. We've got to get out to Route 3 and find out who made that call."

They plowed out into the cold night leaving Millie alone once again to worry about what was happening in their town and to wonder if they would make it back alive.

Route 3 Esso Station, 1:20 am

Doug's mind felt as empty as the road that rolled out before them. The peacefulness of the bright moon overhead belied by the danger that lurked beneath it, just as the emptiness of his mind hid the turmoil in his heart. He couldn't believe all that had happened to them tonight. First, there was his make-out session with Katlin, then someone they knew was killed, it was too much to comprehend all at once. He glanced into the rear-view mirror at Kevin sitting silently in the backseat. No one had spoken a word since they left the dirt road and entered Route 3. Doug reached over and took Katlin's hand in his own. It felt cool, yet she responded warmly by squeezing her acknowledgment, saying a hundred words in one simple gesture, but that serene moment was interrupted when a dull thud came from the back seat.

"Oh no!" Kevin said after thumping his hand on the seat.

Katlin turned in her seat. "What?" Kevin looked pale. "Are you feeling alright," she asked him, worried that he was going to puke in the car.

Kevin shook his head. "No... Yes," he replied. "I'm just stupid, that's all."

"What's wrong?"

"I can't go home," Kevin told them. "I'm supposed to be at Bobby's house. If I go home now, even if I sneak in, I'm not supposed to be there. How am I going to explain that to my parents in the morning, tell them I was homesick and crept back in the middle of the night? God, I'm so stupid." He leaned back and stared at the roof as if the answer would be written there.

"Can't you go to someone else's house then?" Doug suggested.

Kevin sat in silence while he thought. "No, how would they explain that I was suddenly at their house in the morning?"

"Well, what should we do then," Doug asked. They certainly couldn't take him back to the Shaw's house with them.

Kevin didn't say anything he just sat and stared out at the night that was moving past the windows.

Katlin said, "Why don't we pull over at the Esso station up ahead and we'll help you work something out. Is that okay with you Doug?"

"Sure. Kevin?"

"I guess so," Kevin replied morosely.

They passed the next few miles in silence, each wrapped in their own thoughts of what had happened at the party and what would happen should they get caught out after curfew.

Doug pulled the car into the deserted gas station and moved closer to the building so they wouldn't be easily spotted from the road. As soon as the car stopped, Kevin said he needed to pee and stepped out of the car. Doug started to tell him that it wasn't a good idea to be alone in such an isolated place but Kevin was already out and slamming the door behind him.

Katlin and Doug both watched Kevin as he moved around the side of the small building. Katlin placed a restraining hand on Doug's arm as he moved to open his door. "He'll be okay," she whispered.

"I wish we stayed in," Doug said resting his head back and looking at the dingy material overhead.

"Me too."

"What do you think we should do with Kevin?"

"I don't know. Maybe we should take him to Bobby's house, that's where they were going to end up anyway," she suggested.

"Yeah, I'll ask him," Doug said swiveling in his seat trying to spot Kevin. "Damn it, where'd he get off to?"

Katlin just scanned the darkness saying nothing.

Doug wasn't able to wait any longer, he hated to leave Katlin by herself, but at the same time, he wanted to find Kevin and get them all out of there. "Stay here and lock the doors, I'll be right back and…" he paused not wanting to worry her, but feeling the need to be cautious, "If I'm not back in ten minutes leave." And before she could protest he was out of the car and walking towards the edge of the building.

Doug warily watched the dark tree line of the forest that lay just beyond the parking lot of the old gas station. He wondered if whoever had killed Sheila was lurking about, and goose bumps traveled up his spine. It was dark around the back of the building, and he didn't see Kevin anywhere. He wanted desperately to call out to him but was afraid to raise his voice and attract any unwanted attention. Keeping a close eye on the tree line, he crept along the gravel drive. He stayed close against the wall and just when he was about to round the corner, voices stopped him dead in his tracks. He pressed his back tighter to the wall and listened. He heard two male voices and a female. Inching forward he peeked around the edge of the wall. Relief flooded through him when he saw the familiar black Charger with Bobby, Mindy, and Kevin all standing near the payphone talking.

As Doug moved out from behind the building, the threesome stopped talking. He could tell, even in the darkness, that Mindy had been crying again, or maybe she hadn't stopped since the last time he'd seen her. Bobby raised his hand in greeting.

"Hey," Doug said to Kevin, approaching group, "why didn't you come and let us know what you were up too? We got worried waiting for you."

Kevin shrugged. "Sorry man. I got caught up in what these two were doing over here," he waved his hand angrily at Bobby and Mindy. "Why don't you fill him in?"

Doug looked expectantly at Bobby who stood close to Mindy. Bobby picked at the silver piercing beneath his black lips. It had turned into a nervous habit when he wasn't smoking. "Fine man, don't throw a fit." He glanced at Mindy who was crying silently beside him. "Uh - we called the cops man."

"Yeah, right," Mindy shrieked at Bobby, "you called them, but I'm the one who had to tell them what happened to Sheila!"

Bobby raised his hands as if to ward off the verbal blow. "Hey, it's not my fault. I couldn't take the chance of my dad answering the phone."

Mindy lowered her head and kicked at the gravel under her sneaker and chose to ignore Bobby. She felt like hell and just wanted to go home to bed.

Doug shook his head. "Did you ever stop to think that this is the only road to Bear Lake? Now how are we supposed to get home without being spotted?" They'd surely be seen by the cops as they drove home. Then he remembered that he'd left Katlin back at the car and swore under his breath. "Well, you guys can figure it out. I'm getting out of here now. Kevin you'll have to go with Bobby and follow your original plan, stay at his house it's the safest way." Doug lifted his hands defensively after noticing the look of betrayal on Kevin's face. "Sorry pal but we've got to get home too." Then he turned his back to the group and went towards his own car. He didn't stop when he heard footsteps come up behind him.

"Wait!" Mindy called out. She caught up to Doug and matched his quick stride. "Can I ride back with you?" She implored wiping the tears from her face.

"Yeah, that's fine with me." He didn't really care for Mindy, but in light of their situation, it wasn't what was important at the moment. What they needed right now was to get off the highway. Besides he felt sorry for her, how was she going to get by without Sheila anymore?

When they reached the car, they could clearly see Katlin's puzzled face through the window. She popped opened the door and gave Doug a questioning look. Doug quickly explained the new situation. Katlin's expression went dry. "Oh shit, that means the cops are coming this way?"

"Yeah, thanks to Bobby, the dip shit. I don't know why he didn't wait until he got home before he called them," Doug replied while quickly sliding in behind the wheel, throwing the car into gear and flooring it. "It takes fifteen minutes to get to town from here; I hope we can hit a safe turn off before the cops arrive." Doug glanced at his watch and cringed, wondering how much time they had wasted at the gas station.

Mindy sat silently in the back seat full of guilt; it was her fault that Bobby had called the police from the gas station. She begged and cried until he stopped to make the call. She wanted to be there when he did because she didn't trust him and she wanted to make sure that Sheila's body was found. She stared out at the dark highway. Suddenly the car slowed down and began to turn. Mindy sat forward to see where they were going, she didn't recognize the road. "Where are we?"

Doug looked at Mindy in the mirror wincing at the state of her red eyes. "It's somebody's driveway I'm going to pull up as far as I can until we can't be seen from the road. That's one nice thing about farmhouses, long driveways. We'll turn around, kill the lights, and wait until we see the cops go by then we'll head on home."

Mindy sat back again. "That's a good idea," she said relieved.

Katlin slumped down in the front seat not saying anything; she trusted Doug, but she just wanted to get home.

As soon as the dark house came into view, Doug turned off the lights, drove a bit closer then turned the car around, so they faced the highway again. There were no trees along the driveway to shelter them, but he figured they were far enough away that, with the cover of darkness they shouldn't be seen. He slowly pulled as close to the ditch as possible, and when he was satisfied, they were far enough over he shut off the engine. "Well ladies might as well get comfortable." Suddenly all heads turned as Bobby's charger sped past and Doug shook his head. "I don't know what his plan is, but everyone knows his car, especially the cops."

They watched Bobby's taillights trail down to the Highway.

"Oh look, they turned away from town," Katlin tsked, "you have to admit that's kinda smart." She slid closer to Doug, and he took her in his arms and hugged her tight, ignoring the fact that they were stuck here for a while.

Mindy adjusted herself in the back feeling uncomfortable in the presence of two apparent lovers but said nothing to deter them from finding solace in one another.

Fog formed on the windows from their breath, but they could still see out well enough not to worry about turning on the heat. The minutes stretched by, and yet no sign of any vehicles crossed their path. Doug's heart thumped hard in his chest, but it wasn't so much from fear, as it was from having Katlin so close to him again. He could feel her warm breath blowing across his chin and longed to lean down and kiss her, but he dared not with Mindy sitting in the back seat. He tried to ignore the stirrings in his body and concentrate on the road ahead. Then he saw lights coming off the highway.

"I think they're coming," he warned the girls, who didn't need a warning, they saw it too. They all scrunched down a little further in the seats and watched the headlights grow brighter on the highway. A car shot past the driveway.

Katlin sat forward. "Do you think that was them?"

"I don't think it would be anyone else," Doug said.

They watched the brake lights come on, the car pull and U-turn car and slowed to turn into the driveway. "Um…guys, I think they saw us," Mindy whispered fearfully.

CHAOS

An incessant meowing woke Margaret from her
drunken sleep. She squinted into the dim living room
where she had passed out. Unfamiliar shadows
hovered over the floor, and the mewing started up
again. So, she wasn't dreaming after all. Margaret got
off the couch and headed towards the kitchen where
it sounded like the cat was going crazy. It was
meowing and scratching at the door. They had finally
gotten the cat to come inside as the constable was
leaving, and now it wanted out again. "Stupid cat,"
Margaret growled.

"Sneezer," she whispered, not wanting to wake
up Brenda. "Come here kitty." She made kissing
noises at the cat and waved it toward her invitingly.
The cat meowed louder and rubbed its face roughly
across the bottom edge of the door. "What do you
want kitty?" Margaret asked and reached down to
pick it up. When her hands closed over its body, the
cat freaked out. Claws extended, it slashed and hissed.
Its body twisted in her hands so unexpectedly that she
let go, and the cat flew across the room. It smacked
into the bottom cupboard so hard that the door
popped open, and the cat slid around the floor in a

circle, all four legs spread wide. Then scrambling for a foothold, the cat dug its claws into the linoleum and took off out of the room.

"What the hell?" She wondered what was wrong with the cat. Sneezer was always such a quiet, pleasant animal she had never seen it act like this before. She returned to the living room watching the shadows to see if the cat was lurking anywhere, but it didn't seem to be around. So, she tucked herself back under the blankets on the couch and kept a watchful eye open. Now wide awake, she hoped that the cat wouldn't start up again. She would hate to have to hurt it.

□

Martha King jolted upright in bed. "Bill!" She shook her husband's shoulder. He rolled away from the movement and grumbled. Martha made a fist and whacked him harder. "Bill, wake up you old fool," she said in a loud whisper.

"What?" He asked keeping his eyes shut; he could tell by the darkness that it wasn't time to get up yet. "What is it?"

"I heard something, it came from the kitchen," Martha informed him as she slid out of bed and pulled on a tattered old terry robe making sure to keep a close eye on the doorway.

He was just about to ask if she was sure when a loud bang came from the front of their house. Bill jumped out of bed, pulled on his robe and picked up the baseball bat that he always kept nearby. "Stay here," he whispered. His heart pounded fiercely in his chest, and he took a deep breath to steel himself against the fear before slowly walking to the closed bedroom door.

Martha whispered, "Be careful Bill, your heart." She touched her chest as if he needed reminding that he just had a triple by-pass.

He waved her off and gripped the doorknob. He listened intently for any other signs of intrusion. Hearing nothing, he slowly opened the door and peered through the narrow crack. All he saw was the dark hallway and a thin strip of light from the kitchen window at the far end of the house. Nothing moved, so he ventured out into the hall holding the bat up high in both hands ready to attack. He crept as quietly as possible along the hallway with his back against the wall. Each step closer to the light in the kitchen, his heart hammered harder in his chest. He wondered if the noise had come from outside because not a single sound had been made since he stepped out of the bedroom. *Unless whoever was in the house heard me come out of the room and was now in hiding, just waiting for the opportunity to pounce on me and crush my skull.* Bill stopped two feet away from the square of light on the floor wishing he hadn't thought of that. Sour smelling sweat dripped from his underarms. The bat felt loose in his grip, as well. He drew in a deep breath, thinking, *I've got to check it out.* He steeled his will, straightened his back, and rushed into the kitchen yelling as he went. Hoping the loud yelling would scare off any would-be intruders. Rounding the wall to the kitchen, he entered the empty room.

He swiveled around, but there was nobody there. He clicked on the lights and checked the small kitchen. The old Formica counter gleamed, and the two-seater wooden table sat in the center as usual.

There was nothing out of place here. He looked in the broom closet and the living room, but everything was as it should be. "Huh, I wonder what the ruckus was."

He walked back through the house and turned off lights as he went. It wasn't until he reached the closed bedroom door that he wondered why Martha hadn't come out to snoop around too. He reached for the doorknob and paused. *Why was the door closed? Maybe Martha felt safer that way,* he thought as he opened the door.

Martha lay across the bed in the darkness, her arms flung out at odd angles across the bed. Bill stopped in the doorway, he looked over his shoulder. There was no possible way for anyone to have gotten past him. Or so he thought, having missed saw the small dark shadow that darted up the hallway when he was in the living room.

He stepped towards the bed. "Martha?"

No answer came, so he sidestepped around the end of the bed. He glanced warily at the covers that hung down obscuring his view of the space underneath. He lifted the bat out and prodded at her hip. Something didn't look right as the bat pushed into her flesh. It sunk in too quickly.

"Martha? Hey, you alright?" He stepped a little closer reaching out to touch her and see if she was still breathing.

A growl came from under the bed. Bill quickly drew his hand back and cried out. He jumped back from the bed, his weak heart beating too fast. Keeping his eyes on the blankets that trailed on the floor, he pushed the bat under one corner and lifted it slowly. The blanket came up off the floor, and he leaned down watching the darkness under the bed. Two deep red eyes peered out of the black at him.

"Come on then!" He yelled. "Let's get this over with."

He was not going to let his wife of twenty years go without him.

☐

Constable Jim Crow turned down the dirt drive, moths fluttering past his headlights. He never minded riding alone, in fact, he usually preferred to be alone, and he enjoyed the silence. People talked too much, they liked to clutter up life with a bunch of nonsense. As the car rounded the last bend, he had to hit the brakes quickly.

Parked in the middle of the driveway was a patrol car, Baker's unit. Crow threw the car into park and scooped up the mic all in one fluid motion.

"Come in Unit 1," he spoke into the mic while watching the area for any signs of movement. The area surrounding the car was dark. He could see the trailer up ahead, and his own headlights illuminated the back of the patrol car leaving a large shadow looming off to the left.

Salinger responded to Crows call immediately. Crow told the chief of his location and that he found Baker's car, but there was no sign of the two missing constables, yet.

"Do you feel secure enough to handle the situation?" Salinger questioned Crow.

Crow looked around the dark woods around him, he had no idea what could have happened to both of the other constables. There wasn't much point in waiting until more help could arrive because he figured he could handle the situation himself, and if things looked to rough, he'd take off. At least he knew he had to keep an eye out for trouble. "I'm good Chief. I'll check it out and get back to you."

"I want you to beep in every five minutes, and if you miss a call, we'll be right out there. Do you copy?" Salinger said with genuine concern, unable to get away from his own situation to help him at the moment.

Crow gave the affirmative and made sure the microphone on his uniform was turned up. He removed the gun from its holster and stepped out into the night. Overhead the moon moved in and out of the clouds causing shadows to play hide and seek around the car. Crow kept the headlights on to help light his way towards the trailer. He also clicked on his flashlight aiming it at the ground in front of him. He shined the light inside of the other patrol car, afraid of what he might find, but seeing nothing, he was relieved. He wondered what had happened out here and how it was possible for two men to disappear so quickly. Moving cautiously around the car and watching the trailer and at the same time. The swaying grass that surrounded him bothered Crow the most, it constantly moved with the wind, rustling and distracting him as he tried to listen for signs of life.

Nothing other than the grass moved. The trailer remained half dark and motionless, as Crow walked the perimeter shining his light over every inch of the driveway. Looking a few feet ahead he spotted a dark form on the ground. He aimed his light at the form, but it was too far away to see. He walked slowly towards it, watching the ground as he went keeping an eye out for clues. As he came closer to the form, he noticed that it had the outline of a person, but it was flat on the ground, so he figured it was a pile of clothing. Why clothes would be left lying out in the middle of a driveway, he had no idea. However, nothing about today had been ordinary so he'd take this in stride along with everything else.

Crow saw as he got closer that the clothes weren't empty as he first thought. He saw the back of a head. Both hands were stretched out above the head, fingers spread as if reaching for something, but it wasn't right; the body appeared deflated like a ball that lost its air. He hadn't been at any of the other murder scenes, but he'd been told of the condition that the bodies were found in. At the time, he couldn't picture it - or he just didn't believe it was real. Now that he was standing near one of these bodies it terrified him to see the reality of it.

He bent down examining the back of the head the hair was black and short. The clothing was obviously one of their regulation uniforms. Crow knew who it was that lay on the ground before him, he didn't have to turn the body over – it was Wiley. He stood up and shined the light towards the trailer, and sure enough, there was another body laying a few more yards away. It would be Baker.

Crow clicked the button on his mic. "Chief?"

"Go ahead?"

"Wiley and Baker are dead. I'm going to check the perimeter. You'll have to get out here."

Salinger came back clearly exhausted. "I have a situation here too, I can't make it. Call in Dr. Woodhouse, and I'll see what I can do."

"Yes, Sir." Crow surveyed the scene, he was on his own, and that was fine too.

☐

Sally padded across the bedroom in her slippers; she just stepped out of the shower, and she heard her scanner squawk in the background. She grabbed the scanner out of her purse and turned up the volume, but she was too late there was nothing but silence.

"Damn," she put it on the kitchen table deciding to make a cup of tea. She went through the motions, put the water on the stove, got out the honey and waited for the water to boil. The entire time she kept looking at the scanner, waiting for it to bring her some excitement. Nothing happened. She made her tea and sat with a magazine resigned to the fact that she couldn't make the news. When finally, a voice came over the airwaves.

"Yes," she said grabbing it off the table. Constable Crow's voice entered her home as she listened intently to his description of the situation and heard Salinger's reply.

Sally jumped up and raced back into the bedroom. This time, she was going to be smart. She tossed on a heavy sweater and jeans, then she grabbed her purse throwing the scanner back into it and ran out of the house. She didn't know where Salinger was, but she knew that he'd sent Crow to find the missing constables. He distinctly said West and seeing as there was only one highway in this podunk town, she'd cruise it and find Crow.

Salinger flashed his lights as he pulled up next to the station wagon that was parked precariously. Constable Duncan gave the Chief a quizzical glance, and Salinger nodded to the house up ahead. "This house has been deserted for a few years now Constable, yet there is a car in the driveway?" He turned to the young man with a confident look. "That's called detecting son, learn it." Then he put the car in park and stepped out.

Doug opened his door and stepped out, knowing that they were already in trouble, and there was no point in making it worse by running away. The Chief knew right away who he was. He even knew exactly where he lived.

"Mr. Bowan," Salinger said. Nothing about the situation made him uneasy, but training drew his hand to rest on the hilt of his pistol anyway. He assumed the call he received came from Doug and whoever was with him. Duncan got out of the car and walked around to see who else was in the station wagon.

Doug stood before the chief not quite knowing what to do. He knew they were in deep trouble, and he wanted desperately to find a way out of it. He just wasn't sure how to go about doing that. Inside the car, the girls sat anxiously watching the men to see what would happen. Duncan peered inside at them but made no moves to remove them from the car.

Salinger looked Doug over and saw no signs of drug or alcohol use, which was at least a good thing. "I know that your mother is aware of the curfew, care to tell me what you all are doing out here at this time of night?"

Doug was terrified and trying hard not to show it. "Hello Sir," he said respectfully. "I do know about the curfew Sir, and my mother will kill me when she finds out about this." He looked down at his feet. "You see we had - the girls and I that is - had a rendezvous with a couple other friends planned weeks ago," he shrugged, buying time to collect his thoughts. "I know we were wrong in still going out, but you see Sir, we were afraid that with the curfew just being put on today that the girls may not have heard about it. So, I decided to come out to check on them. And as you can see they surely did show up." He finished pointing a thumb over his shoulder at the car and prayed that he didn't go overboard.

Salinger frowned. "Mr. Bowan," he said touching Doug's elbow, "we received an anonymous phone call, and I don't know if you had anything to do with that, but you are going to show me exactly where the body is, and then we'll talk. Now you lead us in your car, and we will follow. Are we clear?" Salinger turned without saying anything else or even waiting for a response and climbed into the cruiser, motioning his constable to follow suit.

Doug stood with his mouth hanging open and watched the chief get back into the cruiser. With little choice, he climbed back into the station wagon with the girls.

Katlin sat stiff and staring ahead. "So? What's going on?"

"Um...I..Uh..." Doug started the car, not even wanting to tell them. He felt Katlin's hand over his own, and he looked at her. "We have to take him to the - uh- to Bear Lake."

Katlin's eyes widened, and she gasped. "What?"

While in the back seat, Mindy began to hyperventilate.

☐

North Falls General Hospital, 1:30am

Lucy Walker lay in the hospital bed thinking about the creature that had attacked her. She saw the cat vividly in her mind. How the glowing red eyes glared at her. She shuddered. No wonder she couldn't sleep, even with the light sedatives they'd given her. She ran her hand gently over the stitches; she received five of them in her head. It was tender but did not hurt as badly as she thought it would. The wound on her ankle, however, pulsated as though the thing was still attached suckling. Bile rose in her throat at the thought of its suction filled mouth.

She checked her watch and was frustrated. The doctor told her she had to stay the night for observation because she may have a concussion. She had been hoping that the police officer would have come back already to let her know that her house was safe, but so far, she hadn't heard a word from them.

She sat up slowly and, when no dizziness occurred, swung her legs off the bed. If the cops weren't going to let her know what was happening in her very own house, then she was going to go out there and find out. She knew she'd have to sneak out of the hospital but wasn't too worried; night shift was light on staff. She figured getting out would be the easy part. Getting home without a car, and no coat in the cold, was a different matter altogether, but she was sure she'd get around it somehow.

Once Lucy had her bloodied clothes back on, she opened her door an inch and peered out into the hallway. After waiting a minute and seeing no movement, she made her move towards the hall stairs. She reached the stairwell exit without seeing, or being seen by, anyone. She sighed with relief as she slipped behind the door

When she reached the ground level, she decided to try her luck in the staff parking to see if maybe she'd find an open vehicle, with keys to borrow. She was not a thief, but it was too cold to walk, and all she wanted was to be in the comfort of her own home. Always a loner and an outcast, Lucy's only solace were her figurines, and she needed them now more than ever.

She spent 25 minutes hunched over and checking cars for keys. She looked in cars that were open checking glove boxes, and visors. She checked the fenders of locked cars, for the magnetic key box. The last car she checked, a red Ford Taurus with a dented fender and peeling paint job, had not only an unlocked door but also had the keys hanging from the ignition.

"Murphy's law," she reasoned with confidence. "If I checked this car first it would have been locked."

She rolled out of the hospital without confrontation. As she turned away from the lot, she decided to go to the police station first and see if they found anything. She needed to know if they found the cat, that was not merely a cat.

Sally drove out past Lucy's house and the Mercer's house, both places she'd been earlier that night. She knew that constable Crow had to be close by and she slowed her vehicle to a crawl. She watched the tree line for any signs of driveways; it wasn't easy without street lights. The moon was now deep behind dark, ominous clouds that completely blotted out the night sky. She turned down a few logging roads, only to have to backtrack. Finally, she spotted a dirt track on the south side and carefully navigated the turn onto weed laden road.

Sally bumped down the old dirt track, which didn't appear to be a real driveway. She hoped she was on the right track and didn't have to turn back and start searching all over again. Relief washed over her as her lights reflected off the rear end of a parked police car. Pulling in behind it, she shut off her Rover. She grabbed a flashlight from the glove compartment and slammed the door loudly. Usually she would sneak around these situations, but tonight she didn't want to be a statistic from being shot by a cop accidentally.

Sure enough, she was rewarded with the flash of light in her direction and a voice yelling out. "Who goes there?"

She stepped behind the police car just as a precaution and yelled back. "It's Sally McKinney, Constable!"

Constable Crow's large form came into view. "What are you doing here?"

"I came to help."

Crow narrowed his eyes his jaw visibly grinding. "Go home."

"Sorry, no can do. The chief personally said he needed my help, and so here I am." She lifted her shoulders and smiled at the big man. "Hey you've got a walkie-talkie, call him up and ask him yourself. I am here to help you, and I promise not to get in the way or mess up your scene."

"Get out of here right this instant. Before I arrest you, and stick you in the back of a freezing cold cruiser, and leave you there until I'm done with my investigation."

Sally backed up realizing that she was not going to get anywhere with this man. She looked up into his stony face. She decided that being frank for once might actually have an advantage. "Please? I talked to Salinger earlier, and he told me about the two constables disappearing. He said that he might need my help, because of how short-handed you are. I can do extra legwork that you're not going to have the time for." Sally smiled kindly up at the man, ever aware of his ability to make good on his threat, trying to show him that she had no other intentions and just wanted to help out.

Constable Crow held up his hand to warn her not to move and stepped a few feet away from the reporter. He dipped his head and spoke quietly into his Mic. He let out an audible sigh and stood tall. "He says it's okay but," he turned to her and held up a finger, "do not touch anything, and none of what you see here tonight gets out to the public unless approved by the chief."

Sally nodded in agreement and followed the constable as he led her towards the trailer. A lump rose in her throat the closer they got, and her palms clammy. As they reached the front of the first cruiser, which naturally belonged to the missing constables, Sally wasn't so sure she'd made the right decision. If the bodies were as horrible as she heard they were, and from the far away portion she's seen of Alice Mercer, she did not want a close-up. She swallowed the lump in her throat and proceeded behind Crow.

The smell hit her first, like rancid meat, her stomach turned. Ahead of her, constable Crow continued on seemingly unaffected by the growing odor. When he stepped around the dark blanket that lay in the middle of the driveway, Sally stopped. He didn't warn her the bodies were right here, he hadn't said anything to her since they started walking.

Crow, noticing that Sally stopped, turned to her. "What?"

Sally gulped down the saliva that threatened to prime a full-on hurl. "Well…" she hesitated not wanting to complain, or sound like she was whining, after all, she was the one that pushed to be here. "I was just wondering what job you want me to do?" She kept her eyes locked on Crow's so she wouldn't have to look down at the ominous sight on the ground.

"I'm taking you to the trailer to help collect evidence," Crow paused furrowing his eyebrows at her. "Are you afraid, Ms. McKinney?"

Sally's face flushed, one of the unfortunate side effects of being a redhead was the accented blushing. She shook her head holding back an angry retort. After all, she did hesitate before the body, and she was afraid that she'd have to see one of them, but she didn't need the constable to rub her face in it. "I'm fine," she said crossing her arms over her chest, "I was just curious as to what I should do. That's all."

"Let's stop wasting time then and get inside," Crow said shifting his eyes nervously around the deserted area, causing shivers to race up Sally's back. He just reminded her that she was out in the middle of nowhere with two constables dead and only one other to protect her. She stepped in place behind the big man silently signaling her submission.

He recognized her hesitation immediately but continued towards the trailer anyway. A few feet before the square of light that lit up the ground outside the trailer, Crow stopped and turned slightly so Sally could see half of his face. Now that she knew her place, he felt he should be more considerate of her feelings. "I'm just warning you that there are two bodies up ahead, they are covered over, but, just so you know, and don't step on them." He finished then walked on and moved around a large blue tarp and up onto the trailer's steps.

This time, Sally didn't hesitate; she didn't even bother to look down. She walked around the tarp, careful of its edges so as not to disturb anything, and entered the trailer.

From where Sally stood at the front door of the trailer it appeared to have been ransacked. To her right was the kitchen. All available surfaces were filled with stacks of dirty dishes. She couldn't even see the top of the small dinette table because it was so overcrowded. In the living, room clothes were strewn on the couch, floor, and also on the coffee table. The smell was enough for her to want to be back outside with the rotten bodies again. The fumes were that of old cigarette butts, stale sweat, and unwashed... everything.

Crow looked at Sally as she plugged her nose against the smell. He sidestepped a yellowed towel. "They were killed outside where they lay," he motioned to the room before them, "this is how they lived."

Sally nodded, and disgust covered her face, then she asked. "So, what are we doing inside then if they were killed out there?" She hoped that they would go out for fresh air soon.

Crow sighed as he waded through the garbage that littered the narrow trailer. "It's still a part of the crime scene. We are checking for evidence," he waved his arm towards the hallway indicating that she should head into the bedroom. "Go in there and look for anything out of the ordinary."

"What would out of the ordinary entail?"

"You'll know it when you see it if you see it."

"Are you shitting me? This is how you do your forensics?

Crow set his mouth tight, and his eyes bore into Sally's. She knew she was pushing her luck, so she shut her mouth and kept her thoughts to herself.

How weird, though, look for anything out of the ordinary? Well, what if I find a twelve foot, vibrating, neon dildo? Is that considered out of the ordinary or should I take it in stride? Jeez, maybe it's a good thing I am here to keep an eye on the system. Sally thought wryly to herself as she moved around the crowded bedroom.

After searching the filthy home, they came up with nothing that deemed itself worthy of clue status. Crow lead Sally back outside where she breathed deeply for the first time since entering the trailer.

"Well, now what?" She asked the stone-faced constable.

He shrugged. "We wait for the Coroner; he hasn't arrived yet as you can see by the bodies lying all around."

"Ha-ha funny." Sally retorted, not at all impressed by his dry humor. "If I'm not needed then, I'll just mosey on over to where ever Salinger may need me."

Crow shook his head. "You're here with me until he calls and tells me otherwise."

Anger rose in Sally's cheeks. *How dare he tell me where I can, or cannot, go!* She was about to yell this, and a few other choice words, when she remembered where she was, and why she was there. If it weren't for Salinger, she wouldn't be in the middle of the investigation, to begin with. She shut her mouth again and pushed her anger down.

To distract herself she concentrated on trying to keep her feet warm while they waited for the coroner to come and take away the bodies.

The Longest Night

Salinger followed the old station wagon as it led them out to Bear Lake over the old shut down route. The dirt road was rutted with large potholes, and the bushes were so overgrown that the two-lane track had narrowed down to one lane, and the tree branches scraped his cruiser. He cursed the kids under his breath for coming out here tonight.

"How'd you know they were the ones that had called in about the body?" Duncan asked as he cringed while branches hit the car.

Not taking his eyes off the road Salinger quietly said. "Mindy."

"Mindy?"

"Yes, Mindy. First of all, you never see her without Sheila, and she had also been crying. I could see the red circles under her eyes and the snot running down her chin even in the dark." Salinger told his young constable. "Although," he paused thinking. "I'm not sure about Mr. Bowan's involvement in all this."

"What?" Duncan asked wanting to get a bead on the chief's thoughts. "You don't think he was with the other girl? But, Mindy is in the car with them."

Salinger shook his head. "No, that's not what I meant. I don't think he was with Mindy when she called into the station. You haven't been in this town long enough. Doug is a good, honest kid. If he was at the payphone with Mindy, he would not have made her speak. Crying as hard as she was, he would have taken responsibility for himself." He shot a quick glance at Duncan, "I know others are involved in this mess, I don't know yet if it matters or not, but I intend to find out."

"You must really know this Doug kid well, to think he would have called himself, and not just be trying to save his own hide."

Salinger shook his head. "That's something else that has been gnawing at me. I'm pretty sure that Doug is a quick thinker, and he would've thought about the fact that this is the only road leading out from the lake. Now, why would someone who wanted to make an anonymous call do that before they got clean away." Salinger shook his head. "Nah, something just doesn't ring true here."

Duncan thought about everything the chief had just told him, but he had no answers as to what was really happening. He kept his mouth shut deciding it was best for the chief to work out the problem and he'd just be there for backup and to learn on the job.

Police Station, 2:00 am

Lucy Walker drove the stolen car slowly through the sleeping town. She was headed to the police station, but she wasn't going to tell them she stole a car. She crinkled her nose at the irony of the situation. *What a weird spot to be in*, she thought. Bypassing the main street, Lucy pulled into the police station parking lot from the back alley. She parked the stolen car away from the building so it would be harder to make out clearly. Locking it up now she pocketed the keys, she didn't want someone stealing her stolen-borrowed car; she'd feel responsible if that were to happen.

As Lucy approached the building, she realized how dumb her actions had been since leaving the hospital. Here she was at the police station with a stolen car, she'd never taken anything without permission in her life, she had blood on her shirt and no coat, and she wanted to go back to the very place she'd been attacked. Lucy stopped and rubbed her head, did she hit her head harder than she thought and had all her senses knocked out? She wasn't sure she wanted to think about that too deeply, but Lucy knew that she wasn't acting rationally. She looked up at the small building, *oh well too late to turn back now*, she told herself and headed into the building.

Millie stepped out of a side room, and the depression lines on her cheek told Lucy that she had been in the break room lying on the couch. Lucy stepped up to the counter and smiled politely.

Millie tilted her head, her unruly hair standing in all direction. "Ms. Walker? What are you doing here?" Knowing that Duncan had taken her to the hospital and that she should still probably be there, recovering.

Lucy gently probed the swollen area around her stitches self-consciously. "Did they find anything at my house?"

"You know I can't answer a question like that Ms. Walker," Millie told her and came out from behind her counter trying to take Lucy's' arm into her own. Lucy pulled away before she could touch her. "Please," she motioned to the break room, "come and sit down in here and rest with me."

Lucy backed away further from the counter all she wanted to do was go home and crawl into her own bed. She shook her head, and the sudden motion made her stomach clench. She closed her eyes for a second, but that only made the sickness feel closer. She was going to heave, and she placed a hand over her mouth. A small belch escaped her lips. "Oh…" she backed up further until the backs of her knees hit a chair, and she sat. "Excuse me. I…um," she opened her eyes and looked at Millie who had now moved closer.

"Just sit there dear," Millie waved at her, "I'll get you a glass of water."

Lucy watched Millie waddle off. *What am I doing here?* She wondered again and decided that she was a complete idiot. Lucy stood up leaned her head on the cool wall for a moment then stumbled out of the station.

She walked as quickly as she dared back to the stolen car. What she needed to do now was find a suitable place to dump the car and still be close enough to get home without having to walk too far in the cold. She thought about the route home visualizing the way she'd go. Then it came to her, the old logging road at the bottom of Jasper hill; she could leave the car there and then walk up the hill back to her home. It was still quite a trek, but it beat getting caught with a stolen vehicle. Having decided that she felt better about going back to her home, she set off determined not to be afraid anymore.

☐

Bear Lake, 2:00 am

Chief Salinger followed close behind and to the side of Doug. His hand ready at the hilt of his pistol, as the two of them, followed the treeline around the clearing. He had his constable stay back in the car with Katlin and Mindy. So far Doug had kept silent, but Salinger knew the boy was holding back; every few seconds he caught the shifting glances that Doug threw his way. He'd wait the boy out feigning nonchalance. Getting a suspect to talk was an art form that he had perfected over the years, and in some cases, silence worked far better than browbeating.

Suddenly Doug stopped. He looked off into the trees ahead then turned and looked back towards the dying fire. After doing this several times, Salinger knew that Doug was trying to get his bearings as to where the body lay. Now Salinger was sure, Doug didn't know where the body was; he was not the one who made the anonymous call. Plus, the circumference of the bonfire, suggested a bush party had taken place. Salinger could only stew, knowing that many teens had snuck past his constables and made it all the way out here.

Salinger shined the flashlight into the dense Forest ahead of them. "Is this where you last saw Sheila?"

~ 219 ~

Doug's eyes narrowed as he thought of how to respond, then he shrugged. "It's really hard to tell sir." He wasn't sure what else to say. He wanted Sheila's body to be found, but he hadn't come near the body earlier.

Salinger nodded. "Alright, I understand son. Why don't you go back to the car and get warm? I'll look around here and see what I find."

He stepped away and shined his light along the edge of the tree line hoping to find her body soon so they could wrap this up and move on. He still could not believe that Baker and Wiley were dead, but even though that weighed on his mind, he had to concentrate on this right now because these deaths were somehow connected and he needed to put a stop to it quickly.

As Doug moved away, he spotted something. "There!" He stopped and pointed into the bushes.

Salinger swung the light in the direction that Doug was pointing, and saw her running shoe first, cocked in a strange position. Its sheer whiteness lit up against the night. *Damn*, he had hoped somehow it would not be true, but it was another body to contend with.

"Don't go any closer." He waved Doug back and went into the brush to see for himself. It came as no surprise that the body was sunken, her mouth a gaping black hole. If the kids had not told them who this was, Salinger wouldn't have known who he was looking at. There was nothing about the body that identified who it used to be, other than perhaps her long flowing blonde hair, that lay in tangled wisps among the underbrush.

As he flashed his light into the open mouth, he heard gagging noises from behind him. "I told you to stay put," Salinger said without turning around. He knew that Doug was standing nearby and looked over his shoulder. He ignored the boy as he ran the light over the clothing. She had a lot of scratches along her arms. Twigs and leaves were stuck in her clothes. Something shimmered as he passed over the body with his light and he leaned in for a closer look. It was another green scale like the one he found in Lucy Walker's bathroom. He took a baggie out of his pocket and scooped the scale into it.

Doug had turned away when he saw the body, but he had turned back in time to see Salinger examining an iridescent scale through the evidence bag. "I've seen that before," he said in an excited, yet puzzled tone.

Salinger turned. "What?"

"I've seen that scale before."

Salinger got in Doug's face so quickly that he almost toppled the boy. He grabbed the front of

Doug's jacket with both fists and pulled him close. "Where!"

"Here..." Doug stammered, pulling away from the chief. "I mean, I've got it right here. I found it earlier today." He proceeded to reach into the pocket of his jeans. He held up a green scale, exactly like the one the chief just lifted from Sheila's body.

Salinger took the scale from the boy's hand. It was identical to the scale he just found. Holding the two up together they were the same size, shape, and density. He dropped the second scales into another baggie. Holding his flashlight, so it lit up Doug's face the chief questioned him. "Tell me exactly where and when you found this?"

"I...we...I mean I found it this afternoon sir," Doug stammered afraid of getting Katlin in more trouble than they already were.

"Where?"

"Off the logging road at the bottom of Jasper hill. I took a spill there today when the brakes failed on my bike. There was this big depression in the ground and that," he pointed indicating the scale, "was on the ground."

"Okay Doug," Salinger said reassuringly. "First things in the morning you are to come back to the station and have a long talk with me. You understand." He took Doug by the shoulder and led him back to the car.

Salinger's words caught Doug off guard. He never expected to have to explain anything beyond showing them the body. The trip back to the cars went too quickly for Doug, as his mind was chocked full of thoughts of how to keep from implicating Bobby and the others.

Jasper Hill, 2:30 am

Lucy turned down the dark lane at the bottom of Jasper Hill. The tires crunched over the gravel sounding like thunder in the quiet night. She clicked off the headlights and slowly coasted along the road until she could no longer see the highway in her mirror. Thanks to the curfew she saw no one else along the way. She took comfort in the fact that no one had seen her in the stolen car, she now regretted taking. But it was too late for regrets; she did what she had to do to get home. She placed the car in park and left the keys in the ignition then got out. The cold air hit her hard, her teeth chattering instantly, she opened the back door and climbed inside hoping to find something to keep herself warm. She rifled around in the dark car, running her hands along the footwells until she found what she wanted. A blanket. It wasn't very large or very thick, but it would help to cut the bitter wind.

The blanket now wrapped around her shoulders, Lucy turned back towards the highway and started walking. Free from the vacuous interior of the car, she could hear how loud the night really was, with the chirping of crickets, the wind rustling fallen leaves and the occasional hooting of an owl. She found the noises quite soothing as it helped her know she wasn't alone out there in the dark on a cold night, and her step got a little lighter.

Her spry step and lighter mood was short-lived, however, as she suddenly heard a different sound. It was an ordinary and familiar sound, but because of her harrowing incident only hours earlier, it drew shivers up her spine.

It was a cat's meow.

Lucy stopped dead in her tracks and listened again. *Did I really hear that, or was it my imagination? Could it be the drugs distorting something less threatening?* She held her breath and listened intently. A rustling off to her left drew her eyes. As she turned her head to look there was more movement from the road in front of her. She looked up and could see nothing in the darkness, just trees, and road. Standing as still as a statue with the blanket held tightly she waited, one minute, three minutes, five – nothing moved but the wind. She let out a sigh of relief, it was just her nerves after all, and she resumed walking.

The first step she took was accompanied by a howl nearby. Lucy jumped, her breath caught in her throat. Suddenly the road ahead of her was lit up like a Christmas tree. Hundreds of sets of red eyes glowed in the night blocking her passage to the highway. They stretched across the road, and more were coming up behind them, they appeared to be flowing out of the bushes. They no longer resembled the cats that they once used to be. They took on their real form. Standing two feet tall, straight-backed, with green scaly skin, glowing red eyes, flickering tongues - through suction cupped mouths, and ready to tear claws clacking on their powerful hands.

Letting the blanket fall to the ground Lucy turned and ran as fast as she could into the trees.

☐

Logan's Residence, 2:30 am

Sally watched as the coroner and his aid loaded the bodies into the two overhauled station wagons. And thought she'd never be able to get into one of those vehicles again. Constable Crow had helped Dr. Woodhouse, and his aide Hal Clement, with the removal of the bodies. Sally wasn't permitted to be close to the bodies. She was thankful for that because no matter how much she wanted to be a part of the investigation, she hadn't planned on getting involved as far as touching dead bodies went. Especially these ones that were little more than limp pools of flesh. She shuddered at the mere thought.

Exhausted, she wanted nothing more than to go home and sleep. Even so, Sally didn't regret promising Chief Salinger that she'd stay and help. She found out the hard way how difficult crime scenes were to investigate, and hoped that he had better luck at finding clues then they did.

With the last body loaded into the vehicle, Dr. Woodhouse patted Crow on the shoulder and left, with his assistant following behind in the second vehicle. Sally was alone again with the stoic officer, a smelly trailer, and a dirt road she longed to be heading home on. She shrugged her shoulders deeper into her coat and hunched her back against the wind. "What now?"

"Go home."

"Constable Crow, is your given name 'Man of Little Words'?" She taunted him, sensing that beneath his big, quiet exterior, he had a sharp sense of humor.

Crow's teeth showed clearly against the distinction of his face, as a smile parted his lips. She couldn't help but notice how distinguished he looked as he smiled.

"Better than Babbling Brooke, as they would have named you." He teased back. "Go home and get some rest," he said, as he placed a friendly hand on her shoulder. "You were a great help tonight, thank you."

Sally nodded, glad to have made a friend in Crow. A reporter's life is often a lonely one, as evidenced by her lack of friends, she had a few back in Vancouver, but no real deep connections. In fact, the last 24 hours in the small town was beginning to make her question the need to return there. The walk back to Sally's Rover was comfortable enough to solidify the notion that he was now her friend, at least in her mind. Crow waited for her to dig out her keys and get into her vehicle safely, but Sally still had other things on her mind. "Shouldn't we go out and give the chief a hand?"

"Just go home. The chief said he's fine, he may even be headed back to the office anytime now, and besides," he shrugged at the helplessness of the situation, "there is nothing we can do for any of these people but find the killer."

"Please let him know that if you need anything, anything at all, I'll be there," she said while starting the engine, then, with a wink, she pulled around in the drive and headed for home.

☐

Police Station, 3:30 am

Short-staffed, Salinger had no choice but to send constable Duncan off with Doug, Katlin, and Mindy in the Shaw's car, to return them home safely. He had stayed back to wait for the coroner to arrive. Then, though it was the wee hours of the morning he still had to inform Sheila's parents of her murder.

The night had been long and arduous, but he sighed with relief after leaving the crying family behind. Facing mutilated bodies paled in comparison to telling parents that their only daughter was dead. He had yet to inform Wiley and Bakers' families that they were gone too. But as far as they knew the men were still on duty. Until he had more information on their deaths, he would hold off telling them for as long as he possibly could. His emotions were too close to slipping over the edge, and he needed to keep his sanity, at least until they caught the murderer.

Now he had to get back to the station and meet his remaining constables whom should both be there by now waiting for him. Everyone needed to get a few hours of sleep, and then he had to formulate a plan of action, he needed more manpower.

Checking his watch, he saw that it was three-thirty in the morning and as he passed through town, he saw no signs of life anywhere. He felt alone and suddenly wished Ms. McKinney had been with him. Then the thought subsided, the last thing he needed in his life right now was a woman, he was just tired of everything, especially of being alone. He shook his head fighting off the weariness that threatened to take over. *I need a strong cup of coffee*, he thought as he pulled into the station.

Inside the station, he found Crow behind Millie's desk with the chair tipped back, his feet up, and his hat pulled low over his eyes. Duncan was sprawled across three of the hard-plastic chairs in the waiting room. Understanding how tired they were, he tiptoed, so as not to disturb them, and, peeking into the break room. Millie on the only sofa sound asleep as well. Salinger wanted to catch a few winks himself but sat behind his desk and stared at the phone instead. He had the desire to check on Sally to see if she made it home safely, but at the same time, he didn't want to disturb her. Running his hands over his face, he decided that he'd best wait until morning; after all, he really didn't want her to know that he was thinking about her.

A New Day

Rays of sunlight reflected off the water in the sink and bounced around the tiny washroom. The weather was not in tune with the heaviness that weighed upon the town.

Salinger rinsed his face under the cold tap water. He scrubbed at the sleep resting in the corners of his eyes and, as he blinked, his eyelids felt like sandpaper. At least the phone had stayed silent in the last hours of the dawn, and they were all able to rest. Now that he was fully awake the night's events plagued his mind. His first job of the morning would be to notify Baker and Wiley's relatives of their deaths. He sighed and felt a hundred years older under the burden. Glancing at the clock, he saw that it was just after seven and decide to check on Sally first.

When Sally picked up the phone, her voice heavy with sleep, Salinger felt his mouth go dry. He cleared his throat as she repeated her hello.

"Yes, sorry. Good morning."

"Oh…hello chief."

Salinger adjusted his tie suddenly not at all sure of what he was doing. He had no clue what to say. He wanted to slam down the phone as if it was a wrong number, but it wasn't possible she knew who it was on the other end. "Did I wake you? I mean I didn't want to wake you, but…" he stumbled over his words and hoped she thought he was just over-tired. "I wanted to ask for your help today."

"Yes of course. This is what I asked you for in the beginning remember?"

He nodded, and then realizing she couldn't see him through the phone, said, "Yes, Ms. McKinney and I wanted to thank you for last night you were a great help to Crow. Without you, his job would have taken twice as long. What time can you get here?"

"How's eight? Is that soon enough?"

"Yes, yes. Eight, um…eight's good. I'll see you then and thank you." Salinger's face flushed. He felt like an old fool. Here he was in the middle of his townspeople's being mutilated, and he was flirting with a city girl. She didn't even bother to answer him; all he got from her end of the phone was a click, then empty air hissing in his ear.

Just then, Millie entered his office with a light wrap of her knuckles on the wood. "Here's some coffee for you." She placed the steaming brew down before him on the desk.

"Ah, Millie, what would I ever do without you?"

She grinned and shrugged. "What's the plan for today sir," she asked him, her clothes wrinkled and her hair now flat on one side and sticking up on the other. She looked a mess but didn't take notice. She was only concerned with being ready to serve her town.

Salinger took a sip of the hot liquid, barely waiting a moment for it to cool, eager for the feeling of the life-pumping elixir to hit his tired veins, and he sat back cradling the mug against his chest. "Well, I think we have no choice but to call an emergency town meeting today." Turning his chair slightly he could see the sun resting above the horizon. Daylight had barely awoken upon his town, but the coffee must have awakened something in him, or maybe it was a second wind. His eyes drew towards Millie, who stood disheveled before him, and he felt sorry for her, hell he felt sorry for everyone right now.

"Millie," he leaned in towards her as though they were conspiring something big together. "We are all going to pull together on this thing. I can't do it alone. I need help, and I think that the good folk of North Falls are just the people to do it."

☐

Shaw Residence, 7:45am

Doug sat at the kitchen table across from Katlin. Neither of them said a word as Mr. and Mrs. Shaw puttered around the kitchen, completely unaware of everything that had happened to the children just a few hours ago. When the constable dropped the kids off at the house, he hadn't thought to see them inside, or to inform Katlin's parents of what had transpired and yet he had driven off in the Shaw's car.

Katlin wasn't sure what to do. Should she tell her parents what happened and that their vehicle was in possession of the police? Or, should she just keep her mouth shut and hope that they didn't want to go out anywhere this morning. She raised her eyebrows and gave a strained look as if to question Doug with some unspoken language on what they should do. Oddly, he knew just what she was saying without a word spoken and shrugged his shoulders. He was just as lost and helpless as she was, and they both resumed watching the time bomb as it ticked away with the everyday business of the Shaw residence.

As soon as breakfast was over, the two nervously speed away from the table into the den to talk.

"Look at those two," Katlin's mom beamed. "They can't wait to be alone." Katlin's dad just winked and smiled.

"What are we going to do?" Katlin half whispered half mouthed her question.

Doug sat on the leather couch to think and knocked on his head lightly with his knuckles, his mind was a jumble. He hadn't called his mother yet this morning, because he felt guilty about last night, and he didn't feel like lying to her first thing in the morning. If that wasn't enough to drive him mad, behind him the sun pierced through the window and laid its burning hands on his shoulders. This made him feel as if he was in the hot seat already. *Christ*, he thought, *I can't believe a person died last night and here we are worried about getting caught sneaking out.* "Come on," he said, holding out his hand to her, "let's go and get the car back." His stomach flipped at the prospect of having to speak with the chief but decided the truth would be his best route. And hoped it'd be over quickly, then they could get the car and come home.

"Huh?"

He quickly asked, "Do you think you can act like we're going out to the store and pretend like we're taking the car?"

Katlin thought about it for a second and nodded her head yes.

"Good, then let's give it a shot." He put his arm around her to let her lead the way.

They both smiled as they looked one another in the eye knowing that no matter what comes out of all this, they would always be together and they walked confidently out of the room.

☐

Police Station, 8:00 am

Sally pulled her Rover into the police station's lot a few minutes before eight o'clock. Not wanting to appear over anxious, she shut off the engine and sat staring towards the building. The streets had been quiet this morning, most of the towns' folk it seemed decided to forgo the typical Saturday hustle of shopping or visiting and stayed indoors where they would be safe. It felt like a ghost town to Sally, and as she watched the silent streets, she wondered if this was the calm before the storm. Finally, she steeled herself and entered the station.

All heads turned in unison as she placed two large boxes mixed with muffins and donuts on the counter. "I figured you all would be starved."

Millie's gaze filled with contempt; her lack of sleep only fueled the fire of what she felt for this woman.

"Good morning," Crow welcomed her, lifting his hand. Duncan looked up from his paperwork and nodded.

Sally looked everyone directly in the eye, "Morning." She moved smoothly through the waiting room and into the station's bowels and took a seat right behind the counter with the two constables and Millie.

"Chief Salinger asked me to come in, is he ready for me?" She asked Millie with a deadly and intentional stare to give a direct sign no one was going to push her around. She had seen the look Millie gave her earlier and wasn't about to be intimidated by a backwoods glorified secretary.

Millie stood and pulled her wrinkled shirt down, trying unsuccessfully to straighten it out, and stalked off towards the chief's private office, her head as high as ever.

Sally leaned in towards Crow, "Hear anything yet?" She questioned gently.

"No, nothing yet," he glanced at his watch, "too early I'd say."

She nodded, not sure what else to say. What do you talk about in such a situation; the weather seemed a bit trivial at this point. She shifted uncomfortably in the hard seat, grateful when the chief's door opened, and he motioned her in.

Salinger held out his hand, and Sally took it in her own feeling his strength as he gave her a quick, gentle squeeze. She longed to feel that same grasp around her waist, and a momentary vision of his lips on her mouth danced across her mind. Sally shook her head to dislodge the thoughts. She wasn't here to have sex with the man after all. She forced a smile as he sat behind his large desk his hands folded.

"Thank you for coming out so early," he moved restlessly in his seat. "I asked you to come because I need your help."

Sally nodded for him to continue. She wanted to hear what he had to ask, without feeling as if she had to force every word out of him.

"As you saw last night something unusual is happening here. No, it's more than that, it's downright horrifying." Now he stood up and began to pace behind his desk. "I need help. I can't solve this alone, too many people have died already, and I don't want to have more deaths in my town."

Sally took her notepad from her purse. "Okay. What can I do to help you? Just point me in the right direction, and I'll go. No strings," she finished smiling at him.

Salinger cleared his throat. "Alright. I'm going to hold an emergency town meeting this evening at the Civic Center. I want everyone to be there it's imperative. And I want you to get them all there for me."

Sally's pen hovered over the blank page, and she looked up at the chief. "What? Me? But how am I…" Setting an announcement up a broadcast was one thing, but gathering an impromptu town meeting was something else altogether.

"Oh, I'm sure you can think of a way to wrangle them all together." He smiled at the incredulous look that pulled her mouth down into a frown. "I never thought a little task like that would put a damper on the hot reporter from the city."

"Are you kidding? It'll be a walk in the park." She teased, with a lilt of sarcasm in her voice.

"The meeting is at five sharp. I'd like for it to be sooner than that, but it should take you at least that long to get the word around. I'm sure your boss, even though he's a hundred years old, will help you. I'll have Millie call in the Legion women to set up tables, food, and coffee. That will help spread the word too, all those loose lips," he said without sarcasm. "And…" he paused, and a slight blush colored his cheeks. "I just wanted to tell you how much I truly appreciate your help."

"You will have plenty of time when this is over to make it up to me," she said not taking her eyes off his. Then without pause as though the flirtation never happened she went on. "I'll report in at say noon-ish and let you know how it's going, sound good?"

"Yes, fine. In case I'm not in, I'll leave word with Millie to be sure to patch you through to me."

"Alright, till noon then," Sally stated, dropped her notepad back into her purse and left the office.

Chief Salinger laid out his idea for the town meeting to his staff. Part of his plan was to recruit some locals and deputize them. He had his picks in mind but solicited ideas from Millie, Crow, and Duncan. Then he asked Millie to get together a list of legionnaire ladies to contact. She was in charge of directing them to set up the meeting hall with tables, quick snacks, and a children's area that would be monitored, and also with spreading the word. On top of all that she still had to remain in the station and take care of any local concerns, dispatch the calls and watch the station. After the short meeting, Salinger sent both Duncan and Crow off in their own patrol cars to continue the lookout for strangers, trouble, or anything out of the ordinary. He also asked them to spread the word about the town meeting at the local coffee houses, and other places where people gathered.

Now that the command stuff was dispensed, he hopped in his car to hit the streets. Priority one was to get to the hospital to see Dr. Woodhouse and find out what the hell happened to his people last night. He was going to talk to the constable's families, but first, he needed some answers. He needed to know not only for his own peace of mind but also to be able to communicate tonight with the townspeople.

"Oh, Shit!" He exclaimed smacking himself on the forehead as he passed Mulberry Street. He had forgotten to call Bobby this morning and check up on him. How could he be so involved that he didn't even call his own son? He was ready to slam on the break as he contemplated turning around and popping back to his house for a minute. Then he remembered that Bobby said he was staying with his friend Kevin's last night.

Salinger picked up the Mic and radioed Millie asking her to call his house and leave a message for his son to check in as soon as he arrived back home. This allowed his thoughts to go back to the task at hand, knowing that Bobby would check in later.

Entering the hospital, Salinger leaned his arms on the countertop so the receptionist, who was busy typing on the computer, would pay attention to him faster at the sight of his uniform.

"Yes," she asked politely. She recognized the chief of police but hadn't interacted with him on a personal basis.

"Morning," he touched the brim of his hat in greeting, "would you be so kind as to inform Dr. Woodhouse that I'll be popping down to visit with him in a few moments. I'd like to see Ms. Walker first if you'd find her room number for me."

The nurse nodded turning back to her computer terminal after hitting a few keys she frowned.

Salinger leaned further over the counter; he knew a problem when it was brewing. "What?"

"There is a note on the screen, sir," she told him tapping the top of the computer. "It says' here that any inquiries about Ms. Walker are to see the head nurse - that'd be Mrs. Dougherty – on the third floor." She shrugged to show that she had no idea what it was all about.

Salinger left the bewildered nurse and headed directly for the elevators. Once on the third floor, he went over to the nurse's station and requested to speak to Mrs. Dougherty. Just as the other nurse was headed off to find her, Mrs. Dougherty came down the hallway from one of the rooms. She saw Salinger standing at her station and waved for him to follow her into the small office.

Mrs. Dougherty turned behind the chief as they entered the space and closed the door. "Seat?" She indicated to the one guest chair opposite her tiny workspace.

Salinger shook his head. "Not to be short, but I am busy can you just tell me what happened?"

She crossed her arms over her chest, in an annoyed stance. "Ms. Walker seems to have snuck out of the hospital during the night. I hate to point fingers at anyone Chief," she said, "but one of our night janitor's cars was missing this morning, and I think she was responsible."

Salinger was taken aback by the news. And he wondered why he hadn't been informed of this sooner. "How bad were her injuries? Would she still be in deep shock or delusional?"

"No, nothing like that at all. She had a little bump and a cut. Nothing more, she was medically sound. The doctor wanted to keep her for observation just to be sure there was no concussion. But her reports in no way showed disorientation or confusion."

"Thank you for your time, Mrs. Dougherty. May I use your phone?"

She waved for him to go ahead and left him alone in her office, while she resumed her work.

Millie picked up the phone after three rings which wasn't bad considering how busy he knew she was. "It's me," Salinger said into the receiver. "How are things shaping up this morning?"

Millie tried to hold in a sigh of exhaustion but didn't fully succeed. "Busy," she answered.

"Did anyone call in this morning to report that Lucy walker left the hospital and may have stolen a car?"

"OH! Oh...no." Millie gasped.

"What is it?"

"Well with all this going on, I completely forgot to tell you that she came in here last night. Oh, Chief I feel terrible!" Millie huffed into the phone.

"Calm down, it's okay Millie. We have a lot going on, I understand, heck I forgot about my own kid. Now I want you to contact the men and let them know that Ms. Walker left the hospital sometime last night. She's not under arrest, but we want to be sure she's alright. Have one of them stop by her house and check it out, and watch for a Red Taurus. Keep me informed as to what they find out."

"Yes Sir," Millie was nearly in tears from her error, even though she wasn't in trouble, she had never forgotten a single detail in the past.

Salinger hung up then went directly to the stairwell and headed straight down to the basement.

Reaching the lowest level, the smell was the first thing that hit him. He hated being in the morgue, especially to see his own men laid out, but bracing himself against the horrible sights he knew were to come he pushed open the swinging doors.

Dr. Woodhouse glanced up when the doors opened just as he was replacing the phone's receiver and the look on his face portrayed more than enough meaning to Salinger that something else bad had just happened.

Salinger raised his eyebrow in question.

"Come on in, have a seat, Charles."

"That bad?"

"Worse than you think," Dr. Woodhouse replied stoically as he pulled up a wheeled office chair and sat beside Salinger. "That was the Vancouver's Medical Examiner he had many questions for us," he took a deep breath before resuming, "unfortunately they have learned nothing more but…" he leaned back removed his glasses and rubbed at his tired eyes.

"They're coming, aren't they?"

Woodhouse nodded. "Yes, they are coming, and they are going to be taking over. The head M.E. called the Government into play; he claims that whatever is happening here is not related to human circumstances."

"What? Not human? What the hell does he mean by that?"

"As I've said they have no more answers than us. If they do, they are keeping us out of the loop. Whatever it was that killed those people," he paused. "It wasn't human. Or, well, at least there is no possible way for a human to remove the organs and bones in that fashion. What a mess." Dr. Woodhouse leaned back in his chair rolling his eyes to the ceiling and shook his head. "You'd better warn the town Charles; once the Canadian Armed Forces arrive you'll be locked out just like the rest of us."

"How long do we have?" Salinger asked the doctor.

He glanced at his watch and mentally calculating the driving time between the army base and North Falls. "Noon - one o'clock - at the latest."

"Well, I'd best get a move on then. Did you find out anything that might be of help to me?"

"Only one thing," the doctor stood up moving back into the examining area and picking up a folder off his desk. "All the bodies, we collected last night had traces of feline hair. I found it on and, even inside of them. I'm talking hundreds of different breeds of cat hairs. Something bad is happening out there Charles, and it somehow involves the ordinary house cat."

"What? Why didn't you tell me this earlier?" Salinger started to pace the room, running his hands nervously through his hair again. "Why...," he looked up at Dr. Woodhouse before looking down, his eyes racing wildly back and forth in confusion remembering the story Ms. Walker told him. "I... I... Do you know what happened? What the hell am I to do? I don't even know what to think or what questions to ask! I'm lost here."

Dr. Woodhouse crossed the space between them and placed his hand on the chief's shoulder. "I'm sorry, I only got the results a little while ago, and I just don't have any more answers for you. I have no clue if it's a band of raving mad cats or an epidemic that is affecting their brains." He stopped and scratched his head. "Even still, that can't explain how the people died. Well regardless it's a start; I'm going to send Hal out to find me a cat. I'll examine it and see if I get any answers. Don't worry I'll contact you if it turns up anything."

"Please let me know A.S.A.P.. Until then, I'm going to have to try and bump the town meeting up. I have to get the people informed before the army shows up and scares the bejesus out of everybody. They're scared enough as it is."

He left the doctor, his mind a whirl, thinking about the quickest way to gather the town after he had already sent people out with an agenda. He barely waved at the doctor as he left, his mind churning through the possibilities. As he raced out to his car, he realized that he still had to tell Baker and Wiley's family that they were dead. "Shit!" He banged his hand on the steering wheel, he didn't have enough time. Even though he hated to pass something this important off to a subordinate, he got constable Crow on the line and requested he do that immediately on his behalf.

Brenda turned on the radio and danced around the cozy kitchen. She was preparing breakfast for Margaret, who was busy polishing her nails at the table. Both women had slept in that morning, relaxing after drinking too much the night before. Brenda didn't worry about Doug last night knowing he was safe at the Shaw's. Then an emergency news broadcast came over the radio, and her heart flipped. She raced over and turned up the volume as the high-pitched beep ended.

"This is an emergency broadcast." The woman's voice said over the airwaves. "The Chief of Police is requiring all North Falls residence attend a meeting tonight at five PM at the Civic Center. There he will address recent events. He hopes to help those in need of support and to gather information that might lead to the identification and apprehension of the suspect in the recent murders. I repeat this is a mandatory emergency meeting."

The broadcast ended then the piercing signal returned, and the message replayed again. It blared twice before Brenda finally made a move to turn the radio off. Her face was pale and her cheerful smile, long gone.

"This is worse than they were saying," Margaret said, moving to attend the frying pan that Brenda had suddenly forgotten.

Brenda nodded in agreement. "Yeah! Jeez, I wish Doug was here with us instead of over at Katlin's."

"How about you call, and we'll pick him up after breakfast," Margaret looked at the clock. "It's still early we can finish up here and spend the rest of the day with the kids."

Brenda picked at her upper lip with the tips of her fingers. "Yeah, I suppose you're right the meeting's not until five." She pulled a chair out from the table, sat across from her friend and continued with a smile. "I'm glad you came." Then she picked up the phone and called the Shaw's house so she could talk to Doug. After a few minutes talking she replaced the receiver, Margaret looked up from the frying pan.

"Doug and Katlin went to the store they said they wouldn't be gone long. Jean just heard the announcement. She said they are going tonight, so I guess we'll see them there."

Seeing the worry on her friend's face, Margaret comforted her. "Don't worry its daytime and they're good kids, they'll be fine."

"I know, but it's hard not to…" Brenda shrugged, unable to express the fear she felt not having her son there with her. "I just have this feeling," she tried to calm herself, but her hand went over her heart, before looking for strength in her friend's eyes. "If I don't hear from him by the time we've eaten, then I'm going after them."

As they had planned on their way home from the busted party, Kevin stayed over at Bobby's house. Kevin was upset and didn't sleep well, so at first light, he took off for home. Bobby paced the floor, missing the solace of having someone with him and wondering why his dad hadn't checked in with him as he promised. He moved around the empty house and tried to break up the silence with the television, but that didn't help, so he replaced it with some music. In both cases, the noise just bothered him because he kept hearing a phantom phone ring. After going from room to room looking out of the windows, pacing from the living room to the kitchen, then into his bedroom and back out again, he gave up and decided to make the call himself.

Bobby stood and picked at the pegboard while he waited, dropping the little balls of cork onto the floor. Millie answered the phone after what felt like ten minutes. "Hi Mill," he said as cheerily as possible not wanting the worry to show through his voice. "Is my dad around?"

"Oh, not right now Bobby. I can patch you through to his squad car if you'll hold on a minute son."

"No, nah! It's okay. I guess he's just really busy huh? He didn't call me when he said he would, and I was just making sure everything was cool."

"Yes, no…I mean he's fine, but I was going to call you soon anyway. There is going to be a meeting at five, have you heard yet?"

"No what's going on?"

"Oh gosh, I'm sorry. I've been so busy here trying to organize things that I simply forgot to tell you." Millie babbled while she flipped through papers on her desk. "Why don't you come to the station this afternoon and then you can head over to the hall later with one of us. We'll be happy to take you to the meeting."

Bobby looked down at the pile of cork on the floor in front of him and realized what he had been doing subconsciously. "No, I'm alright Mill, I'll see you down there later okay," he paused, his face fighting off the hurt and frustration. Then he said. "If dad asks, tell him I'll see him later too." Then he hung up the phone.

"Bobby wait, I think it's…" She tried to stop him to insist that he come down, but the line hummed its tune in her ear, and she just slammed the receiver down, mumbled something about kids these days and went about her business. She had neither the time nor the patience in this time of crisis to worry about someone else's kid, she'd just page the chief and let him know his son was at home and get on with business.

Bobby went to his room changed into his black jeans and T-shirt then, fighting back the emotions, put on his black makeup with a quaking hand, spiked his hair and decided defiantly to hop into his car to see what was happening around the town. Maybe he'd see his dad, maybe he wouldn't, but he just couldn't say which he wanted.

Hal Clement drove around the town scanning left to right, keeping his foot an inch over the brake pedal in case he had to stop suddenly. Driving around town looking for a cat wasn't anywhere close to what he pictured himself doing as a coroner's assistant.

"It doesn't exactly take a college degree to catch a cat," he grumbled under breath, "where in the heck am I supposed to find one anyway?" He wondered for the umpteenth time since being sent on off by Dr. Woodhouse on this wild goose chase. "Shoot, this ain't even a wild goose chase, it's a wild cat chase," he chortled at the cleverness of his own joke. Too bad there was no one in the car with him to share it with. He made a mental note to tell the joke to the doctor later on.

He had already checked the main streets and was going through the residential area when he spotted a cat as it darted down a back alley. He turned the wheel sharply pulling the car into a U-turn. His tires squealed on the pavement, and he winced realizing it wasn't a good idea to make overly loud noises when you're trying to catch a cat. He drove slowly into the gravel alley keeping his eyes peeled for the animal. It didn't take long for him to spot it walking along a fence up ahead. Hal pulled up as far on the opposite side of the lane as the narrow space allowed and parked. He left the engine running, pulled on some heavy-duty work gloves, then picked up the cat carrier from the passenger seat before stepping from the vehicle.

The cat had moved behind some garbage cans and, as Hal approached, it began hissing and pawing at the air. Hal moved slowly not wanting to get bitten by the cat in case it had rabies. He set the carrier down with its door wide open as close to the cans as he could. Then he placed his foot up to the lifted paw as he tried to distract its attention away from his hands. It worked. The cat beat rapidly at his tough work boot its claws nicking the suede surface while Hal swiftly, grabbed it by the scruff of its neck and tossed the unsuspecting animal into the carrier.

"Hah! I did it," he hollered into the empty alley proud of the quick work. He scooped up the carrier, which was now seven pounds heavier, tossed it into his car, and headed back to the lab where Dr. Woodhouse was waiting for them both.

☐

Police Station, 9:30 am

Doug stood on the opposite side of the counter trying his best to look like a happy-go-lucky kid with not a care in the world. He smiled his brightest smile and looked over at Katlin who was there smiling brightly right beside him. He put his arm over her shoulder to amplify how beautiful teenage love was, but Millie was having none of it. She shook her head again, standing her ground.

"Please Millie, we just want the car back." Doug nearly whined, but stopped himself short, not wanting to look the fool in front of Katlin. His plan for just walking down to the station and getting the car wasn't working as well as he thought it would.

Millie crossed her arms over her ample chest. "Sorry folks but you have to talk to the constable that brought it in," she leaned in as if to share a secret with a good friend, "and he is not in."

"But Millie you know me! I didn't do anything. He just gave us a ride home last night because we were out past curfew and then he needed our car to get here. It's not like it was impounded or something."

"I know," she said warmly and reached out to pat his hand. "I'm sorry, but the constable has the keys anyway so even if I could…"

"Can't you call him?"

"Well...I can call him up, but I can't promise that he'll be able to come in right away. We are short staffed you know with only two constables left so..." as soon as she saw both the youngster's jaws drop, Millie realized what she said. She mentally kicked herself for having such a big mouth. "Ignore that, you didn't hear what I just said," her face flushed with embarrassment.

Doug turned to Katlin. Her face had gone pale he squeezed her hand for reassurance. "Don't worry we won't tell anyone, but will you help us then?"

"Well." Millie wrung her hands. "I'll radio Duncan and see if he can come in, but you just have to understand the situation here. We have a crisis to deal with," her eyes teared and she was visibly shaken by the ordeal.

"Of course I understand, I just want the car, and then we'll be out of here." Doug smiled politely.

Millie went over to the radio and called constable Duncan. He answered her almost immediately and stated his location. He was still within the town limits just cruising around and informing people of the meeting. Millie let him know that the kids were in to pick up their car. Duncan agreed that he would head back towards the station to return the keys but said that it would still take him the better part of an hour.

He didn't want to rush past anyone that he knew may not have access to radio or television. Millie told him to take his time; they sure didn't want to be responsible if anyone got forgotten about.

Then she told the kids that they'd have to wait awhile for him to return and they agreed to wait across the street at the coffee shop. Doug tipped an imaginary hat on the way out, receiving a swat on the butt from Katlin.

The Hustle

Doctor Woodhouse peered into the dark animal carrier. "I'll need a light tranquilizer. I want the cat drowsy but not totally out of it."

"Why didn't you call Dr. Carlton in to do this?"

"What do you think a vet will do that we can't-do? We're the real doctors here," Dr. Woodhouse waved angrily at the carrier. "Now quit stalling."

Hal filled the syringe with what he hoped was a small enough dose of tranquilizer for a cat. He didn't regularly use tranquilizer because the things he worked with were already dead. He passed it over to the doctor, who stood watching the animal through the narrow bars.

Dr. Woodhouse took the syringe. "Okay pull it out and hold it still for me."

Hal dreaded taking hold of the cat and couldn't keep it from showing on his face. It was bad enough that he had to capture the animal; now he had to hold the wriggling angry thing down, while it got stuck with a needle. He was bound to get scratched, which was not his idea of a good time, but he had no choice, Dr. Woodhouse was the boss. Doing as he was asked, he opened the door and reached into the cage. The cat moved back hissing and pushing itself as deep as it could into the farthest reaches of the cage. Hal ducked his head down nearer to the table peering into the shadowy box trying to get a bead on the cat so he could go straight for it and pull it out.

"Damn, it's dark in there. Can you pull the light over," Hal asked Dr. Woodhouse who stood off to the side waiting impatiently for Hal to retrieve the animal.

With an audible sigh, he reached up bringing the overhead spotlight down and forward as far as its track would allow. "Better?"

Hal grunted his response while concentrating on getting the cat. With the light above him, he could now see a shadow at least, in the back of the carrier. "Why the hell do they make these things so damn..ugh..dense." He complained grunting as he stretched his arm into the carrier.

"Please stop swearing," Dr. Woodhouse commanded. "Just dump it upside-down if you must and let's get on with it."

Hal yanked his arm back out of the cage. "Well why didn't you just say so in the first place," he said while lifting the carrier and tipping it straight up over the table. From inside, the sound of claws screeched over the plastic as the cat scrambled to keep from falling from the cage. With nothing to dig into, the cat came tumbling out of the carrier. It hit the table on its side with a thud, and before either man could move, it got to its' feet and leaped to the floor.

Dr. Woodhouse jumped back as the cat ran past his feet and disappeared under the table.

"Shee-eet!" Hal said, then grinned when the doctor frowned at him.

Dr. Woodhouse rolled his eyes and motioned that Hal was to get the animal out from under the table.

Hal sighed and got right to the job. Crouching down low he looked under the table, and sure enough, the cat had huddled as far back into the darkest corner as possible, up against the wall. "Tsk tsk, here kitty-kitty…" Hal called to the cat rubbing his fingers together like he had food to give it. "Hey you wouldn't have any catnip in your pockets would ya?" He yelled up to the doctor.

"Funny."

"Ah cool! You should see its eyes glowing under here."

Dr. Woodhouse was about to explain to his young assistant about the way that light refracts off the eyes when suddenly Hal cried out. "What the hell!"

As Hal's hand wrapped around the scruff of the cat's neck, it's fur began to slide off. He stumbled back a few steps but had not thought to drop the cat. Its eyes blinked twice, changing from pale orange to a bright glowing red. Its front paws popped forward, the fur dropping away revealing two arms. The four-fingered hands unfurled, and long yellow claws sprung forth. As the new head appeared out of the molting fur, Hal screamed and flung the beast away. It hit the wall with a loud thud and a high-pitched screech.

"What in Gods name was that?" Dr. Woodhouse grabbed the carrier of the table, keeping it between himself and the beast on the floor.

"I don't know," Hal pressed up against the Formica counter, aiming to get as far away from the thing as possible, in the small space. "But let's get the fuck out of here!"

Dr. Woodhouse pushed the carrier towards Hal. "No, we have to capture it. Here, get it back in the cage." Then the beast leaped on Hal's chest, sending him off balance and to the floor. Dr. Woodhouse hollered as Hal rolled under the exam table. All he saw was Hal's legs flailing in the air. He grabbed one of Hal's ankles and started to pull him out.

As Hal's writhing body came towards the doctor, the beast flew out from underneath the table. No longer on all fours, it reared up on its two back legs standing tall. The fur now replaced with iridescent scales. It opened its mouth, bearing back its lips to show off the scores of salivating suction cups.

Dr. Woodhouse fell back, a scream froze in his lungs.

The scaly creature appeared to be smiling as it leaped over the doctor's plump stomach, landing on his chest, its claws extended towards his tender face.

☐

Police Station, 9:40am

Salinger pulled the police cruiser against the curb in front of the police station and ran up the front steps. He banged through the doors so quickly that they swung back and hit the wall with a loud thud. Millie jerked her head up at the noise, just about to yell out at the rude intrusion when she noticed the chief himself striding purposefully towards her desk. "What…" she began when Salinger pushed his way behind the counter and interrupted her.

"I need you to get on the horn now and tell the guy's plans have changed," Salinger sat down in front of Millie's computer and quickly moved through programs muttering incoherently under his breath. He noticed that Millie hadn't moved to carry out his orders yet and realized how crazy he must look right then. Taking a deep breath, he told himself to calm down and stopped what he was doing to turn his full attention to Millie.

"What is it you'd like me to tell the men sir?"

"I'm sorry Millie," he began, "I just found out that the Military are coming in. We are going to probably be quarantined until they can solve this problem." He stopped talking as her mouth dropped open. He reached over and took her hand in his.

Right now he needed her to be strong and help him. He couldn't afford to have his people panicking. "Millie," he gently rubbed his thumb over her fleshy hand. "I need to make the town meeting for right now, so I can let everyone know what's happening. What I want you to do is tell Crow and Duncan about it. I'm setting off the air raid siren, and I need them out there on the streets to help keep everyone calm."

Millie tried blinking out the confusion as she wondered what was happening to their quiet little town, but forced herself over to the radio and began calling the two constables.

"Got it!" Salinger called out when he finally found access to the correct program that gave access to the siren. He turned back to Millie. "Do the guys know what to do?" He asked her making sure they were ready before he set off the emergency sirens.

"Yes sir, they're ready," Millie replied.

"Okay…well here goes everything," he said as he hit the enter key and the siren that sat unused for twenty years began to scream over the entire town. Even though they knew the siren was going to go off, both Salinger and Millie jumped as it started howling.

"What now?" Millie said and bit her lip to help steel her courage.

The chief placed his hand on her shoulder. "I need you to stay here a little while longer Millie," he yelled over the siren. "I'm going out to direct people, along with the constables. First, call the guys at the Fire Dept. fill them in and get them to help wrangle people to the hall. Just tell Chief Fredrick not to worry about manning the station. Then I want you here to field the calls, come over to the meeting hall in about an hour that should give everyone plenty of time to get their bearings and when you're ready to leave stick a note on the door for any stragglers. Okay?"

Although visibly shaken by the recent events Millie nodded to the chief. "I've got it under control."

Salinger nodded his thanks gave her shoulder a squeeze and headed out into the streets that appeared empty right at that moment, but he knew wouldn't be for long.

☐

Sally had gone to the radio station with Salinger's new instructions. She was working with her boss, a withered old man, who would undoubtedly be replaced soon, if not by his death, then for the good of the town's only radio station. That was if anyone had any sense in the small town. Currently, only three people were running the place, and Sally was one of them. The other was a forty-year-old drunk, Tom Danechuck, who had come to North Falls to drink and fish. He hadn't been around at all since Sally started, and he wasn't there today either.

Sally had to set up the automated recording, similar to the one she aired just the night before, with the help of her crotchety old boss alone. They both were trying to figure out what to do next when the siren sounded. She had left her purse, with her police scanner in the break room, and now was kicking herself for it.

"What is that?" Sally screamed over the siren.

Wilfred mumbled unintelligibly.

"What!"

"It's the air raid sirens," Wilfred called back as loud as his 87-year-old vocal chords would allow.

"For bombs. In the old days! Everyone is to go to the Civic Center for safety."

Sally thought about the implications of that. *Okay, so I was already broadcasting for the townspeople to meet there at 5pm, something big must have happened.* She touched Wilfred's shoulder, "Let's go to town, I'll drop you at the center."

"Nope," Wilfred shook his head, his sagging cheeks flapped oddly, "this building is concrete. I'm safe here."

Sally didn't have time, nor the desire to argue with the old man, she left Wilfred locked in the small cement building and raced back into town. As she rolled into the middle of the traffic jam, she saw the chief leaning into a car window ahead. She waited until the vehicles inched forward enough to say something. Pulling up behind his rather enthralling tan-clad behind, she tooted the horn lightly.

Salinger, startled by the horn bumped his head on top of the window edge. He turned, rubbing his head, and smiled when he saw the black Rover with the redhead sticking out the window.

"What's the deal Chief?" Sally yelled over the noise.

"It's an emergency I needed to bump the meeting up to now, and this was the only way to get everyone to the hall quickly."

"Well, it certainly worked," Sally replied motioning to the flux of traffic that seemed unbelievable for such a small town. "I left Wilfred up at the radio station alone, is that safe?"

"Yeah, that's good. He won't open the door to anyone, and he's too old to run around town in this melee."

"What do you want me to do now?" She asked him without preamble knowing he would fill in the details later.

Salinger ran his hands through his hair thinking about what had to be done to ensure the town's safety. He already had both constables, and the firemen, out going door to door to the old folks, and people they knew wouldn't be bothered by such a fuss. Millie was guarding the station, and he was monitoring the main street. Then the thought came to him, no one was in the hall to assist or direct people. He hoped the auxiliary ladies would be heading out there all ready to set up food and chairs, but he couldn't be sure that anything so organized could have happened so fast.

"Listen," he said and leaned tiredly in the open window of her truck. "I really need someone to go out to the hall and check up on what's happening there. If you can get some volunteers to help set up the chairs? Just try to keep everyone calm and patient until I can get there, that would be wonderful."

Sally nodded. "Yes, okay." She bit her lip, wondering how to get out of the traffic jam.

Salinger read her mind. "Get over to that side street and leave your truck there. It'll be faster to walk to the hall."

"Alright, see you later." She inched away from the chief as he resumed poking his head into cars and telling them what to do.

Sally finally made it around the corner and parked. She was in such a hurry that she accidentally opened the car door on a couple of kids. "Oh, I'm so sorry," the embarrassment obvious on her face. "Are you two alright?"

"I'm ok ma'am," Doug replied. "How about you Kat?"

"Oh, I'm fine. Sorry about not seeing your door opening. We were in a hurry to get to the Civic Center, we're supposed to meet our parents there."

Realizing the opportunity at hand, Sally quickly asked, "Can you two assist me when we get to the center? The chief has asked me to help set up things there, and I could use a few more hands."

"Depends," Doug said warily, putting an arm around Katlin to show that he was going to protect his girl first and foremost. "What is it you want from us?"

Sally didn't have a definitive answer, they were all winging it at this point. "Well I was going to head to the hall and see if there are people there setting up chairs," she shrugged, "just keeping everyone calm and preparing for a meeting." She leaned into them to make sure they could hear her, "I'm afraid no one really knows me here, so locals on my side are a big help."

"I guess it wouldn't hurt to help you if we'll be at the center anyways," Doug nodded, and Katlin followed his lead.

"Thank you so much, we can use level-headed kids like you, so if you know, anyone else willing to chip in let me know. Maybe even your folks?" Her green eyes alight with the adventure.

That's when Katlin realized who the lady was. "Hey, are you the new anchor lady from TV last night?"

Sally smiled wearily. "I'm Sally McKinney," her smile faltered, "I would say pleased to met you –

but." She raised her hands at the situation. Of course, the kids understood, after all, it was their town.

They all turned together and headed towards the center. More people had moved out onto the sidewalks and were all heading in the same direction. The sight reminded Sally of the Pied Piper.

Civic Center 10:30 am

They arrived at the meeting hall along with a crowd of people who had also abandoned their vehicles or lived close enough to walk. The double entrance doors were pulled open, and people milled about talking loudly. They questioned each other to see who had the answers to what was happening. Of course, everyone had different ideas, most of the rumors that had no standing whatsoever. Sally shook her head as she passed a group of teenagers talking about a horrible brain-eating monster on the loose. She rolled her eyes and kept on walking. She saw the ladies' auxiliary were already taking control of the situation, some of them were dragging fold-up chairs from behind a stage curtain, while others maneuvered plates of finger foods around large tables.

"Are these people always this quick about things?" Sally asked trying not to yell it out too loudly and offend anyone.

Doug smiled and nodded. "Pretty much." Then he leaned into Katlin, said something to her and pointed towards the stage. Katlin mouthed ok and left his side. "These ladies live for functions. I'm going to help set up the chairs if you need me yell," he told Sally not waiting to see if she approved of his taking charge and walked away.

Sally shrugged; it seemed as though this town knew how to take care of itself. Not sure on where she was able to assist she moved back out to the main doors and decided to try and get the people to start moving inside. They could help finish up the preparations and then they'd be already seated before the chief showed up. That was the plan anyway; whether or not the townspeople would listen to her was another story.

Main Street, 11:00 am

Chief Salinger checked on the shops as he passed by. Most of them were locked up tight, the owners having already left. There were a few diehards inside not wanting to abandon their businesses, afraid to lose even one stray customer that might wander in on their way to the Civic Center. Salinger went in and made them leave, telling them that if they weren't shut up by the time he worked his way back, he'd arrest them. Some of them grumbled and griped, but they all listened to the chief. It didn't take long for the town to have an abandoned feel to it. The stores were empty, a few stragglers moved along the sidewalks; the bulk of vehicles had driven past a while ago. He just prayed that his men had the same results with the farmers and old folks further out.

As he reached the end of Main Street where it turned, and the base of Jasper hill started, there were no more stores to check. He turned around to head back down the other side of the street. Two steps later he stopped, cocked his head, and listened. *What was that?* He wondered turning around and facing the hill. He didn't see anything, and the Siren was still pretty loud. He waited to listen anyway, not sure that he actually heard the faint scream he thought he heard.

Just then Crow's patrol car stopped a few feet in front of him. "Everything alright?" Salinger asked leaning in the open passenger window.

Crow nodded his head. "East end is done sir; I just dropped off a few of the stranded folks. How about you, need a lift?"

"Nope I'm going to run back and shut off this siren before I get in, why don't you head on up Jasper hill and check on Duncan for me. Try to get everyone down here by...," he glanced at his watch shocked to see that it was 11:00 am already, "11:30. The meeting should get started as soon as possible."

Salinger patted the roof of the car to signify that he was done. Crow sped off and roared up the hill. He looked at his watch again and prayed that they would be able to get the meeting over with before the Army arrived. He didn't want them scaring all his people before he had the chance to inform them properly.

☐

Civic Center, 11:30 am

Children, oblivious to the stress and fear that their parents felt, ran, yelled, laughed and played in the rows of seats and behind the stage curtains. Parents ignored the children's cries as they huddled in groups, or stood off with their friends and whispered about what was happening. The rumors were rampant and had very little to do with the truth. It was plain for all to see that they were afraid, and they tried desperately to cover it up with nervous chatter.

Salinger stood in the doorway watching the people, no one had spotted him yet, or he would have been bombarded with questions already. He was glad for a moment's peace even though it would be short-lived. A flash of red caught the corner of his eye, and he turned his head in time to see Sally directing people towards the seats trying to make sense of the chaos. He couldn't stop the smile that formed on his lips; she was quite a woman. With a quick deep breath, he braced himself and moved through the crowd towards her. He nodded to people as they opened their mouths to question him, but merely touched their elbows, and shoulders, giving quick moments of comfort, he hoped would suffice as he pushed on in her direction without stopping.

The stress left Sally's face as soon as she saw him coming. Her lips curved into a welcoming smile.

"I see you've taken care of everything. I could have gone on home to rest," Salinger teased.

Sally blushed in spite of herself. "Actually, you have quite the town here chief, these people know how to handle a crisis. And, thank God that siren has been shut off; I was beginning to go mad."

"Yes, I figured most of the townsfolk are here now or at least the ones that want to be, so I turned it off. I can't thank you enough for helping out here." He frowned as a thought came to him. "By the way have you seen a teenage boy with black hair and a pierced face? He wouldn't be hard to miss since he's the only town kid that dresses that way," he asked Sally while scanning the crowd half expecting his son's face to appear any second.

Sally shook her head. "No. I haven't seen anyone like that here. Why, are we supposed to watch him or something?"

"He's my son," he said.

She raised a hand to her lips to cover the faux-pa of unintentionally assuming the pierced kid a hooligan. She wouldn't have thought the police chief had a child, the way he dealt with his business and seemed whole-heartedly engulfed in his job.

"Please don't worry about it; I just never thought to tell you about my little black sheep. Well, he's not so little anymore and he kind of stands out like a sore thumb. Everyone copes in different ways I guess."

"What about his mother? Wouldn't he be with her?" Sally asked innocently.

Salinger's brow tightened, "She passed years ago…" he held up his hand as he saw the look that everyone gets when they hear a loved one died. Now was not the time. "Don't say sorry, it's been years."

"Well I'm sure he's here somewhere, do you want me to ask around?"

Salinger shook his head, "Don't worry about it, he'll turn up. I wouldn't be surprised if he's mad at me for neglecting him these last few days, but you know," he sighed running his hands through his hair, a nervous habit that Sally found attractive. "I'm the whole town's father right now not just his, and sorry to say I guess that does mean I kind of neglect him."

Sally simply nodded; she knew nothing about kids, so she had no idea what to say to the chief to make him feel better.

"I think I'd better get up there and address the people, they're getting restless." He turned and started to walk away from Sally then stopped and turned back to her again. "By the way why don't you call me Charles from now on?"

"Only if you promise not to call me Ms. McKinney anymore."

Salinger turned away wanting to laugh, but that urge was nothing in comparison to his desire to go back, take her in his arms and kiss her maddening lips, but he knew this wasn't the time or the place. He turned back at that thought and smiled at her, hoping they would get through this crisis soon. Then maybe they could get to know each other better.

The Forest, 11:30 am

      Lucy peered between the decaying leaves that made up the mound in front of her. Seeing nothing, she slowly pushed her hand through the mess creating a wider hole. She sat and watched the surrounding leaves flutter in the wind. Her back was beginning to ache, and her stomach growled fiercely. She was cold, hungry, and tired, but her fear of the creatures was greater than all that put together. She patiently huddled in her hidey-hole watching to see if she was being watched by them and waited.

      After what must have been at least an hour of just scanning the Forest before her, she made her first move. Pushing more leaves out of the way Lucy slowly crawled out of the hollow tree. The Forest had been silent all night long, she had run long and hard for hours. Stumbling through the dense woods, getting scratched and poked by the bushes and low tree branches but she had survived, and that was the vital part. Now she just had to find her way back into town and safety. That thought brought to heart a considerable regret for leaving the comfort and safety of the hospital. Suddenly pulled from her reverie, she heard the sound of the air raid siren and hoped it meant the town finally understood the danger they were in. It did help her get her bearing's, and she aimed back towards Jasper Hill.

At first, she walked cautiously as her eyes darted from bush to bush in case those things were nearby. But after seeing nothing out of the ordinary, she began to move faster. The day wore on, and she watched the sun dip behind the clouds as the afternoon was slipping by. A couple more hours and it would be dark. She had gone a lot farther into the woods than she thought, or she was lost and circling. Lucy was worried that she'd have to spend another night in the woods with those creatures. That was enough to set her pace faster. Soon she was running again, only this time she had more than a mission to just live.

Civic Center, 11:45 am

Chief Salinger worked his way through the crowd and up onto the stage. People began moving to their seats when they saw him. All attention drew his way as they were eager to find out what was so important that the town had to be shut down today. Total silence descended over the hall after one last squeak of an old wooden chair leg against the wooden floor. Salinger cleared his throat before beginning. His voice was loud and full of command as he addressed the town. "Thank you, everyone, for coming here in a quick and orderly fashion. You all deserve to know what is happening, and I called this meeting just for that purpose."

"Yeah! Why are we here?" Someone from the crowd yelled out. "What's going on?" Another voice said, then others piped up, too.

Salinger raised his arms motioning for quiet. "Please let me speak, and then I promise you we will have an open question session afterward. I will answer whatever I can for you."

People squirmed nervously in their seats, while others leaned over to their neighbors to say a word under their breath, but the room soon settled to listen.

"Okay then," Salinger resumed, "I called you all here today because of the recent deaths…" the crowd began talking at once, and a loud din soon filled the air.

"SILENCE!" A voice came from the rear of the hall.

All heads turned to the back of the room as constable Crow stood upon a chair. "Let the Chief speak!"

Salinger lifted his hand to Crow in thanks and continued. "Due to the unexplained deaths here in town, and there have been more than a few, the army have been notified and are on their way. They will, I expect, place us under quarantine until they can discover the reasons behind these events."

Someone shouted angrily from the crowd. "Why you gotta' bring the Army into this. Cain't you handle this yourself." The crowd chimed in with their agreement, and suddenly Salinger felt very uneasy and angry at the same time. He never thought he'd see his town come to this.

"QUIET!" All eyes turned his way, and he motioned with his arms at the people to sit down. "Please calm down, sit, sit down please," he yelled over the noise and through his embarrassment of having lost his temper publicly. "I didn't call the Army in. The Vancouver's Medical Examiner tipped them off after we sent some aaa..." Salinger chose his words strategically, not wanting to raise the level of anxiety. "Well we needed their help in testing some things, and they took matters into their own hands."

One voice rose above the others asking a bit sarcastically, "Well, what do you know?"

The silence was instantaneous. Heads swiveled to see who was brave enough to ask that question, especially in that tone.

Salinger didn't bother to search out who said it, he only wanted to move on with keeping everyone calm. "Only that I want everyone to stay safe. I want everyone to stay here and hunker down until the army moves out again."

A farmer in the front row yelled up from his seat. "How long are we supposed to stay locked up?"

"Yeah?" Some voices rang out.

"Why should we?" Another asked. "Was it a virus that killed those people? Should we be worried?"

"That is a good question. No, it was not a virus," he raised his hands again to squelch the noise. "I can't tell you what killed those people, or why. However, I personally know for a fact that it was no virus AND!" He yelled over the roar, his voice was starting to get raw, more from simple exhaustion than from his speaking. "All I know is that whatever killed those people is still out there, so we'll let the army worry about it. And we can all stay safely together, and I also ask that you have patience."

Just as the crowd was beginning to move about and get restless again the back doors of the hall flew open banging against the wall. The entire room turned, startled by the sound.

Hal Clement stood bleeding against the doorframe, his hand clutching his throat. A harsh whisper came out, and then he collapsed into constable Crow's massive arms.

"He's dead." A woman cried out. Someone screamed, and the voices rose into a cacophony once again.

Constable Crow turned and shushed the woman standing beside him. "He is not dead," he growled at her. He gently lowered the injured man to the floor. "Step back please," he shoved at the people that crowded around, "give the man some air."

Salinger pushed his way through the crowd and got down on his knees beside his constable. He placed his finger on Hal's throat checking his pulse, it was weak, but at least he still had one. Salinger whispered to Crow. "What did he say to you before he passed out?"

Crow's chestnut eyes were dark pools of worry that spoke more to the chief than the words he was about to say. "He only said, the cat."

"The cat? No, it can't be." Salinger recalled what Dr. Woodhouse had told him about there being cat hair inside the bodies and Lucy Walker's story about the cat Missy – who had belonged to the now dead Judith Barnes. *Was there truth to her story after all?* He dreaded the implications of that thought. "Well, we best keep this between us for now."

Crow nodded. "Not a problem sir."

The murmuring crowd grew noisy as they pushed and shoved trying to all get a better look at the injured man. Some people, especially the women, cried out in shock of what they saw, and now some of the children, who before had been so oblivious earlier, were crying.

Salinger stood, "I need a doctor or nurse over here please," he yelled into the crowd. A wave rippled through the people in the wake of Dr. Samuel as he moved toward the group.

"I'm here," Dr. Samuel said. The doctor moved in and immediately knelt down beside Hal and loosened his clothing. He checked the pulse and wounds. Next, he yelled out orders to the nearest able bodies. "You there," he pointed to a strong looking young man, "go into the supply closet and find the emergency kit. There should also be a stretcher strapped to the wall nearby, find help, and bring those to me. Go!" He waved the man away. Then he ordered an elderly lady and her daughter to bring him clean water and any sheets, or even drapes if they had to and rushed them off.

Sally slipped through the people and stood near the chief's shoulder. "What can I do?"

Salinger sighed running his hands through his hair; things were not turning out as he had hoped they would. He turned to her staring into her bright green eyes, her red hair a tangled mess of curls and he took her hand into his. "One thing," he said to her.

"What's that?"

"Promise me you'll stay close. I think I need you."

"Promise," she replied smoothly.

Salinger smiled at her, squeezed her hand tightly, then let it go as the ground underneath their feet began to rumble. Instinctively, she grabbed onto him as a deafening roar filled the hall. "Nothing to worry about," he answered her frightened stare. "They're here."

As if the weather was tuned into the army's plans, dark cumulus clouds rolled in, blocking out the bright autumn sun. A cold wind whistled ominously through the deserted streets.

☐

Civic Center, Noon

Salinger stood out in the chilly gray weather, his arms crossed waiting silently for one of the trucks to stop and acknowledge him. People from the meeting milled around behind him watching in awe as the giant green army vehicles drove through their peaceful little town. Their eyes were full of wonder and shock as the trucks rolled past, seeing the open back trucks with their flaps rolled up filled with armed men.

A Humvee drew itself out of the line of thundering vehicles, swerved quickly into the lot and came to a quick sliding stop. The door opened, and out stepped a sizeable gray-haired man with a determined look about him.

Salinger stood his ground and did not offer his hand as the man approached. "What do you want?" He asked bluntly wanting to get this over with, so he could go back to his people.

"I'm Colonel McCollum," the man said stepping in front of the chief, "and I suppose you must be Chief Salinger since that's what your nameplate says."

"I am Chief Salinger, and I'd like to know why you and your men are barging into my town like a war is about to begin?"

The colonel eyed the crowd behind Salinger, his eyes hard, cold, emotionless. "Let's move into my vehicle and discuss this," he said motioning to the Humvee behind him with just a flick of his head. A younger officer had stepped out to hold open the colonel's door and was awaiting their entry. With a simple twitch of his own head in reply, Salinger agreed, and the colonel turned and hopped into the Hummer. The young officer closed the door behind him and stepped to the back door waiting for Salinger to get in.

Sally touched her lips to Salinger's earlobe, startling him from his thoughts. "Let me come," she whispered.

Salinger turned his head just enough to see the subtle red hair that graced her brow and had to suppress the impulse to press his lips to its softness. It had been a wearisome few days; he was tired and needed it all to end. With the army coming in, this was his opportunity to walk away from the responsibility. It was their puppy now, and he could leave it to them without feeling like he was abandoning the situation. Now that this great weight had been lifted from his shoulders he turned, took Sally's arm gently and responded. "Not now. Let me talk to this guy alone," he pointed his thumb over his shoulder, "and then I promise to fill you in on all the details over a hot lunch." He gave her arm a reassuring squeeze, turned, and with a nod to the soldier stepped up into the Hummer.

Salinger pulled the door closed and got right to the point. "So, what exactly is going to happen here?"

The Colonel bit off the end of a cigar, spit it out the window and popped it into his mouth. His eyes narrowed into slits, and his mouth was set in a grim line as he grunted through the cloud of smoke he exhaled, "Where's Mayor Wainfleet?"

"Away," was Salinger's curt answer. He wasn't about to let this guy get away with avoiding his question.

Smoke billowed toward Salinger, filling the back of the vehicle with its pungent aroma. "What kind of answer is that? I want to talk to the top authority here."

Salinger turned to face the man, his eyes narrowing with irritation. "Look I don't know exactly what is happening out there, or why you all are involved, but I think I deserve some answers here. After all…"

The colonel cleared his throat loudly interrupting Salinger, turning his steel gray eyes towards him. "I don't have to answer anything to anyone. What I want from you is to get all these people back inside that building, set up camp and stay there until I, give the go-ahead to leave." He took another deep drag on the cigar exhaling a thick blanket of smoke before he resumed speaking. "If you promise me not to tell the other yokels, I'll tell you what we know."

Salinger clenched back the anger, his teeth momentarily grinding away the personal attack. The anger then gave way to concern for his friends and family that make up this town. He looked out the window at the people. They had started to push out of the Civic Center in their attempt to see what's going on. Armed guards had actually gotten out of the trucks and were standing along the street facing the people like they were controlling a riot. This was one thing he never imagined he'd see in his lifetime. He turned back to the colonel – who had sat back smoking as if he had not a care in the world – and realized the difference between them; he did care. He cared about his town and his people, and he wasn't going to sit back and let these strangers take over; it was still his town after all.

"As the Chief of Police in this town and the highest ranking official present, I have every right to know," he said. "Now, you'd better rethink how this is going to go down. We 'yokels' don't take kindly to uncooperative folks."

Shocked to see that Salinger had a backbone after all, the colonel took an overly dramatic pause, cocked his head, and responded through his cigar. "Right then, those bodies you sent our way came up with some pretty unusual findings."

"Tell me something I don't know," Salinger scoffed.

The Colonel cleared his throat, not keen on being interrupted. "The insides were liquefied, even the bones were gone, and yet the skin and skull were completely intact," he leaned into Salinger's face. "Something funny is going on around here, and they sent me to find out what."

Salinger leaned against the door to get away from the stench of the colonel's breath. "So, in other words, you don't have any more answers than I do?"

The colonel rolled down his window reached his arm out and banged on the roof. On his signal, the door Salinger was leaning against popped open almost ejecting him onto the sidewalk. Salinger composed himself as best he could, turned to look into the darkness of the Humvee, and said succinctly, "I guess we're done then?"

Colonel McCollum leaned across the seat so Salinger could see his face. "I'd better not see you anywhere near my operations, or I'll have you locked up in your own jail so fast your head won't even have time to spin."

"Oh, you don't have to worry about that none."

Upon hearing that, the colonel's lips began to curve into a triumphant smile, but then Salinger finished his sentence. "I've got better things to do than play army with a bunch of children." He turned and walked back towards Sally, leaving the colonels mouth hanging open in an empty retort.

Sally cocked her head giving Salinger that tell me what's happening look as he walked over to where she stood. He took her elbow gently in his hand and without a glance backward led her into the meeting hall, ushering the town's people in along with them.

Once they were back inside, Salinger was quick to take charge of the crowd. He held his arms up to try and quiet the people. "Listen up everyone," he shouted out and waited for all heads to turn his way. The murmuring died down quickly, and he addressed them without hesitation. "I want everyone pulling together to turn the hall into a temporary shelter!"

People milled around discontent with the situation asking questions demanding to know why the army was here and when they would be able to go home. Others moved about banding together and left the hall hoping to make it home before the army stepped in and made them stay there.

Unsure of just what would get these people on board the quickest, Salinger bared his heart in one last effort to reach them. "Listen, I am just looking out for you. People have died!" He paused to fight back the emotions that arose in him at the thought, emotions that until now he had kept from public display. "My people! Your People! Your friends, your neighbors, and what concerns me most is that you could be next. For God's sake, folks I need your help with this! Please, co-operate!"

Some of the people began nodding their heads and shouting, "We're with you!" Other supportive statements came from the crowd and, as proof, they started moving into groups and organizing what needed to be done to transform the hall as the chief had asked.

Relieved that his emotions didn't get the best of him and that a general riot wasn't imminent, Salinger finally turned to Sally. But then he saw Millie standing behind Sally with a grim look on her face. "Excuse me for one more minute," he said quietly to Sally without waiting for a reply, stepped around her to talk to Millie.

"Millie," Salinger took her elbow, "what's wrong now?"

"I told Bobby to meet us here. I talked to him this morning chief, and he said he would come but," Her eyes pinched tight with worry. "I've looked around and asked his friends, he's not here." She finished, her voice softening at the end as though she felt it was her fault that his son wasn't at the meeting.

Salinger squeezed the bridge of his nose between his eyes, "Goddamn it." When he noticed the desperate look on Millie's face, he reached out and wrapped his arm around her shoulder. "It's not your fault Millie. I should have gone out to the house myself and got him, he's my kid after all."

He motioned for Sally to come over and reached into his pocket to pull out his car keys. As they came out something fell to the floor. He bent down to retrieve it. It was the strange green scale that he had confiscated from Doug Bowan the night before. Even through the bag, the light reflected off its surface as he turned it in his hand.

Both Millie and Sally leaned in for a better look. "What is it?" Millie asked.

"I don't know, but I found others like it too," Salinger looked up from the strange object and over the heads of his towns' people. "I think we'd better get out to the place where this was found and see if we can't come up with any new information." He paused a moment considering everything that he still needed to take care of, his son one of those chores. "Millie, I hate to do this to you now but…"

Millie pulled the keys from his hands and unhooked the house key from the rest of them. "Yes, and don't worry I'll find him."

"You're the best, you know that," Salinger said placing a quick peck on her reddening cheek.

Salinger took Sally by the hand leading her through the crowd. "I need to talk to Crow, do you think you can find the boy I was talking to last night? His name is Doug Bowan, and he's…"

"Yep, I know who he is," Sally interrupted him.

Salinger was taken aback for a second. "Well, good, then I don't have to describe his whole family to you."

Sally nodded her head. "Hey, did you forget I'm a reporter. My eyes and ears are always open," she smiled, and Salinger smiled back.

"That I do believe," he squeezed her hand. "I'll meet you out front in say," checking the time he frowned at the lateness of the afternoon, "twenty minutes. Okay?"

"Sure thing Charles," Sally said brightly, with a quick salute then turned and disappeared into the crowd so quickly that Salinger only caught a glimpse of her flaming red hair

Shaking his head, he walked off in the opposite direction searching for Crow and Hal Clement. So far Hal, and the M.I.A. Lucy were the only known survivors of this crazy ordeal – that he knew of.

Trouble

Colonel McCollum puffed on his cigar rapidly shooting stern glances to anyone that even so much as looked in his direction. He was still pissed at the way that police chief had spoken to him and yet unless the man actually stepped out of line, officially, there was nothing he could do about it. Typically, other officials kissed his ass and did his bidding. He was accustomed to those around him wanting to please and impress him; even if it was to serve their own selfish little lives. He paced and seethed while thinking about how best to handle the situation.

A young officer still green around the ears raced up to him and lowered his gaze. "Sir?"

"What is it? I haven't got all day," the colonel bellowed into the man's reddening face.

"We picked up a teenager sniffing about the camp sir and…"

"What do you need me for," the colonel said putting his face almost right on top of the young man's; he was so close that he could see the sweat forming on the man's brow.

The young man took a deep breath making sure to keep his eyes straightforward over the colonel's shoulder. "It's his name, Sir! He says he's Bobby Salinger, the chief's son."

The colonel's face cracked into a broad grin, his eyes lit up like a child on Christmas morning, and he clapped his steel grip on the young man's shoulder. "Well, why didn't you say so sooner! Lead the way." He chuckled under his breath. *Now I really have something on the chief, his son*, he thought wryly.

☐

Civic Center, 12:30 pm

Doug and his mother Brenda had been sitting with the Shaw's; deciding on where they should all spend the night when Sally came rushing over. Smiling politely and trying not to look too nutty, Sally worked her way into the group.

"Excuse me. I'm sorry to interrupt, but Chief Salinger asked for Doug's assistance on something."

Brenda Bowan looked puzzled and turned to Doug. He shrugged and turned to Katlin, who was just as confused. Of course, a little voice in the back of Doug's mind was saying, oh no now he wants to talk to me about last night. They had gotten away with neither of their parents discovering that they had snuck off without the car when the air raid went off. Katlin had called home and said they were going to park near the police station. Then walk to the Civic Center, and met up there. The siren actually saved their necks. Now fear gripped his stomach thinking it would come out that they were at the party the night before.

"What is this about?" Brenda asked.

Sally shook her head. "Sorry Mam, he didn't say, but I'm sure it's nothing difficult. If you don't mind?"

"Mom?"

Brenda looked worried. "Okay just don't leave the hall."

Doug nodded and gave her a quick kiss on the cheek. "No problemo..uh..." he turned to the Shaw's. "Can Kat come with me," he asked secretly hoping that the chief would go easy on him with her there. They approved under the same rules, and the kids took off with Sally.

Finding Doug faster than anticipated, Sally led them to the room where she knew Hal had been taken. When they reached the door that led to the room behind the stage, Sally waved at the kids to stay outside, then she disappeared behind the door.

Katlin nervously chewed at her lip. "Why do you think they want you?"

"It's probably nothing, maybe about the party last night. I don't know?"

Everyone was frightened by what was happening in town. The Army coming through in their big trucks, made the sudden fear of war arise in their young minds, even if that wasn't the intention at all. The kids did not know war and hoped they never would. They waited impatiently outside the door and watched the people move around, setting up cots, and tables, and acting as if this was a slumber party instead of an emergency.

Tired of waiting Doug lifted a finger to his lips and slowly turned the doorknob until it clicked open. Katlin's eyes grew wide at what he was doing, but she didn't object leaning in closer to see.

Through the crack, they saw inside the room. The only illumination came from a desk lamp that was pushed low to reflect off the desk and back against the wall. The chief leaned over a body that lay prone on the stretcher, while Sally and constable Crow stood near the feet listening intently to the chief and whomever he was speaking too.

Doug could faintly make out a man's voice talking in slow whispered huffs - obviously from the man on the stretcher.

"Huh…no. It changed," a pause then the voice continued, "the cat…uhh…not cat. Body slimy wet, fur gone. Eyes red... glowing…uhh," another huffed breath of pain, then silence and the chief offering quiet placations. Then the voice resumed. "The mouth…oh god! It was - it was the mouth! Grover's dead – like the others – sucked dry." The man on the stretcher began to weep.

The people inside began shifting their positions around the table and away from the stretcher, when Doug gently pulled the door closed.

Katlin stood back. "What the hell was all that about?"

"I don't know, but I think it has something to do with why we're all stuck in here." He took her arm and pulled her a few steps further away from the door, so there was no way anyone would suspect they were listening.

Just then the door opened, and Salinger stepped out with Sally behind him. "Ah Mr. Bowan," he said seeing Doug and Katlin. A smile plied his lips, but the strain and weariness were evident in his eyes.

"Sir," Doug replied not knowing what to say.

"Come over here with us so we can talk privately about that scale you found?"

"Yeah? I told you exactly what happened," he replied defensively.

Katlin nodded her head in agreement with Doug. "I was there. He's telling the truth."

Salinger pulled the scale from his pocket, "Where exactly was it that you found this?"

"It was at the bottom of Jasper hill, Sir. Just as you come to the end of the hill. You know, where it curves, and there's that dirt road. That's where...," he blushed at the memory of wiping out on his bike with Katlin and was caught for a moment in the realization of how much his life had changed since then.

Katlin added, "That's right Sir. We were coming down the hill and lost the breaks on the bike. Doug swerved onto the dirt road to keep us out of the traffic, and we found a crater... and that," she said pointing at the scale he was holding in his hand.

Salinger closed his eyes in silent relief that he was getting somewhere in this investigation. That was what Doug had told him last night, and he just needed an exact location so he could go out and see what was there. So far it was his only lead in the case, and he wanted to check it out before that blowhard colonel found out about it. "You said there was a crater? Is it tough to find?"

"Well…" Doug scratched his chin in thought, "it doesn't really stand out because we never even would have seen it had it not been for where we happened to crash."

"Huh," Salinger thought tapping his fingers on the scale, "well I'm sure I can find it. Thank you for your help Mr. Bowan, Ms. Shaw. You can return to your families now before they get too worried about you," he dismissed them quickly and turned to Sally. "Want to go for a ride?"

☐

Army Camp, 1:00 pm

Bobby had been out cruising around trying to find something to occupy his time when he had spotted the army trucks rolling through town. He decided to follow them to see what was happening. He watched curiously as they set up a roadblock and figured that they must have one at the other end of town as well. Then he followed the trucks as they entered the elementary school's grounds and began turning it into their base of operations.

Everything was going smoothly as Bobby was satisfying his curiosity, not to mention his rebellious streak until an army guy stepped out to take a piss and almost stepped right on him. After an hour of tedious questions that he refused to answer, he finally said that they'd all be up shit's creek when his father found out that they were holding him against his will. That seemed to do the job because the army guy's face flushed when Bobby said the word chief and the interrogator excused himself in a nervous hurry.

Bobby imagined himself gloating at the thought of his dad ripping these losers a new asshole when the colonel walked in. He watched as the large man stepped into the oversized tent and knew for sure that any chances of getting out of this mess scot-free were getting slimmer by the second.

"So," Colonel McCollum began smugly, his arms behind his back, chest thrust out, and head held high. "I hear we have caught us a spy!" His voice rang sure and loud, even though the ground and canvas walls of the large tent were quite dampening.

Bobby pursed his lips in defiance, knowing full well this man would not chance harming him in any way considering who his father was. Nonetheless, rebellion gave way to the steel gray eyes that bore into Bobby's soul, and he couldn't help but shift his gaze away. These were the eyes of madness. The colonel's grin revealed perfect white teeth, sharp and threatening as knives, and made the man before him look even more menacing and maniacal, though Bobby could not imagine anything more soul arresting than those eyes alone.

Colonel McCollum didn't bother waiting for the stuttered responses, and lies he expected would pour forth. He reached out and grasped the black ball of the piercing, which jutted out from underneath the kids' matching black lips. Bobby strained forward in his chair wanting to reach up and clasp the hand that pulled on his lip piercing, but all he could do was sit back in his fear and try to blink out the tears that pooled in his eyes.

"What were you doing sneaking around my base camp? Did your father send you out to spy on me?"

"Juth lookin man," Bobby managed to say through the pain. His eyes widened as he watched his lower lip being pulled further away from his face. It felt like his skin was going to give at any minute, and all that would be left of his lower jaw would be a gaping hole showing off all his lower teeth.

McCollum growled in the kid's face. "That's not the answer I was looking for!" He pulled the ball out a little further. "Now, what were you doing here?"

Bobby felt the tears that he was fighting off, fall from his eyes. He couldn't stop them from watering. Gritting his teeth tight together he talked through the pain. "I alreathy toth you! Juth lookin, I like tankths."

McCollum let go of the kid's lip allowing it slap back into place. There was a significant red circle haloing the piercing, but he knew that mark would disappear soon enough. He watched as the kid defiantly rubbed the tears away with the palms of his hands. It was apparent the kid was just like his father. He'd have to think of a different way to use the kid.

Bobby thumped his chair back onto its rear legs. "Am I free to go now?"

McCollum harrumphed in his face. "Not bloody likely punk! We caught you trespassing and spying on military operations. That is grounds for arrest." He turned to the private that was guarding the tent entrance. "You hear that Solider?"

"Sir! Yes, Sir!" The young soldier replied with a tight salute.

Colonel McCollum turned away from Bobby. "Good, then keep him here under close watch until I give you further instructions." Without looking back, he stalked out of the tent leaving the boy to stew.

☐

Civic Center, 1:10 pm

Chief Salinger left his remaining two constables in charge of the meeting hall and led Sally discreetly out a side door. It felt odd for him to be sneaking around his own territory but he trusted his gut when it told him the colonel was a conniving fellow and was probably having him watched.

With a darting glance around the building, Salinger spotted an army jeep parked near the hall's entrance. "He's not even trying to hide it," Salinger mumbled shaking his head.

"What?" Sally asked peering over his shoulder. She could hardly believe they were conspiring together; after all, it was only a couple of days ago that they were almost ready to tear each other's throats out. She smiled thinking about it but was pulled back into their current situation when Salinger tugged on her arm.

He pointed and whispered. "Let's take your truck. We'll go around the back of the building and up Sycamore Street. We should be able to get to Jasper hill that way."

Huddled over in an uncomfortable crouch they waddled behind the thick bushes then quietly behind the center. Salinger checked every side street and between alleys as they proceeded slowly across town.

When they reached her truck safely, he motioned for her to drive. He climbed in the passenger seat and hunched down low.

Sally sat up straight and started the engine, her heart pounded with the excitement, and she had to fight to keep the smile off her face.

"You're really enjoying this aren't you?"

Her teeth showed briefly. "Am I that transparent?"

"Like a sieve lady," he replied reaching over and squeezing her knee. It gave a brief tingle up her leg causing her to squirm as she drew her legs together in response.

"Keep that up, and we'll get caught for sure, but I'm not saying what we'll get caught doing," she smiled down at him patting his hand. When he tried to remove it from her leg, she spoke up quickly. "No," she said holding onto it. "but I like the way it adds to the excitement."

"Just drive would you; I'm getting a cramp here." Salinger couldn't help but smile back. Her moods seemed to be infectious, and he cleared his throat trying to keep focused on the situation at hand.

"Would you care to direct me as to where we are headed? Or should I just drive around aimlessly all day?" She asked giving his hand a pat.

"Oh," he said startled and cautiously sat up, "I'm sorry I forgot you're new here. I've gotten so used to you magically appearing everywhere I am, I thought you were omniscient."

"Hardy-har-har, you're a real riot when you want to be, you know that?" Her green eyes flashed at him.

They had already passed the stretch of businesses, and the buildings were getting thinner as the mountain loomed off in the distance. Pointing straight ahead he said, "Just keep on driving until we near that big hill at the end of Main St. There will be a dirt road on your left, turn there. I'll let you know when we're close."

"Okay," she replied, and they both fell into silence now that they actually thought about where they were going and what they may find once they got there.

☐

Civic Center, 2:00 pm

Doug and Katlin hung around a small group of teenagers that huddled in a far corner away from the younger kids and their parents. It was bad enough that they weren't allowed to go home the last thing any of them wanted was to be hovered over by a bunch of worried old folks. Every now and then an adult would wander too close, and silence would fall over the group as if they were hiding big plans.

Which, in fact, they were.

Some of the kids wanted to sneak out and go exploring the nearly empty streets of the town; to them, this was the best thing to ever happen in North Falls. Others argued that the idea was too stupid to even consider. After all, the parents were in the same room, and would eventually notice them missing, and the Army was right outside the door.

Katlin and Doug stood close, arms touching, listening to the stupidity of the group. Neither of them said anything about the plans. They didn't agree or disagree, and they offered no advice either way. Both of their minds were lost in thought on what they had overheard. The only reason they were hanging out with the group was to be away from their parents.

Doug watched his mother as she directed a man pushing cots around. He admired her strength and wished he was small again so he could cling onto her coattails. He wished he could feel as free as he did then without a care in the world to trouble his mind.

Beside him, Katlin felt him shudder. Concerned, she placed a hand on his forearm. "What is it?"

Doug leaned his head down closer to her shining black hair and was able to smell the fruity shampoo she'd used. He thought how far away last night was when they had lain together. He wrapped his arm around her shoulder drawing her tightly to his body. "I just miss you." He smiled when her blue eyes smiled into his playfully scolding him. "Honest, that's all it is."

Just then one of the other kids said accusatively in a playful way, "What's going on here? You two an item now?"

Doug stepped forward, his eyes flashing anger while still keeping a loose hold on her shoulder. The other kid saw the reaction and postured in response.

Katlin was quick to intervene by rubbing Doug's chest with her free hand and reaching up to turn his chin with a crooked finger. "Well, are we going to hang out here until something happens? Or are you up to doing something," she asked mischievously.

Doug looked around the room tracking her parents. "I'm just not sure how to get out of here without getting caught," he said thoughtfully.

Katlin glanced at her watch, it was already two o'clock in the afternoon, and she knew that it would be dark within the next few hours. "If we're quick about it, I think we can get out and back in without anyone noticing."

"But how are we going to get past the Army guys that are posted outside?"

Katlin thought about it but could not come up with any viable scenarios.

Doug squeezed Katlin's arm, gently leading her out of the other kids' earshot. "I saw a few bikes out back. If we sneak out that way we can zip through the trails that lead over to Jasper Hill and no one will be the wiser."

"Okay!" Katlin said excitedly. Now that there was a plan in motion, she could barely contain her excitement. "But how are we going to get out of here," her eyes scanned the hundreds of people milling about the large room.

"You go and sit on the stage stairs," he pointed to the staging area, "do you see that exit?"

She nodded, and he finished telling her his idea. She gave him a peck on the cheek and headed through the crowd of people, being sure to avoid any family members, and sat down on the bottom step of the stage. Her demeanor was a choppy nonchalant as best as she could manage because of nerves, but then she jumped at what she heard next. Expecting it did not prevent the reaction.

Yelling began from the group of teens they had left earlier. Someone had joined them – a friend of Doug's who had been helping on the other side of the room – and pushed the guy Doug had words with. A fight broke out within seconds, and all heads turned to the ruckus. Adults yelled from everywhere around the room, some rushing over to the fight as quickly as they could. The melee enabled Doug's plan to continue without a hitch. He took Katlin's hand and, with a quick check around, they pushed out the side door into the gray cloudy daylight and scrambled around to the back of the hall.

Laughing, Katlin slumped against the rough brick wall holding her side. "You were great!" She said to Doug. "How did you get them to fight?"

"Ah, that was easy," he bragged smiling. "I told my friend to tell Glenn that his girl was seen at the drive-in with Carl…"

"Carl Wallace?" Katlin gasped covering her mouth. "That's gross and mean!"

Doug shrugged. "I know, but they'll sort it out quick enough. Let's roll."

"Okay," Katlin agreed, then grabbed a bike. "Hey check the brakes first! Remember what happened last time."

Trying to contain their laughter, they walked their bikes into the trees where the trails started, then hopped on and began to ride in the direction of Jasper Hill.

☐

Army Camp, 2:00 pm

A young officer ran up to Colonel McCollum stopping a respectful distance away and saluting stiffly.

"Yes, Private," he questioned around the stub of his cigar.

"There is a call for you Sir!"

"Thank you. Dismissed," he bellowed throwing out a half-hearted salute to send the private on his way. He had to hold back a grin as the man almost tripped over his own feet.

McCollum entered the trailer that had been established as the communications center and picked up the receiver. A smile spread across his weathered face, this was the call he's been waiting for. The voice on the other end told him the redhead woman was on the move. He knew from years of well-honed instincts that the chief was in that vehicle with the girl.

While the chief thought he went unobserved, the colonel had seen the few small exchanges that took place between the two. The furtive glances and the way they stood together shoulders almost touching. He knew what those movements meant; they were either already involved or going to be. He had seen enough to have her watched just as closely as the chief. It was only a matter of waiting. And waiting was a game he was trained to play.

Hanging up the phone, he pointed to the man nearest the desk. "Gear up you're coming with me."

The officer came out behind him with his pack flung over his shoulder. Saluting the colonel, he turned and led the way to the Humvee. They both jumped into the vehicle. "Where to Sir?" he asked.

"Head into town, we'll both find that out soon enough."

"Yes, Sir!"

Jasper Hill 2:00 pm

Salinger pointed beyond the trees. "Up there, that's the road," he said.

Sally nodded her head. "I see it." She slowed the truck, then turned onto the dirt track. Parking she asked, "What are we looking for?"

Salinger removed the green scale from his pocket. He held it up to show how it shimmered in the dull daylight. "A crater through the trees," he told her nodding his head down the road.

"Wow, a crater? Did anyone report seeing a meteor, or hearing anything?"

"Nope, not a peep, but small towns do tend to go to bed early," Salinger's gaze traveled to the clouds overhead as he thought about an unseen meteor crashing just outside his town limits.

Sally scoffed under her breath, "tell me about it." She was used to a big city where there was action 24/7 if you wanted it. But she couldn't complain, she had more action in the past two days then she'd ever had in Vancouver, and the people were beginning to grow on her. Her gaze took in Charles' strong features, and her belly fluttered. Shaking the thoughts that crept in, she focused her mind on the task at hand.

~ 324 ~

Salinger walked head down, checking the dirt, projecting how the kids on a bicycle would come flying off the road. Where the trajectory would lead and using his right hand aimed towards the ditch a few feet away. "I would think with the rate of speed, they would have come across the road here," he pointed out his thoughts, "and hit the ditch just over here. Let's start there."

Sally followed him down the deep ditch and up into the Forest. As they stepped through the thin strand of Pine trees sure enough just on the other side was a clearing, which was obviously not man-made, with a wide crater at the core. Trees had been toppled into each other, and the ground was brush free and hard. They walked up to the edge of the crater. Salinger hopped down into it while Sally milled about the edge. He walked along shuffling his feet pushing the hardened dirt with his heel.

"What do you think," Sally inquired.

Salinger grunted, not really answering either way when he raised his head pressing a finger to his lips to keep her from talking. He'd heard something.

Sally cocked her head to listen and shrugged; she didn't hear anything. "What?" She mouthed to him when suddenly she heard it too. There was a rustling noise, like a strong wind blowing through the trees. But there was something else behind it, something that sounded much more disturbing. She watched the Forest beyond where they were standing.

A lone figure moved within the trees. Running and weaving as if being chased, it bobbed in and out of their line of sight. They both saw a white hair and a pale, strained face. As she neared the clearing, the saw it was Lucy Walker.

Salinger cupped his hands around his mouth and yelled her name. She stumbled along turning towards the sound of her name then waved her arms and shouted. Not understanding what Lucy was saying Salinger climbed out of the crater and began jogging lightly towards her. As they got closer to each other, he saw that she was waving him backward, to turn around and breathlessly saying, "run run..." He hesitated for a moment, then without thought pulled his gun out of his holster picking up his pace.

Lucy pushed her tired body as forcefully as she could into Salinger when he put his arms out to aid her. "Go!" She said as loud as she could into his face moving past him, not waiting to look behind, as she already knew what was there.

"What the..." Salinger breathed the words, unable to do more as his breath was lost to shock.

As Lucy shoved him aside, he saw the things that were chasing her. There appeared to be hundreds of small creatures following her. He had never seen animals like these before. They were walking on two legs, no taller than a medium-sized dog. Even in the dull light of the day, he could see their skin reflecting the colors of the rainbow. His hand went instinctively to his pocket, and he realized it was not skin, it was scales. Their eyes glowed a fierce, fiery red and their mouths opened and closed with a loud popping.

"What the bloody hell are those things?" He walked backward aware that Lucy was long gone and those things were getting closer, but he could do no more in the state of utter shock that overcame him.

The nearer the creatures got, the more he could see, and the less he wanted to know. Their small hands were tipped with long sharp claws, that clacked greedily. He lifted his gun as the things scampered within ten yards of him. He began firing into the mass of flowing bodies. They hissed and screeched, but whether in pain or anger, he did not know, and he was not going to hang about to find out. He turned away and bolted towards the road. He saw that Lucy had reached Sally and she was helping the tired women through the stand of trees. Now all he had to do was make it there himself.

Shivers raced up his spine as he thought about what these creatures had already done. He knew without a doubt now who had killed the townspeople. He hitched his legs up higher as the noises behind him reached a new level of strangeness; the things made a gasping slurping growling sound that his brain could not define. He reached the edge of the ditch and jumped across.

Lucy nearly screamed as Salinger came up on her left side flinging her arm over his shoulder. Sally dipped her head forward to talk to him past the exhausted face between them. "What were those things?"

"I don't know what they are," he answered her, "but I am positive that they are what killed all those people."

Sally looked fearfully over her shoulder. The creatures were now flowing out of the ditch and up onto the road.

"Hurry!" She said picking up speed herself.

Reaching the truck, Salinger braced Lucy up against the side while Sally grappled with her jacket pocket to retrieve the keys.

Salinger yelled "hurry, hurry," and Lucy, finally able to stop after a long ordeal, closed her eyes to rest. Once the locks were sprung, they flung open the doors; Salinger tossed Lucy into the back and clambered into the front seat.

Sally gunned the engine spraying gravel at the creatures as the truck roared off leaving the things in their dust.

Creatures

Doug skidded to a halt, and Katlin barely stopped in time to avoid running into him. They arrived just as chief Salinger was hauling Lucy into the vehicle. Katlin stood up on the bike pedals to see over the tops of the bushes that lined the ditch, steadying herself by holding onto one of the bushes beside her. The path they had ridden in on did not continue straight through. Their only options were either down alongside the road to the left, which led deeper into the woods, or to the right towards the highway.

"What the heck are they doing," Katlin asked, struggling to see through the thicket in front of her and past Doug.

Doug shook his head. "I don't know, but they look frightened. I've never seen a grown man look that scared." He was watching them peel off down the road when he heard an odd noise and craned his neck toward it. "What the hell is that," he wondered aloud, ducking low to peer between two branches. A flash of red caught his eye, and he squinted at it then reared back.

"Whoa," he shouted, startling Katlin.

That's when the first creature came ripping through the undergrowth at them. Katlin screamed in fear slipping off the pedals and coming down hard on the bicycle seat. "Oaf," she huffed as the wind knocked out of her.

"Kat! Go, go, go right towards to the highway!" Doug, yelled, then turned to see more creatures climbing into the bushes after them.

He yanked the handlebars of her bike to start her in the proper direction and gave her a shove. As she began to pedal away from him, he turned and watched the first creature tumble out of the bush and hiss open-mouthed at him. Doug's heart felt like it was going to explode in his chest. Never before had he seen anything more hideous. The thing's mouth gaped wide showing off the hundreds of tiny suction cups that pulsed and salivated as if ready to feed. Its small sharp claws curled in and out, waiting to bring down its prey. The scaly body shimmered even in the dull afternoon. Doug pushed hard on the pedals and tore off after Katlin, he'd seen more than enough.

The nearest creature flew after him, diving, just as his foot left the ground, it clamped onto his leg. Doug let out a loud screech, and Katlin turned her head to see what happened. "Keep going!" He yelled at her. "Don't stop for anything!"

The front wheel of Katlin's bike swerved when she turned around, and she had to fight the perpetual motion of the swerve to keep upright. Her breath burned in her lungs as she pumped her legs faster than ever before. She kept her eyes focused straight forward praying that Doug would be able to rid himself of the thing that was hanging off his leg. All she could do was stay ahead and not slow him down. She stood up on the pedals and pumped even harder, keeping an eye out for low hanging branches as she whipped through the woods.

Staying close behind her, Doug shook his leg, but the thing had too good a hold on him. He could feel blood trickling down his leg from where its claws had pierced his skin. So far it was only holding on and hadn't tried to climb higher yet, but he knew it was only a matter of time before it got tired of waiting and would come up for the kill. Glancing down he saw that another one had been able to latch onto the first one's leg; two creatures were actually hanging off him. The sight of them up close made him gag; they were grotesque and slimy with wide set mouths. He pedaled a few beats, then lifted his leg and shook it, but to no avail, the things weren't letting him go. Ahead of him Katlin turned a bend and disappeared. We must be getting close to the road, he thought wanting to be able to stop and get the things off of him, but he wasn't sure how far behind the others were.

As he turned the corner, the loose fabric of his jogging pant leg rubbed on the chain. That gave him an idea. Slowing the bike down enough so he could maintain control, he looked down at the creatures, and he lifted his leg backward. It was difficult to do with their weight, but he managed to get the bottom creature close enough to the wheel that its back leg flung outward rubbing it against the spinning tire.

The beast screeched as it tore away from the top one, its foot was drawn between the tire and splash guard, snapping like a twig then spinning the creature along with it. The bike slowed further as the body bounced off the tire, ripping off its leg. Doug pressed the pedals as hard as he could. Gore spurted up the backs of his legs and what was left of the thing fell to the ground.

Katlin was just ahead of him looking back fearfully.

The remaining creature, still making the disgusting hissing gurgling noise, began to climb Doug's leg. The pain was excruciating. Doug clenched his teeth in pain, then spotted a fallen log that Katlin had just barely missed running into. The thing was up to his knee, and he knew he had to get it off. He swerved towards the fallen log.

The creature hit the log at full speed. It tore the beast from his leg, taking half his pant leg, and a lot of skin with it. Doug hollered in pain but didn't stop.

Katlin reached the highway and stopped to wait, keeping her pedals in the ready position just in case.

"Are you alright?" She asked breathlessly when he reached her.

Doug stopped and looked back; he didn't see any more of the creatures, just the one that lay motionless on the ground. He couldn't tell if it was dead or not, but it hadn't moved, and that was all that mattered at the moment. Taking the edge of his pant leg, he lifted it up looking at the battered leg underneath. "I owe your dad a pair of pants," he laughed at the absurdity of it all. Then seeing the open wounds frowned, "Yuck, I hope that thing doesn't have rabies."

Katlin sneered at him. "Yeah, you must be fine if you're making jokes at a time like this."

"Who's joking? I most certainly don't want to catch a disease from that thing…whatever it was," he replied seriously. "Come on let's get out of here."

As they moved the last few feet to the paved highway, they saw the black rover sitting in the middle of the road a green camouflaged Humvee, and a group of people shouting at one another.

The Rover skidded from the stone road onto the hard asphalt, leaving black marks across the pavement as the ass end swung out. Sally gripped the steering wheel tight holding the vehicle tightly to the road as it lost the centrifugal force and righted itself again with a quick whiplash back in the opposite direction. Meanwhile, Salinger kept his gaze out the back window, hoping those things couldn't run as fast as the truck. They hadn't gone far when suddenly he was flung forward in his seat almost whacking his head on the dashboard.

"What the..." he yelled as he quickly braced himself with his forearm. He turned to face forward and saw why Sally had stopped so suddenly. "Great," he murmured.

"Should we try and go around," she asked Salinger, not sure of the legal ramifications if she tried to outrun an Army vehicle.

Salinger huffed, wondering what else could go wrong. "Honestly I don't trust this guy not to shoot us if we try to run." He turned around to check on Lucy and saw that she was fast asleep. He nodded towards the back seat. "We'll leave her sleeping," he said then opened his door and stepped out into the darkening afternoon.

The colonel approached their truck, his head held high, a cigar jutting between his tight lips and a smirk in his eyes. "So!" Smoke streamed from his nostrils like some kind of angry beast. "I see you left the area without permission endangering the lives of innocent people."

Salinger stepped closer to Sally, feeling the need to protect her from such an ugly man. "This is still a free country," he countered, "excuse me if I have a job to do."

Colonel McCollum chose to ignore the chief's remarks, knowing full well that he had no real precedence to detain the man in any way. "Where are you going in such a hurry?"

Salinger flicked his eyes toward Sally unsure whether or not he should tell the colonel what they had found. Her only reply was a slight shrug of her shoulder and a sideward tilt of her head, accompanied by raised eyebrows to indicate she thought he had no choice but to answer. His downward glance revealed his agreement with her unspoken reply. He didn't see how they would be able to keep this from the Army. Considering that it was what they had come to town for and having just been chased by some terrifying creatures, he didn't want to face alone, he gave in to the demand.

"We went to look for evidence in a crater back there..." Salinger nodded over his shoulder. "When a whole group, gaggle, whatever, a lot, of troll-like little creatures attacked us."

Colonel McCollum let out a hearty laugh. "You expect me to believe this crap," he roared. "I've heard better excuses from a private late for training! Creatures! Hell man, what do you take me for an idiot?"

Salinger held up his hand in mock surrender. "Fine," he said, "go back there and see for yourself."

The colonel's eyes narrowed, and he stepped into Salinger's space. "Oh, you'd like that wouldn't you?" He whispered in Salinger's face his rancid cigar breath going straight up into the chief's sinuses. "Well, I have a little surprise for you. Are you missing something? Maybe someone who you'd like to say hello to?"

Salinger's face twisted in confusion.

"I found your little punk son, or should I say, spy, snoopin' 'round my camp."

Salinger sucked in his breath, his anger overriding the smell it drew in. "You son of a bitch!" He yelled pushing the colonel with both hands.

Sally yelled out and was about to step in-between the two men when two teenagers came speeding toward them on their bikes hollering excitedly.

The kids rode up to the group. "What the chief is telling you is true," Doug called out.

Salinger was shocked to see them here. "What are you doing?"

"Sorry Sir," Doug said, not really concerned with getting in trouble at this point. "We were just bored and wanted to investigate for fun. But then we got attacked by those things, you were running away from."

Colonel McCollum was fed up with these mountain folk. "You got to be kidding me. Did you plan this conspiracy to throw us off the real trail, Salinger?"

"Look." Katlin pointed to Doug's chewed up leg.

"That could be from a fall, I want more proof than that."

"I killed one back there," Doug said and pointed back the way they came.

"Okay wise-ass, let's go see it then, shall we?" The colonel motioned for Doug to lead the way.

"This is ridiculous," Salinger stated. He wasn't going to let Doug go off with the crazy army guy alone, especially back to where those creatures were. "You stay here," he told the girls. "If we don't come back in ten minutes head back to the Civic Center and let them know what we discovered."

Sally nodded and took both the kids bikes and put them in the back of her truck. Then she got Katlin to climb in the back with Lucy, who was still passed out and pulled the vehicle off to the side of the road.

Doug walked the men back across the highway to the trail. They walked back to where Doug thought he knocked the creature loose from his leg. He stopped a few feet away and pointed beyond the colonel's shoulder. "Right there Sir, that's where I was able to shake the thing off. It hit the log and dropped."

They could all see something small lying on the trail. Colonel McCollum held Doug back with a hand on the chest. Doug had no problem with that at all, worried that other creatures might be nearby. He glanced at Salinger who nodded his understanding without further prompt and stepped closer to reassure the young man.

Colonel McCollum approached the thing slowly. As he neared, he saw that they hadn't been lying to him after all. The creature was like nothing he had ever seen before. It had strange iridescent scales, and with the mouth left hanging open, he could clearly see the suction cups within. Its hands were small but fat fingered, tipped with sharp curved claws. A shiver ran down his spine at the thought of one of these things touching him. He popped the cigar back into his mouth, reset his usual stern look to avoid giving the impression that what he saw actually scared him, and turned back to Doug and the chief. His mind turned to one thought – the glory it would bring him to be the man who stopped an alien invasion.

"Well then," he stated matter-of-factly. "You say there are more of these things out there?"

"I believe so, yes, hundreds more" Salinger answered.

"I'll take care of it then." The colonel stated without another thought. "You get the kids and that fine-lookin' girlfriend of yours out of here and back to the hall."

They walked back to the vehicles in a silence that lasted the short drive back to where Sally was waiting, each with his own self-motivated reason toward his silent thought. Salinger couldn't help but notice Sally's worried expression through the windshield as she waited patiently for them to return. He turned to face the colonel after he exited the vehicle. "What about my son?" He asked gritting his teeth.

"I'll keep him safe until I can return him to you. We wouldn't want him to distract you from your duties, would we," he said evenly; the chief knew instantly the true meaning behind the colonel's words, but the shock of hearing it in such an even, and blatantly cryptic way left him speechless. "You have my word on it." His voice never changed, and Salinger never responded. After a moment's pause, the colonel continued. "But in the meantime, you take care of those townsfolk. I'm about to have a bonfire, and I wouldn't want things to get tragically out of control." Then laughing like a man possessed, he saluted lazily, slammed the door and slapped the seat in front of him saying, "Let's go, soldier, we got us some creatures to kill."

Civic Center, 4:00 pm

The Rover sped back toward the meeting hall, but unlike the vehicle, the passengers rode in silence thinking about what they had witnessed and the possible consequences of what the crazy colonel had planned. As they pulled into the packed parking area, the first thing they noticed was that the Army vehicle that had been guarding the area was now gone. Sally parked near the front entrance so Lucy wouldn't have too far to go. After getting out of the truck, she rounded the passenger side to help Salinger with Lucy and placed her hand on his arm to stop him before he could open the door. "What are we going to do?"

Salinger tossed a worried look toward the kids that were piling out of the back seat on the opposite side of the truck. Then he leaned in close and said slightly under his breath, "We have to stop him and find my son."

Sally sighed wishing this would all be over so they could be alone together. She patted his hand reaching past him to open the door. "Then we'd better get a move on." She proceeded to gently shake Lucy awake to get her inside.

Doug and Katlin opened the back of the truck taking out the bikes. As they wearily walked past the chief, he turned to them. "Hey," he called out, "don't tell anyone what you saw just yet, okay?"

They both nodded, and he went on. "And stay near your families. Things could go from bad to worse real quick, and you need to be with them." His eyes hardened to show his seriousness and ushered them off with a wave of his arm.

Katlin lowered her head – she'd had enough adventure for one day. Doug answered for both of them. "Don't worry sir, we won't be going anywhere." As they turned to go, he hesitated then said. "And by the way, thank you."

Salinger smiled thinking of his own son and what he must be going through right now. "Just doing my job son. Just doing my job."

☐

Army Camp, 4:00 pm

Back at the base, the colonel bellowed out orders. He loved watching a well-oiled machine work. "Get him out of here." He yelled to the guard on duty.

"Yes, Sir." The guard took Bobby by the arm and led him down the hallway to the trailers back rooms.

As soon as the area was cleared, colonel McCollum picked up his phone and called back to his headquarters in Surrey, the only people he still had to answer to – for now. He verified what the officials had suspected, even though he had thought them full of crap. An otherworldly species had landed or crashed, they didn't know that aspect, in the small town. He vowed to bring them a sample of the aliens, and they gave him the green light to torch the place. Of course, he would have done that very thing even without their approval. Regardless, he had planned to find a way to make it work, and no one could stop him without becoming a part of that equation. Now, however, that wasn't even an issue. He had played his best role keeping the officious bastards under thumb. He had them believing the wonderful townspeople were far out of harm's way. His lips curled at the thought they could all burn in hell as far as he was concerned, along with the beasts.

"Lieutenant," he bellowed down the hall.

"Yes, sir?"

"Get the closest airbase on the line. I want to order up some napalm. I don't care if I have to burn the whole town to the ground; I'm going to eradicate those creatures from my green earth."

A loud clang rang out from the back of the trailer followed by grunting and a thud. "What the..!" colonel McCollum yelled standing up from behind his desk.

Bobby came tearing down the narrow hallway from where the officer had held him. He pointed an accusing finger at the colonel. "You son of a bitch," he screamed, spittle flying from his lips. "You can't do this! We'll stop you, my dad will stop you!"

Colonel McCollum laughed as the teenager flew at him pounding his small fists into the barrel of his chest. He grasped the small fists into his own and squeezed. The boy's lips pulled back into a grimace of pain, and he dropped to his knees. "And what do you think that pussy father of yours is going to do about it?" He sneered into the boy's face and threw him backward.

The other officer who answered the colonel earlier stumbled out of the back room pausing at what he saw; he knew the colonel to be a cruel man but what he was doing here now was illegal. The other soldier stuttered in fear, "I..I'm sorry Colonel. He...pushed a-a-nd I.."

"Restrain him and take him to my truck. This time, don't let him get away."

"Yes, Sir." Th officer grasped the boy tightly around his skinny arm and hauled him out of the trailer glad to have gotten off so easily.

As the officer pulled Bobby by his arm, Bobby had no choice but to stumble along or risk falling onto the gravel and being dragged. He could see that the man was upset by the episode. He felt sorry for him because they had been sharing personal stories back in the trailer and seemed to have gotten along reasonably well while the colonel was away. Now Bobby was worried that he'd lost his only hope of getting free.

"Look, Bruce, I'm sorry about what happened back there," he explained and was about to continue when the soldier jerked his arm hard wrenching his shoulder. "Ouch! Jeez man, I.."

Bruce turned to him and hissed through his teeth. "Don't you dare say my name here." His eyes darted back and forth to the busy area where other officers were running around barking orders and preparing to leave the site. "Why did you have to go and act like that! Huh? Are you trying to get us both killed? Christ, I'm lucky I'm not on shit duty after a stunt like that."

"I said I was sorry," Bobby complained, "but what I'm I supposed to do, sit there and listen to that maniac talk about burning my town to the ground? I've got to tell my father. You heard him, man!" Bobby whispered fiercely.

Bruce squeezed his fingers tighter around the teenagers' arm willing him to shut-up. He wasn't happy about the situation either, but he didn't know what to do. "Just get into the vehicle," he said pushing his hand on top of the kids' head as he helped him into the backseat of the Humvee. "I'm sure that the higher-ranking officers here won't let him burn the town down." As he stepped into the truck behind the teen, he mumbled to himself. "I hope not anyway."

Civic Center, 4:00 pm

Sally and the chief walked as quickly as possible with Lucy propped up between them. The people had settled in more since they had left and she noticed that the beds were almost completely set out. Families were grouped together working to help each other cope with the situation. The sight made her sad. To think that at any minute their already upside-down world could get even worse.

As they hobbled along, Salinger spoke briefly into his walkie-talkie, but he had spoken in code, not so Sally wouldn't catch what he'd said, but because he didn't want those around them to understand what was being said. Most heads turned as they walked by, wondering what was happening. As they cleared the last of the rows of makeshift beds, Sally let loose of her curiosity and asked, "So, what was that all about? You're not keeping secrets from me, are you?"

Without hesitation, he whispered his response. "The constables are meeting us back here. I was just warning them that we were coming with a new patient," he said pointing to the room off the staging area. Hal Clement was still laid out on the stretcher healing. And now Lucy would be joining him.

As they entered the room, a woman came rushing to them from Hal's bedside. Together they lay

Lucy down on a blanket, and the woman immediately began fussing over Lucy.

"What happened to her?" The woman asked.

Salinger sighed. "She's had a long night in the woods I'd say. Uh, Sally, this is Mrs. Reilly she works at the hospital."

The woman ignored the introduction and continued to check over Lucy. She finished checking the pulse. "I think she'll be fine. A few bruises, lots of minor cuts a nasty bump on the noggin. I'll know more when she's awake which I don't think will be for a while yet, she's zonked."

They all looked up from where Lucy lay as the door opened and the two constables stepped into the room. Crow's eyes darted around the room taking it all in. Duncan was white as a ghost and kept his eyes on Lucy.

"I hope you don't mind that I asked Mrs. Reilly in to keep an eye on Hal, there," Crow said.

Salinger shook his head. "Not at all. I'm glad you took the initiative to get the extra help, we sure can use it." He patted the large Indians shoulder then turned to the other constable. "How are you feeling Duncan? You don't look too well."

Duncan took a shallow breath focusing his dark-rimmed eyes on the chief. "Ah I'm okay," he smiled weakly; "you know how it is. Not enough sleep and tons of stress."

Salinger grimaced wrapping his arm around the young man to give his support. "Well, unfortunately, it's going to get worse," his gaze went from Crow to Sally and back again. "Let's go somewhere private, and I'll tell you all about it." He led them further into the room leaving nurse Reilly alone to attend to the two patients.

As he filled the constables in on what happened to them out at Jasper Hill, they couldn't believe what they were hearing. Salinger was glad that Sally was there with him to back up his story, or they might have thought he'd lost his mind. What was even harder to believe was that the colonel was going to set the Forest on fire.

"Doesn't he know that he'll burn us all to the ground?" Crow rumbled.

"Of course he does, that's the point, he doesn't care. This guy is nuts, I swear. This maniac doesn't care if he murders the whole town."

"But why?" Sally interrupted. "What difference does it make to him if they kill these things with guns and just get out of town?"

"Maybe he has something against us?" Duncan said quietly.

Salinger shook his head. "No. I don't think that's it, but I don't understand his reasoning either, all I know is that we have to stop them."

Crow asked the question that was on all of their minds. "How are we going to stop an Army?"

"I've been thinking about that this whole time," Salinger said to the group "And with everyone's' help I may just have a plan." His gaze traveled to the high windows above them and was drawn back down as Sally spoke.

Sally jabbed her thumb towards the room full of people. "Does your plan include them?"

Salinger nodded. "Yes, unfortunately, it does. They have to be told what's going on. I mean it's their lives at stake, regardless. If the Army manages to start a fire, we have to be prepared for it. Those people out there," he indicated behind him, "they will not stand idly by and watch their town burn."

"Hell no!" Crow agreed a little too loudly.

"But what about the creatures? Don't you think we'll come off sounding nuts if you tell them about that," she asked.

Salinger didn't like the way her worry drew upon her soft brow. He tried to brush it away ever so softly with the edge of his thumb as he cupped her delicate chin in his hand and said, "Even if they don't understand they will be willing to help save the town and that will be enough for them. Believe me, I know what these people are capable of. This is where I grew up and where I'll die, and if you're able to stay and become a part of that, you'll understand too, someday."

Sally blushed as his gaze penetrated hers. The fact that he wasn't embarrassed to talk to her in such a way made her heart skip a beat. Never before had she met a man able to talk openly about his feelings for her and she replied in a mock Mae West voice, "Why Chief, is that an invitation?"

He smiled, his hand still cupping her face, he pulled her close enough to smell her light perfume and pressed his lips firmly against hers. They were softer than he imagined. She kissed him back, surprised that he kept his eyes open. How else could he do anything but stare into her emerald eyes.

His two constables turned their backs to give them privacy, after rolling their eyes in unison. Sally pulled back, her cheeks redder than before, and he rubbed his thumb across a smudge of dirt on her freckled cheek. "Yes," he finally said. "That is an invitation."

Laughing she said, "That's the warmest invite I've ever had. Okay so let's get this show on the road then."

As he was about to turn to take the stage, Millie burst into the room. The front tail of her blouse was hanging loose out of her skirt. Her already frizzy hair was haloed around her head, as though she was emulating Einstein, and her breath came in short bursts as she tried to speak.
"Chei..huh..Bobby…uh…I," she bent at the waist, drawing a deep recovering breath.

Salinger rubbed his hand in a calming motion between Millie's shoulder blades, angry with himself now for neglecting yet another person. It seemed trying to save the entire town meant leaving individuals to flounder. He felt inadequate to take on a job so daunting. "Millie, we know where Bobby is," he said. "I am terribly sorry that I wasn't able to tell you sooner. I know you've been running all over town looking for him." He raised his eyebrows as she straightened, "In light of all this, can you forgive me?"

Catching her breath finally she replied, "Oh thank god! I was so worried," her eyes traveled to the leggy redhead, with her perfectly freckled cheeks and her flouncy ringlet hair. She pressed her sausage fingers against the wrinkled tails of her own blouse and stepped into the chief's shoulder, so he had no choice but to move left and block Sally's view. "I'll go check on the auxiliary gals now," she gave Salinger's muscular arm a squeeze, "thank you, Charles, I'm happy you found Bobby." Millie melted into the crowd holding her head high, knowing that at the very least, she was a damned hard worker.

With that settled, Salinger took center stage once again to address the townspeople. This time knowing the news would be worse and harder for him to get across, left him a little shaky.

People shuffled about in disbelief after he told them about the strange creatures that had tried to attack them and the hushed voices grew to a dull roar.

"Listen up folks!" He shouted to get their full attention. "I know that this is a surreal time for everyone but it is happening and it's happening now!" He moved to the edge of the stage so the people could see his face clearer and the sincerity that he portrayed. These people were his neighbors, his friends, his relatives, and he was going to make sure that they understood where he was coming from. He wanted to reassure them that he wasn't insane, that he was still the man they trusted to protect them. He raised his left hand as if swearing to uphold the law for them. "I was not alone out there, others saw the creatures, too. These things are what have been killing the people around here," he looked into the slack-jawed faces below him. "Some of you even saw the results of the mutilations."

A voice from the crowd shouted out, "What are we going to do about it?" Other voices followed suit yelling out, both questions, and answers interrupting him.

Salinger cleared his throat. "That... people...that... that's what we need to discuss!" He shouted to once again regain the floor. "The Army has also seen these creatures, and they want to set fire to the Forest area where they are."

"Yeah! Burn the sons-a-bitches!" A man hollered. Shouts arose from the crowd once again.

Salinger had to shout out once again to maintain silence. "If they do that, it'll create a Forest fire. Everyone may not remember, but I do, I know the older folks do too. We almost lost this town the last time there was a fire. I have come up with a plan to stop not only the army but the strange beasts as well. But I need your help, and it will be dangerous." He watched as the crowd moved like waves in the ocean. People talked loudly to each other and were yelling towards the stage. Emotions ran high, including his, as he waited for them to discuss the situation knowing that in a few minutes when they settled down he could lay out the plan and they would be with him one-hundred percent.

"Chief Fredrick?" Salinger called out while searching over the mass of heads for the fire chief.

A hand popped up from the back of the room. "Here!"

"Can you come up to the stage, please. We'll need your expertise."

As he waited, Sally came quietly up onto the stage and took his warm hand into her own giving him a reassuring squeeze. "I know your plan is going to work," she whispered.

He looked down into her eyes. "It had better, it's our only chance."

The Revolt

Sally was shocked at the speed in which the townspeople moved from disbelief to action. They rallied between themselves opting on who should stay behind, and who should go out and fight the beasts from hell. Or wherever it was they appeared from.

Salinger informed everyone that if his plan fell through the air raid siren would go off again, only, this time, it would be a town evacuation.

The first thing that happened was all the woman, children, and elderly, had been shuffled off to the next safest building, City Hall. A few strong young men moved the incapacitated Hal Clement, and no one seemed to notice that Lucy Walker was no longer in her cot sleeping and nowhere to be seen.

A group of twenty people milled about waiting for their orders. They had already pushed all the chairs and cots in jumbled piles against the walls.

Salinger hopped up on the stage and drew their attention. "I need you to split into two teams. Half of you must be fast runners and of good health. That team will be heading down the trails behind the hall.

Constable Crow will be with you, and once he gives the signal, you are to attract the creature's attention. I want them all led back here." Salinger watched their worried faces as he laid out his idea. He placed a hand on the fire chiefs shoulder. "You heard it folks, Fredricks, agrees that this is the safest building to use. The walls are solid stone, and with the windows as high as they are, we can safely contain a fire and not worry about the Forest or town beyond."

Fredrick nodded solemnly, he too grew up in North Falls and would do anything to protect his town. "Yup it's the best bet, and I'm looking forward to it."

Salinger wrapped up. "I need five people with me in cars and the rest to stay here with Chief Fredrick. Those who are trained firemen, go to the station and bring out the trucks. I want them prepped just in case."

People began shuffling about deciding who was going to risk running through the woods, who was staying and who would go with the police chief.

Salinger motioned to constable Crow. "I want you to start these people off down the trail. Duncan can follow at the end to watch for anything from behind. Once you get there switch spots, you're the stronger of the two. Let Duncan lead them back, and you watch their asses." He wrapped his arm around the big Indian's shoulder pulling him in close. "I'm counting on you to get these people there safely. I would go myself, but I need to be where the army is to keep an eye on that crazy colonel."

Crow's eyes constantly roamed over the people that would be going into the woods with him. They moved around murmuring, shuffling their feet, and hunching their shoulders in worry. They didn't look like the best bunch, but he knew most of them in one way or another and felt that given the need, he could count on any one of them. "You think they understand the situation," he asked the chief, worried about the consequences if anything should go wrong.

"I certainly hope so. I know you'll handle them just fine."

Sally moved up behind Salinger and asked him quietly, knowing he was probably at wits end and not wanting to startle him, "Are you ready?"

"I'm ready, let's get going."

Army Camp, 5:00 pm

Colonel McCollum was well away from his makeshift camp with his foot intently jammed on the gas pedal of his Humvee. He had one last thing to complete in his mission to become the celebrated savior of the world and he didn't care who got in his way, they were about to be run over. At this point, he didn't care if that was figuratively or literally.

He had the camp shut down in less than an hour after those losers at the Air Command had their last laugh and was ready to leave this hick town far behind as soon as he put his plan into action. He had ordered everyone away from the area except for the few peons who had little meaning to his plans. Three of the larger army trucks followed behind filled with about thirty men and the supplies he needed. No one had questioned his orders as he knew they wouldn't.

In the backseat, Bobby, and the soldier, Bruce, sat in nervous silence. They could only hope that there was a plan in motion to stop the lunatic before it was too late. Bobby was watching for an opportunity to escape out of the vehicle, but it never slowed down long enough to jump. They rode in silence, their heads spinning, wondering what tomorrow would look like, and holding on for dear life hoping the colonel wouldn't crash them into a fiery pile of scrap metal.

City Hall, 5:30 pm

Now holed up in City Hall, Doug and Katlin sat quietly talking on a cot, while his mother, Brenda and her best friend Margaret discussed the situation. "I think I should have gone," Margaret said for the umpteenth time. "I am faster than any of those men they chose."

Brenda grabbed her friend's' hand. "Are you nuts? You have to stay with me. I mean look at those two," she pointed over her shoulder at the kids. "If I don't stay and watch them they'll get into even more trouble." She was mad at Doug for taking off earlier that day, not to mention that he could have been killed and now she didn't dare let him out of her sight.

Margaret bounced on her heels impatiently. "Yeah, yeah, I know that but…"

"No buts!" Brenda wagged her finger. "You are not going out there!" Then as she saw her friends' eyebrows rise in question, she said in a softer tone. "I'm scared too, and I need someone here with me."

Relenting, Margaret hugged her friend close. "Okay I'll stay with you, but if I miss out on a chance for some grand adventure because I was too chicken to stick my neck out, I'm blaming you."

"Hey," Brenda slapped her on the back, "we'll take a cruise after this, or go skydiving, or climb a mountain." They laughed together as they joked around trying to make the best of a dangerous situation. Wondering how long until they would know if the town was safe, or if they'd all have to leave.

☐

Constable Crow moved swiftly in front of the group. He positioned them single file behind him. A few stronger men, he'd picked were riding ahead on mountain bikes to scout out the area. They had speed, so if anything happened, they could get back to him quickly and let him know. Twigs snapped and dead leaves crunched under the men's feet, so it was obvious they were not going to be sneaking up on anyone. Crow wasn't sure if he liked the idea, but he saw the chief's reasoning behind the scheme and knew it had to be done. He just hoped that the chief was correct in his calculations on how fast the things moved; he didn't want to be outrun by something that thought he was dinner.

Meanwhile, on Jasper Hill, Salinger stopped the truck a good twenty feet before the dirt roads entrance. Once he pulled over, the other vehicles behind him followed suit. He motioned with his arm, pointing and gesturing, directing them on how best to block the road. As soon as he had the entire highway blocked he jumped out of the truck and asked the two people that had driven in the police cruisers to flip on the lights.

Everyone gathered around the flashing red and blue lights. Salinger just hoped that the flashing lights weren't a beacon for other unwanted things.

"Okay listen up. I want everyone to move back behind the roadblock. We are going to stay on the road away from the bushes, but we must be on the other side of the vehicles for safety. I'll need lookouts to face either side of the road and watch for movement from the woods. Let's go!"

They jumped into action; whispering amongst themselves. Sally put her hand on his arm. "I'm sure this will work," she said smiling up at him, not a bit of the worry she felt showing through.

Salinger's eyes flitted around her red hair, as it brightened and darkened with the continually moving lights, and smiled back. He rubbed her soft cheek with his thumb and leaned into her lips. She responded warmly. Then he pulled away, hooking her arm through his, and took her around to the safe side of the roadblock without saying a word.

☐

The Trails, 5:45 pm

Constable Crow lead the team of men as quietly as possible through the woods. They had followed the same trail from behind the Civic Center that Doug and Katlin used earlier. It would lead them right up to the backs of the creatures. If they were still here that was. Sure enough, the trail abruptly ended at the crater, and, with a chill and momentary racing of his heart, he saw that they were no longer alone.

The crater was filled with a writhing mass of red eyes, that moved in unison as though they were one rather than hundreds. In the darkness, it appeared as though red glowing orbs were hovering two feet above the ground. But the noise was the worst part of it all. There was a loud humming gurgle, almost like a clogged drain slowly sucking down water.

As Crow's eyes took in the entire scene, he could see the mass of small dark bodies moving as if dancing to their own slurping mix of macabre music. He knew at that point that they were going to be in trouble if they fucked this up.

He motioned to the men behind him that stood silently as they too saw the beasts, their mouths agape. Crow whispered, "Move back, back up, back up." He gently pushed at the nearest man to get them moving further away so he could talk to them without being heard. He formulated the plan. "You guys on the bikes go quietly to the right trail, towards the highway. Let Salinger know that we are on the move with the creatures on our asses." They nodded their understanding and walked the bikes away from the group. "Ok, pair-up men. We'll split off the trails that led back to the hall to make sure that all the things follow. Stay together, look out for your partner and run like hell on my mark."

Jasper Hill, 5:45 pm

Salinger turned as headlights reflected through the night coming towards their position. "Everyone stay back and hold tight," he said raising his hand to steady his people's resolve. No one moved an inch as the large trucks came rumbling up the road. They could clearly hear the gears winding down as the vehicles slowed to a stop just before the patrol car. Of course, the lead vehicle was the colonel's Humvee, but the chief was surprised to see he was the driver.

Salinger stepped in front of the roadblock. He shielded his eyes from the glare and waited for the colonel to get out of the truck. "Go back to where you came from," he hollered, as the Humvee door popped open. "We don't need your help here; we can handle this ourselves."

Colonel McCollum jumped out of the driver's' seat clearly hearing the chief's request, but there was no way in hell he was going to allow a hick town police chief issue him orders. "I think you'd better move your little," he waved his hand at the roadblock as he paused to chuckle, "set up here, Chief."

Salinger took a deep breath to steel his resolve and to keep himself from running right over and ripping the colonel's throat out. He upped the ante by slowly pulling his revolver from its holster. "I think you better reconsider your next move very carefully. I am done playing with you, so why don't you just turn your little convoy around and let me get on with taking care of this town."

The colonel cleared his throat; this man was beginning to irritate him. He turned and made a signal at the Humvee as if motioning for someone to move ahead and the rear passenger door opened slowly. There was a moment of muffled talking then Bobby Salinger was shoved out of the back of the vehicle. His hands were cuffed behind him, and a soldier held him by the arm pushing him forward.

The colonel reached out as the boy neared and pulled Bobby close to him in mock affection; Bobby resisted. "As you can well see, I have something that belongs to you. Now move your people, and you can have him back. If not well…" he shrugged and didn't complete the threat, knowing no further explanation was necessary.

Salinger crossed his arms defiantly with a chuckle. "You're assuming that there is a connection between this boy and me, but this punk broke that a long time ago with all his rebellion. He's been on his own since his mother passed. His life is not worth the entire towns, colonel. Even if I cared, I couldn't make that trade." He dared not look into his son's eyes, knowing it might trigger a response and blow his poker face, so he kept his focus on the colonel. He could not afford to show any weakness at this point. "It's too late anyway. I've set a plan in motion and am awaiting word that the creatures aren't there anymore. So, you might as well let my son go and leave our town. We're not afraid to force you out, we don't put up with people coming in and kidnapping our children. No matter who they are, there will be consequences."

With that statement, there was a chatter of movement behind the chief as the men prepared for a fight and aligned their sights on the colonel's head.

"What do you mean they are not here?" Colonel McCollum demanded. "Where are the creatures if not in there?"

"We've directed them elsewhere, somewhere that they can be dealt with, without endangering our town or its people."

Colonel McCollum laughed. He released Bobby arm pushing him towards his father. "You can have him," he said then casually lit up a cigar, "you're all dead anyway. Don't you know that the Government watches the sky?"

Salinger stepped forward taking Bobby's elbow as he approached. "What do you mean watches the sky?"

"That's right," he nodded puffing his cigar. "those things that turned your people into dinner - they came straight out of the sky." He raised his hands upwards in mock awe as if a miracle had landed. "Oh but not to worry," he continued. "We've gotten our samples. The bodies you sent us plus a few aliens, that thanks to Mr. Bowan, we now have. You see all we needed was to locate exactly where they landed. But you came along and led us right to them. For that, I suppose I should thank you. So, I'll thank you, now if you'd care to call your men off and kiss your…" The colonel never got to finish his sentence as two men on mountain bikes came flying out of the bushes.

Salinger turned around recognizing his town's people. They swerved through the group stopping only when they were close enough to talk to the chief. "Crow sent us. We found the monsters, and it's begun!"

Salinger nodded his assent. "You two better stay with us now, it won't be safe going back that way." He waited for them to move out of earshot and turned to the colonel with a satisfied smirk. "You see the aliens are no longer back there."

"What did you do?" Spittle flew from his lips as instant rage turned McCollum's face red.

Salinger just shrugged; he decided not to help the colonel out in any way. If the man wanted to try setting fire to the Forest still, then he'd have to find a new reason. Right now, what Salinger needed was for the colonel to be out of his way. He turned circling his arms in the air signifying the men to rally up and get ready to move out. His men scrambled back into their vehicles, and with a roar of engines revving in the cold autumn night they slowly began to move around until they were in a single line pointed back towards the town.

Sally had silently stayed a few feet behind Salinger as he had approached the colonel, and now took it all in stride. The snooping was imbedded in her DNA, and she couldn't change that, she wanted to be there for Charles, but she still had the drive to know everything that was happening at all times.

Salinger turned while the colonel sputtered obscenities at him and Sally moved in beside him, matching his pace. He helped Bobby out of the cuffs as the approached his patrol car and opened the back door for his son. Sally slid in the passenger side, as Salinger got in behind the wheel. He smiled and waved confidently to the colonel as he led his convoy of cars past the army.

☐

The Trails, 5:50 pm

Crow gave the okay signal, and everyone began shouting loudly so their voices would carry over the field to the creatures. The whole idea was for the monsters to see the men and want to attack them, then they'd run down the trails making sure that the group spread out enough so they wouldn't get clogged up together. The men were nervous after actually seeing the creatures, and although they were small there were hundreds of them, and they outnumbered the men.

The creatures had heard them and were moving out of the crater. Crow stayed down the road on the same side of the crater but far enough away so they couldn't see him. He hoped they couldn't see him because he had to stay until last to make sure that all the creatures left the area and not just a few of them.

The men turned and began heading into the trails. They moved slowly at first while still making noises. A young man stayed at the end of the line and walked backward watching the crater as they drew away from it. Then as the first creature crested the lip, he yelled. "Here they come!" And the men started running. He too turned when fear gripped his heart, and his stomach tightened as he got a better look at the flat-faced, scaled beasts. Their sharp claws clicked ominously as they began their chase, then hundreds of red eyes lit up the dark Forest.

Crow waited until the last of the red eyes disappeared into the trees and gave it another minute, keeping his eyes and ears open. He saw neither movement nor glowing eyes in the crater; it appeared as though all the creatures had followed his men. He moved slowly from his hiding spot drawing his gun just in case. Cautiously, he crossed through the trees and moved silently in the night until he reached the crater. He peered over the edge and seeing it was empty, turned and slowly walked towards the trail. Now came the hard part, he had to follow behind the beasts and make sure that they stayed their course. One man, one gun, and a lifetime of Indian instincts; he felt safe enough.

Jasper Hill, 6:00 pm

Salinger drove slowly watching his rear-view mirror as the colonel led his convoy of army trucks down the logging road, knowing that it was too late for them to find anything. "Aliens," he shook his head, "do you believe what he told us? Aliens," he said flabbergasted.

Beside him, Sally reached over and took his hand and said, "If I hadn't heard it myself, or seen the bodies," she bit the inside of her lip, the reporter in her wanted to blow this story wide. Her eyes traveled over Charles lean jawline, and she knew in her heart that she would lose him if she told the world about this. She made the instant decision that life here with him would be better than a life alone in the cold city. "You've got a good plan," she reassured. Then she turned looking at the young boy in the back seat; this was the first time she was meeting his teenage son. She offered her hand over the headrest in introduction. "I'm Sally," she said feeling the heat rising off his young palm as he briefly took it in awkward silence. "Did he treat you okay," she asked and nodded her head towards the back window indicating she was referring to the colonel

Bobby's eyes flickered from the fiery red-headed woman to the back of his dad's' head. So far, his dad hadn't said two words to him, and he figured he was in deep shit even though it wasn't his fault. He shrugged not wanting to appear weak in front of a hot older chick. "He got rough, but I handled it," he said quietly while watching for any reaction from his dad.

Salinger's focus moved from the road to the rear-view mirror to catch his son's glare from the backseat. "I'm just glad you're safe...and um...I'm sorry I haven't been there for you the last few years. You know I didn't mean what I said to the colonel right?" Salinger's heart fluttered in his chest, he couldn't believe that this talk was more difficult than dealing with alien beings, but he pushed on. "I had to make him believe that I didn't care about you, so he wouldn't harm you – I do care – Bobby; I'm sorry. When this is over, I promise things will change. And don't say anything to people about what you heard. You know they'll panic if they hear the word Aliens."

Bobby shrugged saying nothing, though silently he was happy that his dad wanted to try again. Perhaps he could change too. As soon as his dad's eyes moved back to the road ahead, Bobby smiled, taking no concern with the so-called aliens.

Salinger watched the forest pass by his window, and it wasn't long before they were back at the Civic Center, and the toughest job lay ahead.

☐

Jasper Hill, 6:00 pm

The roar and lights of the military vehicles invaded the peacefulness of the dark logging road as they came to an abrupt stop behind colonel McCollum. He jumped out of his Humvee immediately yelling and motioning for the soldiers to move out. His soldiers raced through the trees, waving their flashlights. Eventually, a voice rang out, "Here Colonel. We found it."

Colonel McCollum pushed through the brush, and his men lit up the crater for him. Seeing it was empty, he swore out loud. "Goddamn him!" He shouted grabbing the nearest soldier to him. "That bastard is going to pay for ruining my plans."

The soldier stood as erect as possible in the colonels grasp, his eyes wide with fear and his mouth hanging open in shock. He knew enough not to say a word and to just stare straight ahead and wait out the rage. Finally, the colonel let him go and set some work in motion. He had them search the crater and surrounding area in the dark, clouded night, for any scrap of the aliens, or their means of arrival, while he paced, stewed, and chewed on the end of his wet cigar.

☐

Crow walked slowly, gun raised, eyes peeled and gently placed one foot before the other making sure not to snap any dry twigs underfoot. Although he figured that unless there were any stragglers, nobody would hear him. Up ahead on the trails he could faintly hear the rustling of bushes and the men's shouts to each other. He was far enough back that he could not make out what they were saying and he hoped that they were not crying out for any type of help because at this stage of the game if any of them got attacked they would be goners. He couldn't let himself worry about that right now, though and scanned the bushes around him. He had to keep focused and make sure that none of the creatures fell behind or just plain wandered off. There was no way he was going to let any of those things escape, not on his watch.

"Go faster!" Joe yelled as he pushed at Bob's back. He stumbled over his own feet, as he turned and watched the mob of red eyes' rushing up from behind. Their iridescent bodies reflected odd shades of blue and green as the flashlights bounced off their bodies, and their long claws clacked loudly. The creatures couldn't run as fast as the men, but the fear of seeing strange beasts chasing you was enough to freak anyone out.

Bob took long strides not bothering to look back. "Are you okay?" His voice rose and fell with the huffing of his breath. He didn't dare try to turn his head for fear of stepping off the trail. He could see that the trees were beginning to thin out some. "I think we're getting close," he yelled reassuringly.

"I'm good! Just keep going," Joe replied pumping his arms extra hard along his sides to get a better stride. The creatures disappeared behind them as they rounded a bend in the trail, and he knew that as long as they kept up their current speed, the things wouldn't catch them.

Civic Center, 6:15 pm

Salinger checked the hall; it was empty just as he ordered. He returned to the car where his group from the roadblock stood around waiting for the rest of their instructions. Salinger glanced at his watch. "Okay let's get going, they should be coming along soon, and I want everyone in place."

He waved for Sally and Bobby to step aside with him and as soon as they moved out of earshot of the group he turned to Sally and said, "Listen I know that you want to help, but I really need you to do something for me."

Bobby saw his father's' eyes flash from him back to Sally and he stepped back holding up his hands, "Whoa, I know what's going on here," he said so loudly that heads turned and looked towards them. "I do not need a babysitter!"

"That's not it," Salinger said raising his hands in a calming gesture which only exacerbated his son's defensiveness.

"Yes, it is," Bobby spoke through his teeth trying hard to keep the whine out of his voice to prove his point. "I..."

"Wait!" Sally said stepping between the two men. "Listen we don't have time for this. I will take him with me, now get going they're waiting for you," she shoved his shoulder, and without waiting for a response, she turned around and grabbed Bobby's arm.

He sputtered looking back at his father then almost stumbling followed the woman, whose actions led him to believe her temper might be as fiery as her flaming red hair, as she pulled him around to the back of the parking lot. "Where are we going?" He asked as he extracted his arm from her grip.

"To where it's safe," she said, then hunching her shoulders deeper in her jacket as the cold night air finally began seeping through her, she continued, "and warm."

Bobby couldn't help but smile a little, he liked her already, she was tough and cute, and she didn't sneer at his pierced face the way all other adults did. Suddenly he worried about his dad he looked back at the hall. It seemed so lonely, lit up in the night with the forest as its spooky backdrop.

Sally saw the hesitation and concern in his eyes and said, "He'll be fine. No one is going to let anything happen to him; he is essential to them you know."

Bobby nodded, "Yeah I know, but I just know that colonel is going to mess things up." Then he matched her quick stride as she moved them further away from the building.

Finishing It

Salinger moved everyone into position, making sure that they were exactly where he wanted them to be. Then he triple checked the side doors of the hall. They were locked up tight and could not be opened from inside. The only open exits were the front where his people needed to escape, and the back, where the creatures were being led in. He walked out through that very door now. It faced right into the heart of the Forest. Constable Duncan was there leaning up against the wall watching the trails.

"Anything," was the chief's simple inquiry.

Duncan shook his head and took a deep breath, still recovering from his run out of the trail. "Not yet Chief."

Salinger leaned up against the wall beside the young constable. "Okay, keep your ears open, they should be along very soon."

"That's if everything's okay," Duncan said quietly remembering how Baker and Wiley, two seasoned cops, had gotten eaten by the things.

"Everything is fine, or we would have heard something," Salinger said calmly, and then a noise drew his attention. "Shh..." he placed a finger to his lips. Cocking his head, he listened to the night. Sure enough, he could hear shouts coming from the woods.

"They're coming, get ready," he told Duncan, then took the whistle that was hanging around his neck, stepped through the open doorway of the hall and blew it hard. The shrill sound filled the area echoing back at him. Twenty some odd hearts began to race, while more than a few stomachs tensed and turned in anticipation of what was about to happen.

Duncan jammed a broken two-by-four tightly between the push bar on the door and the ground to jam it open. As he saw the first man break out of the trees and head to the light, he ducked left around the side of the building to guard that close corner and make sure none of them took the route.

Salinger waved the man on as he came out of the trail, another man close behind. This was the hard part, the timing of it all. He saw more of the men exiting the woods. They struggled for breath as they slowed down to enter the threshold of the hall. Salinger patted their backs and said good job as they darted past him. He counted two more, and then he saw the eyes of the aliens.

They pierced the darkness before him as if a fire among the brush had been suddenly stirred and their embers released in the heat that rose above them. Barely breaking before them were two figures. Bob was one stride out of the woods, and Joe almost on top of him. The two were oddly silhouetted by the explosion of glowing eyes like black rag dolls shadowed behind a curtain on the macabre stage behind them.

Salinger shouted out to them, "Come on guys you made it! Just a little more!" He stepped towards them then stopped. As much as he wanted to get closer and help, he knew there was nothing he could do; he couldn't help them run faster, all he could do was to encourage them on.

As soon as Bob made it past the tree line Joe stepped out and overtook him, he had been waiting for his chance to get ahead. Now he was finally free of the other man's back and the first one through the open door.

Salinger didn't wait to the see the creatures come out of the trees, their glowing eyes were enough for him to know they were close, and he needed to get into position himself. Inside, the hall was deathly quiet as the men who had raced into the hall only moments before, had already gone out the other side.

To give the runners a rest, new groups had taken up places inside the hall. They were to be the bait when the aliens arrived.

Salinger moved onto the stage, slipping out of sight behind the thick red curtains where he could keep an eye on the aliens, and his people. He gave a silent prayer that if these creatures had a great sense of smell, the thickness of the dusty old curtains would aid as a block against their senses. His heart throbbed in his chest as he waited, knowing that the people scattered about the floor would be even more anxious than he, for they were standing right out in the open.

Salinger knew the aliens were entering the building, as the men's eyes widen at the sight of the little monsters. Next, he heard the clicking of their sharp-clawed feet on the floor and the gurgling sucking noise that they made. His hands grew clammy but his mouth dried up and he tried to control his breath as the excitement of the moment drove his heart to beat faster and faster.

The men began to slowly back towards the doors behind them wanting to give all the creatures time to get inside. Salinger peeked out around the back of the curtain so he could see the door. He saw the troll-like beasts entering the hall slowly, as if wary of the strange room, or maybe they sensed it was a trap. But their hunger must have been greater than their fear because one of the larger ones in front of the group opened its mouth wide and hissed sending steaming spittle out in an arch.

The men backed further away as more of the creatures poured in through the doorway pushing those ahead further into the building. Now that they spotted dinner on the other side of the open space the first aliens moved outwards spreading to block the exit behind them.

Salinger remained motionless for fear of drawing their attention. Now that there were so many of the things inside, if they spotted him, he knew he'd be dinner in mere seconds. He drew a restrained breath as he watched them still piling in the open door. *Come on*, he goaded in his mind as if he could telepathically rush the beasts, *hurry up you slimy bastards.*

The aliens moved across the hardwood floor. Their claws clicked together in unison, to in some insane hungry beat. The sound echoed in the large hall and was just as creepy as the slurping sounds.

"God! They're disgusting," a voice whispered.

"What are they," another asked.

More voices murmured as the things filled the hall. They crept in on their hind legs. They had lizard-like heads, with no visible ears, red glowing eyes and the strange scaly prismatic skin, unlike anything people had ever seen before. Their arms reached out, tipped with clacking claws, as though drawing prey to them. All their mouths opened, revealing the layers of suction-cupped innards.

"Holy-fucking-hell. Let's get out of here," someone shouted.

The men that stood around the walls near the main entrance backed up further as the creatures continued to push forward, and more were still pouring in through the doorway. Suddenly one of the front men screamed in terror as the largest of the creatures unexpectedly jumped out of the group landing on his leg.

Men yelled scrambling both forward and backward depending on the height of their fear.

"Get it off!" The man cried out shaking his leg, but the creature remained firmly attached.

The fire chief raced over and, using the heel of his heavy work boot, slammed his foot down on the creature's' head. The thing dug its claws in deeper drawing blood then was forced by the weight of the boot down onto the floor. Another foot came down onto its scaly head, and before the creature could scream with pain, boots were kicking at its face and body.

The other aliens let out a shrill whistling screech that pierced the men's ears, and then they rushed towards the men.

Hands grabbed at the fire chief's back as his foot rained pain on the creature. "Come on!" Someone else yelled, and people began to push him away from the monster.

Chief Frederick looked up and saw that the creatures were coming for him now. With one last kick at the still body of the alien, he headed for the door along with the others.

Salinger held his breath as the creatures attacked and watched as the men retaliated against the aliens. He moved slowly behind the curtain and pulled it back so he could see the rear door, the last exit. He would have to time this right so that the men in the front would all get out as well. He could see that the aliens were all jammed up in the back door. He'd have to try and get the men to do something to get the aliens to move further inside.

The aliens began to shriek a cacophony so loud that everyone had to cover their ears. Salinger wondered if this was a part of their defenses, a way to render their prey helpless. Hands over his ears, he looked out around the curtain again and saw the front doors slam shut, and all the men had already gotten out. But there were still aliens too close to the back door. "Damn," he muttered and looked around for a distraction when suddenly an interior door opened and Lucy Walker came rushing out.

Lucy slammed the door hard, drawing the attention of the aliens. "GO NOW GO," she screamed at Salinger. "Come on you bastards," she taunted the aliens, "you took away all I loved; well now I'm here to make sure you die!" She was pressed up against the wall between the main entrance, that was now locked and barred, and the back door that was standing wide open. "Run Chief, never mind me," she called out again, knowing that the chief wouldn't want to leave her there, but she had nothing left to live for and was ready to give herself for the town she loved. Her early fear dissolved into seer hatred and she resolved that she would see these monsters die.

Salinger jumped off the stage not bothering to use the stairs, his boot heels reverberated with a loud thud. Lucy gave a shrill whistle to keep the aliens attention on her. And it worked, their mouths pulsating with hunger closed in on Lucy. Salinger didn't wait around to see what would happen. He hit the open doorway at a run, skidding on the loose gravel. Then, scrabbling for traction, he spun and kicked away the two-by-four that held it open, and it slammed shut. As the clasp clicked in a place, he leaned his back against the cold metal to be sure that it was closed securely.

Alien bodies banged against the metal door, and their piercing screams continued. Salinger leaned into it wanting to back away but afraid that if he let go it would open, and they'd be all over him. His head dropped in shame at leaving poor old Lucy Walker behind. After everything she had already been through, he prayed it would be over quick for her. He almost screamed when a hand clapped him on the shoulder.

"You're safe now Chief," Duncan said patting Salinger's back. "That was a good idea y…AAHH.," he screamed stumbling backward.

"Duncan?" Salinger raced towards his young constable not sure what happened. As Duncan leaned forward, he saw one of the aliens clinging to the constable's back, its long sharp claws piercing not only his uniform but also his flesh. A stain of red quickly forming around the area.

Duncan spun in crazy circles trying to get the monster off his back. His arms swung madly trying to grab it.

Salinger grabbed the two-by-four that they had used to prop the door. "Stop turning," he yelled and pressed pushed the chunk of wood between the alien and Duncan's back.

The beast opened its sucker filled mouth and latched onto Duncan's neck.

Salinger pried back hard, and the thing flew off Duncan's back landing in the gravel. It hissed and kicked, its legs flailing about, trying to regain footing. Constable Crow flew out of the woods his gun raised. A single shot rang out exploding the beast's head, and it dropped to the ground.

Salinger could do nothing but duck out of the line of fire.

Crow stood over it and fired his gun until it clicked. Only then did he stop to check on Duncan who lay face down and still. "Jesus," he whispered.

Salinger moved over to Duncan knowing it was too late. His jugular had been emptied in the mere seconds that it had taken for him to react and another one of his constables was dead.

"It's my fault Chief," Crow said closing Duncan's eyes. "I was following it, and I lost sight of the thing when it left the trail. I was waiting for it to move, to give itself away." He sighed lowering his head. "I should have tried harder to hunt it down."

"No Crow, it's not your fault. He wasn't supposed to be here, not right now. It was no one's fault," Salinger squeezed his shoulder, "come on we still have much left to do."

A thundering sound filled the cold night air, and the ground rumbled beneath their feet. They looked up from Duncan's still body.

"They've made it," Salinger said standing up. He tripled checked the door was securely barred, so no aliens would escape and motioned for Crow to head behind the parked cars.

Colonel McCollum was out of the Humvee and striding towards the hall entrance as Salinger came around the corner.

"Stop," Salinger called out, "I wouldn't go in there if I were you."

The colonel puffed out his chest. "How dare you run my men and me off on a wild goose chase like that," spittle flew from his lips as he strode forward to confront Salinger.

Salinger didn't back down, this was his town, and he was determined to save it. "My townspeople and I have trapped the aliens inside the hall. I had my reporter friend, Sally McKinney, you know her," his eyes narrowed slyly, "call the Governor Generals Office and the Prime Minister. Neither of whom are going to sit by and let you destroy our town." Salinger poked a finger into the colonel's hard chest. "In fact, I hope you are prepared for early retirement."

The colonel's mouth opened slightly, just enough to show his surprise at what the chief had accomplished, then it snapped close and his arm came out and shoved at Salinger's chest. "I think we can handle it from here," he turned and waved to his troops. Engines roared at the signal, and the parking lot was flooded with light. His back to Salinger, he said, "If I were you I'd keep my mouth shut and get out of here." Then he strode back to his Humvee and disappeared inside.

Salinger hurried off to the patrol car where Crow was waiting, and as they sped out of the parking lot, he said, "We'll have to come back for Duncan's body later, I hate to leave him, but it's safer to not be near the building when it blows." Crow nodded his understanding.

The colonel radioed his men into position around the hall. He was disappointed that he wouldn't have the opportunity to torch the town. But if he got lucky the fire might still spread. The only difference was that this time, they were setting a building on fire, instead of the Forest.

"Colonel, we have something around back," his radio squawked.

"Hold your positions," he commanded the troops and jumped from his truck. He walked quickly around the back of the hall keeping his eyes warily on the doors as he passed. From inside the hall, the creatures were making an awful racket and the sooner he had them taken care of the better.

"What is it?" He asked gruffly as he approached an officer down on one knee inspecting something.

The officer pointed to the ground. "Here Colonel, we've found one of the aliens' dead."

Colonel McCollum approached cautiously; he had seen the results of what these things had done and did not want to make any mistakes. He could see easily enough in the bright beam of the soldier's flashlight that the thing was dead. It was more than dead it was mangled beyond recognition. "Looks like this one almost got away," he said with a tsk. "Good work. Scoop up as much of it as you can and bottle it. Now get back to work."

The alien specimen was safely within his Humvee, he gave the order to bust out the windows and use their on-hand flame-throwers. He stood stock still, hands behind his back, poised with confidence and strength, waiting. With a simple nod of his head, flames roared from the metal barrels aimed into the building. The wooden interior of the old building, popped with the heat, as it began to smoke and catch fire. The shrill screams of the alien creatures could clearly be heard as they shrieked and scrambled to escape.

The townspeople milled around the sidewalks a few blocks away from the hall watching as flames licked the roof and reached for the sky. Sally McKinney and Bobby were at the head of the group. As Salinger walked towards them, Sally threw her arms around Salinger's neck kissing his cheek.

"You don't know how glad I am that you made it," she whispered in his ear.

"Unfortunately, we lost Lucy Walker and Constable Duncan," he sighed, "I'll fill you in later," he finished and smiled wearily, looking into her gentle green eyes he pressed his lips to hers. From behind them, a throat cleared. Salinger lifted his lips from Sally's and nodded to his son. He braced his hand around the smooth skin at the back of his son's' neck. "Are you okay?"

"Yeah dad, I'm good," Bobby pulled away, unaccustomed to receiving affection from his father.

"Do you think it's over?" Sally asked bringing his attention back to her.

He turned around putting an arm over her shoulder and the other over his sons on the opposite side. "I certainly hope so," he said quietly, "I need a nap."

She laughed and whispered, "Are you ever going to tell them?"

"That they were aliens?" he pursed his lips watching the fire. "Nah, I can't see how that will help."

☐

North Falls, 3:00 am

Colonel McCollum stayed listening as the aliens bellowed in their death throes. Since this was the last hurrah of his career, he planned on enjoying it. The Governor-General had called on his SAT Phone and informed him to clear the area and pull out. He waited for the fire to rage and the already prepared fire department, moved in to cool the embers, as per chief Salinger's orders.

As soon as it was safe enough, colonel McCollum had his men comb through the hollowed out building to make sure there was nothing left alive. Once he was satisfied that all trace of the alien creatures was eliminated, he waved his troops on, and they left the small isolated town as they had arrived, on the rumble of heavy motors.

He went alone in his Humvee; his two Alien carcasses stashed away in the back. As soon as he got away from the watchful eyes of the Government, he had some plans of his own. He puffed his cigar and laughed as North Falls fell away in his mirror.

Three Days Later

Doug adjusted his pants back into shape and yawned, tossing the blanket over the back of the couch. Outside the sun was shining, and he could hear birds singing. From the kitchen, the smell of freshly brewed coffee filled the air.

Katlin popped out from around the kitchen doorway a smile plastered on her face. "Good morning sleepyhead." She entered the room with two cups of steaming coffee.

"Hey," Doug smiled. "I still can't believe everything that's happened in the last couple of days."

He and his mother had been staying at the Shaw's house ever since the night of the fire. Doug was thoroughly enjoying himself; even though he and Katlin barely got five minutes alone, they had grown much closer in the last week.

"I know and lucky us we get to return to school tomorrow," Katlin said.

"Gee I wonder if it's safe?"

Katlin laughed swatting his arm. "You'll pray for anything to get out of school for another few days." She had enjoyed the few days off herself they had needed some time to recover from the weird events. Now, however, she was ready for life to get back to normal.

"Yeah well, I just want to forget this whole mess," Doug sighed taking her in his arms.

They leaned in to kiss each other and Brenda walked into the room. "Now now," she interrupted. "With school starting up again tomorrow, I think we should return back home today."

"We're safe to go back home," Doug asked, trying to hold back the disappointment.

"As safe as it ever was," she wrapped her hands tighter around the hot mug of coffee. "I hope Sneezer checked out okay. We'll have to stop at the vet's first. From the talk of the town, he is the last cat alive around here." Brenda sighed, it was all so weird.

Doug wondered if Sneezer did check out, as the thought of the scaly creatures flashed in his memory. He was curious if anyone knew what they were and why, or even how, they got inside of the cats. Next, he wondered if he would he ever trust having a pet again and rubbed his throat.

Sally was in a half asleep – half awake euphoric dream state when the shrill ringing of a phone drew her into reality. She rolled over wrapping her arms around the warm body beside her, making sure that he wasn't just a dream as well.

A muffled voice called out from downstairs. "Dad!"

"Mmm…" Salinger moaned and rolled into Sally's embrace. "Good morning beautiful."

"You haven't made it a good morning yet cowboy."

He nibbled her neck then pulled back, "As much as I'd love to take you up on that offer I do have to answer the call."

"I know," she said and rolled out the other side of the bed to avoid the temptations herself.

Salinger heaved himself out of the warm bed pulling on his robe. "Getting voted in as the Mayor of North Falls has its downfalls you know. It's not just all prestige and awards, I actually have to work for a living."

Sally groaned and threw a pillow at his head missing by inches. "You're not Mayor yet smarty pants. You still have to wait until Friday to see if the actual Mayor returns from his fishing trip before they can hold a re-election."

Salinger walked around the bed wrapped his arms around Sally's warm body and planted kisses all over her freckled cheeks. "I think something's happened to him anyway. He's usually back from his weekend getaways by Monday night, and here it is Wednesday, and there's been no sign of the man," staring into Sally's bright green eyes he pondered aloud, "I do wonder what happened to him, though."

Sally slipped out of his embrace, tossed on her robe and together they went to the kitchen to have breakfast with Bobby. He had changed drastically since the events on the weekend. He was already at the stove cracking eggs, his hair no longer gelled up and all his piercing removed, he greeted them warmly.

Later that morning Salinger stopped at what used to be their Civic Center. He still reeled from the hard choices he had to make only a few nights ago. Looking at the still standing concrete walls, he was glad that he was correct in choosing this building for the fire. He knew from history that it was built as the bomb shelter, the safe haven in a time of crisis, and chief Fredricks backed his theory. The building should burn inside only and not spread to the Forest or the rest of the buildings. He was saddened that somewhere in the ashes lay Lucy Walker, and made the decision right then to dedicate the new Civic Center to her.

With a sigh, he returned to his patrol car, along with the thought that he wasn't sure he wanted to give up being the chief, he loved his job. Of course, regardless of what was to transpire, his first order of business was to hire some new constables. After everything that happened, he knew the first person he wanted to ask was Doug Bowan. If he would agree to the extra schooling, of course.

☐

December 1992
Bear Lake, 11:00am

Tom Danechuck removed the chunk of ice from his new fishing hole and brushed away the light snow that formed on his glasses. He peered down into the dark water below.

"I hope the fishes are biting today."

Suddenly a wrinkled, pale face floated into view, it bobbed and caught on the lip of ice where it came to rest. Empty eye sockets stared up at the falling snow, the skin rippling loosely with the tug of water.

"What the…," He jolted back from the ice hole, his heart thudding in his chest. Tom leaned back in for a better look.

"Ah shit," he spoke to the empty air surrounding him on the secluded lake. "I guess I better hook'em up and call the chief. Just my luck, out for a relaxing weekend and I find the missing Mayor."

A cold breeze blew across the forest and, deep in the trees, too far for Tom to hear, a cat meowed.

Thanks for reading, I hope you enjoyed the book. Please be kind and leave a review.

https://www.amazon.com/Theresa-Jacobs/e/B01BAS13T2

Check out Zane Dowlings superb novels

https://www.amazon.com/Zane-Dowling/e/B00A5VA4V4

Find me on Facebook
https://www.facebook.com/Theresajcbs

Or Twitter
https://twitter.com/writerTheresaJ

Read free stories on Wordpress
https://authortheresajacobs.wordpress.com

Made in the USA
Columbia, SC
10 August 2018